"I was so incred̶ ... **k̶a̶y̶,**
Zoe said, her voice low and sincere.

"And I...I care about you, more than I thought possible in such a short time," she admitted, her gaze locked with his, vulnerable and searching.

Their fingers intertwined naturally, as if they were meant to fit together all along. The distance between them on the couch was gone.

The softness of her fingers and the sweetness of her breath forced Noah to acknowledge how bad he wanted her. He felt a shift within him. The barriers of their professional relationship, now gone, left them standing on new, uncharted ground. "We're not working together anymore," he said, the reality of their situation dawning on him, both liberating and daunting. "But our jobs, they're still...complicated."

"Maybe we're reckless to even consider this," Zoe whispered.

"Maybe," he conceded, the depth of his feelings for her breaking through the last of his reservations. "But I can't let you go. Not without exploring what this is between us."

Dear Reader,

Siblings are both amazing and frustrating. My brother is one of my best friends and also the person who can antagonize me more than anyone else. His antics occasionally make me wish for a sister, a wish that inspired the creation of twin sisters Allison and Zoe Goodwyn. Allison is focused on getting ahead in her job as an investigative reporter, while Zoe, an elementary school teacher, drops everything to help out both her sister and their father. In *The Twin's Bodyguard*, Zoe takes on Allison's identity in order to save her sister's life.

She transitions out of her role as a teacher into the world of television news. She not only takes over her sister's wardrobe but picks up a sexy bodyguard, Noah, along the way. While Noah's protecting Zoe, his belief in her shifts her self-image and allows her to step out from her sister's shadow.

This is book two of the Fresh Pond Security series, which can be read as a stand-alone. However, this book does expand on some plotlines introduced in book one, *Protector in Disguise*, Fiona and Jason's story.

I love hearing from my readers, so feel free to visit me at www.veronicaforand.com and leave me a message.

Enjoy the thrill!

Veronica

THE TWIN'S BODYGUARD

VERONICA FORAND

ROMANTIC SUSPENSE

Harlequin®
ROMANTIC
SUSPENSE™

Recycling programs
for this product may
not exist in your area.

ISBN-13: 978-1-335-50271-1

The Twin's Bodyguard

For questions and comments about the quality of this book, please contact us at CustomerService@Harlequin.com.

TM and ® are trademarks of Harlequin Enterprises ULC.

Harlequin Enterprises ULC
22 Adelaide St. West, 41st Floor
Toronto, Ontario M5H 4E3, Canada
www.Harlequin.com

MIX
Paper | Supporting
responsible forestry
FSC® C021394

Printed in Lithuania

Veronica Forand is the award-winning author of romantic thrillers, winning both the Booksellers' Best and the Golden Pen Award for the novels in her True Lies series.

When she's not writing, she's a search and rescue canine handler with her dog, Max.

A lover of education but a hater of tests, she attended Smith College and Boston College Law School. She studied in Paris and Geneva, worked in London and spent several glorious months in Ripon, England.

She currently divides her time living between Philadelphia, Vermont and Cape Cod.

Books by Veronica Forand

Harlequin Romantic Suspense

Fresh Pond Security

Protector in Disguise
The Twin's Bodyguard

Visit the Author Profile page at Harlequin.com for more titles.

For Steve

When they handed out older brothers,
I hit the jackpot.

Thanks for the laughter, the scotch
and always having my back.

Chapter 1

For as long as Zoe Goodwyn could remember, she'd put the needs of her twin sister, Allison, first, even if it meant sacrificing her own needs. She'd given up career opportunities and even let go of a boyfriend or two to remain in their hometown to care for their father. Her latest sacrifice seemed mild by comparison—abandoning plans with friends to catch the ferry from Nantucket and watch her sister's dog.

Stepping off the bus into the heart of Boston, Zoe shielded herself from the city's loud energy, a sharp contrast to the meditative qualities of waves breaking on a sandy beach and the call of seagulls darting across the sky. The salt air in Boston felt invigorating, but the bags of trash waiting for pickup added a somewhat sour city smell that wrinkled her nose. Although Zoe enjoyed visits to Boston, she preferred when Allison traveled to Nantucket so Zoe could remain in her zen place. Not that she entirely disliked the city. Just city people. People acted differently in large groups. They had more of a survival of the fittest mentality. She preferred any groups around her to be under the age of ten. In fact, her third-grade students were her favorite people. Everyone else brought too much with them. Too much noise, conflict, gossip, expectations, and superiority. She slipped away from the crush at the bus station while texting her dad that she'd made it into the city.

Zoe relaxed as she reached her sister's neighborhood. Few cars ventured down the one-way cobblestone road to the three-story brownstone. Pausing in front of a florist, she bought a bundle of white and pink peonies before traveling the final block to her destination. Flowers always made everything a touch brighter and more fragrant.

A woman, dressed in a pale blue shirtdress and walking a large white dog, waved from across the street. "Allison, I loved your report on stolen pets. Keep up the good work." As a young and energetic investigative reporter for a local news channel, Allison had minor celebrity status in the city. She thrived among people and could persuade anyone to hand over their most personal stories. She also loved getting in the middle of complicated issues.

Normally, Zoe would ignore people confusing her for her sister, but she couldn't make her sister appear unfriendly. Trying to explain that she was not, in fact, Allison, was always too much of a chore. Not many people knew about Allison's sister, and Zoe liked it that way. Her baseball cap, ponytail and sunglasses should have kept her identity hidden. This was her sister's neighborhood, however, so perhaps, people could see through a disguise here. She waved and mouthed thanks to the woman, who smiled and continued down the street with her dog.

Once inside the building, Zoe heard howling. Marlowe. Mrs. Peterson, an older woman with a tousled, pewter bob and a charming disposition, never disciplined Marlowe when she watched him. She preferred the bribery method in restraining him. Zoe entered the apartment and was greeted by one very excited beagle. As soon as the door closed behind her, she let go of her suitcase, kicked off her red Mary Janes, never allowed on the perfectly waxed floor, and headed to the kitchen to put the flowers in a vase. Marlowe's intensity didn't slow. His tail wasn't wagging. Instead, he appeared distressed. He was always happy to see her, so his behavior caused her to pause and crouch down to his level.

"What's the matter, little man?" Zoe asked the shaking beagle. Normally, he'd greet her between blistering romps around the foyer, into the kitchen, over the living room furniture and right back to her side. Now he didn't leave her side.

She dropped the flowers on the counter and scanned the room. The kitchen and living room seemed as sterile and minimalist as always, but quiet, except for Marlowe.

"Mrs. Peterson?" she called out, as Marlowe continued his barking. He nearly tripped her as she tried to walk into the room. "Go to bed." She pointed to Marlowe's bed and looked around for Mrs. Peterson. She paused and stared him down. He popped into a down position on his bed, but as soon as she walked further into the apartment, he bounded to her side.

Turning away from him, she took a deep breath.

The energy inside the apartment felt unfamiliar. Something was off. Whatever created the tension in the room lifted the hair on her arms and made her almost turn around and run back out the door. But Mrs. Peterson had to be here because Zoe could smell hints of the jasmine perfume she always wore.

Marlowe rushed ahead, barking and winding up again. Zoe stalled at the door to Allison's study. Papers and drawers and files had been tossed all over the floor. Marlowe skittered back into the hall away from Mrs. Peterson, who was face down on the floor.

Zoe rushed over to her. It appeared as though she'd fallen or maybe collapsed. A good-sized gash was on the back of her head, matting her hair with blood.

"Mrs. Peterson, are you okay?" she asked, knowing she wasn't. Marlowe rushed toward her, barking louder. Zoe wanted to comfort him but had to focus on the unconscious woman in front of her.

"You're here?" A gruff voice came from behind her.

Before she could turn, the stranger's hand reached around and covered her mouth with a cloth. She tried to push him away, but his grip was strong and her ability to fight was fading. Her eyes closed, the barking grew faint, and everything went black.

Chapter 2

Noah Montgomery sat inside his car, listening to Vivaldi and snacking on M&M's, almonds, and raisins for hours. He'd already placed two discreet cameras at the back entrances to the apartment complex he'd been assigned and had parked near the front entrance to watch for anyone coming and going.

Allison, the woman whose apartment he'd been tasked to watch, had already walked by his car, carrying flowers and a duffel bag with her brown hair up in a ponytail covered with a baseball hat and wearing sunglasses. Even with the attempted disguise, he'd recognize her from the news. She'd strolled along as though she had no worries in the world, but according to their client, she had a target on her back. Allegedly, she'd uncovered a bribe in the local government. Although the source of the bribe was unknown, there were rumblings in underground channels placing Allison at risk. Not that she'd appeared anxious or even more cautious than the average person. Perhaps she was unaware of the risk or welcomed dangerous assignments.

When he called Jason, the operational leader, to tell him that she was back, Jason seemed incredulous.

"She is? Meaghan last tracked her to Rhode Island," Jason said.

Rhode Island was only an hour from Boston, so she could have easily driven back from wherever she'd gone.

"I don't know where she was, but she's here now."

"Fine, keep an eye on the door. I'll send Meaghan to stay on her," Jason said.

Noah had spent years at a desk as an analyst for the NSA—he wanted fieldwork, not more sitting. "I can enter an apartment just as well as Meaghan can."

"You're on the building, she's assigned to the person. If Allison leaves again, I still need someone watching all the exits. Keep an eye on the outside for anything unusual."

Noah's gaze had remained on the front entry and on the camera feeds of the back of the building. "Understood," he said, through clenched teeth. This was supposed to be the year he took on more adventurous assignments. As soon as Jason approved his request.

Having been stuck at a desk for the past few months after a gunshot wound, he'd been happy to get out of the office to handle surveillance work. Granted, he'd prefer interacting with people in more direct fieldwork, but at least he was no longer in his office twelve hours a day. Having arrived at 1:00 p.m., he couldn't be certain who had come and gone in the morning, but Jason had made it clear that he remain outside the building in the background.

This was Noah's first assignment with their client EON, the Eclipse Operations Network, a shadow agency that stepped in when a case needed specialized teams outside of regular law enforcement channels. When

Fiona, a former member of EON, joined Fresh Pond Security, EON saw an opportunity to use the team as an alternative arm of their group. It paid much better than security guard and protection work, but the assignments often had vague instructions and unclear goals.

The team had been hired on this case to investigate bribes running between City Hall and some sort of criminal enterprise. EON wanted the name of the entity making the bribe. After years of monitoring these types of organizations when Noah was an analyst at the NSA, he understood how difficult it would be to find enough evidence for charges to stick, but he'd do his part sitting inside his car, watching the comings and goings of Allison Goodwyn, the investigative reporter who had broken open the case.

But ten minutes later, everything changed. A food delivery guy carrying two bags entered the building when a woman and a young kid exited. He was dressed in jeans, a gray T-shirt, and heavy leather work boots that nobody in their right mind would wear for Uber Eats deliveries. The muddy boots seemed more appropriate for a construction site. His suspicions raised, Noah contacted Jason again and explained the situation. Although he didn't have the actual field experience of his colleagues, the majority former law enforcement or military types, he could analyze a situation better than most. And his instincts screamed to follow that guy.

"I can wait for Meaghan or go inside and get a closer look," he said, trying not to overstep his position, but knowing damn well that something was off. "All of the cameras are recording and Calvin has the feedback at the office, so we shouldn't miss anything on the outside."

There was a pause and then Jason replied, "Meaghan's delayed. Go ahead and check on Allison's well-being."

Noah didn't have time to feel relieved. He left his car, only to be stopped by the locked front door. "Damn it," he cursed under his breath.

As he stood and waited for someone to let him inside, he tried to listen through the door for anything that sounded off. The only sound coming from the building was a barking dog. After what felt like forever, he lucked out when some business suit of a guy exited the building more focused on his phone than on whom he was letting inside the building. Noah bolted past him. Too much time had lapsed for a simple food delivery. He dashed upstairs and could hear the muffled sounds of a struggle in the location of the barking dog.

He tried the apartment door. After rattling it enough to know it was locked, he backed up a few steps and then used his stronger leg to kick in the door. His hip throbbed with a sharp pain that shot through him as every muscle propelled him forward, but the door burst open. As the door slammed into the wall, he paused at the scene inside the apartment. The fake delivery man, a huge guy with a scowl on his face, stood with an accomplice, another burly guy in jeans and a T-shirt, who must have entered the apartment before Noah had been sent to monitor the place. Allison was unconscious and being dragged across the rug toward the front door. A beagle ran around the men, barking and growling.

Noah pulled out his weapon. "Stay where you are." He pointed his gun but didn't have a good enough shot to guarantee he wouldn't hit Allison. Although he seemed the same height as the men, he had more lean muscle than pumped-up gym muscle. But he'd handled burly guys in hand-to-hand combat in training, outwitting them in tactical situations when his strength wouldn't match his opponents.

Instead of rushing them, he grabbed a large blue vase from a side table with his free hand and tossed it at the man closer to him.

The guy deflected it toward the wall where it smashed into an explosion of glass fragments. To avoid the glass, the men dropped Allison. The beagle bit into the pant leg of one of them, who kicked back and forth trying to get free. His partner pointed a weapon at the dog, which sent Noah rushing forward to the asshole. With his focus on rescuing Allison and saving the dog, one of the men came from behind and clocked him in the head with a very large fist. He fell, curling under his shoulder to limit the impact of the fall. By the time he righted himself, the men had rushed out the door. Allison, her hat knocked off and part of her shirt ripped, remained out of it in the middle of the floor on top of bits of glass.

He knelt by her and checked her pulse. She was alive. Phew. That would take a whole lot of explaining if he'd failed her, although he had an even bigger question. Where the heck was Meaghan? She was supposed to be trailing and guarding her all day. Meaghan had fantastic instincts when it came to the protection of her subjects. Yet, in this instance, she wasn't in sight. Instead, Allison had been left alone to be attacked and almost kidnapped.

The beagle's incessant barking started to push Noah's last limits. Exasperated, he shouted, "Quiet!" To his surprise, the dog obeyed. "Good dog," he whispered, his heart still pounding from the rush of adrenaline.

He called Jason and updated him on everything that happened. "Have you heard from Meaghan?"

"She's been caught up in something going on in Rhode Island." Jason provided no more insight into Meaghan's failure to be there, so Noah didn't question him further. He had enough going on.

"Do you want me to call an ambulance or take Allison to a hospital?" Noticing a rag next to her, Noah lifted it. Soaked. He could smell the sweet smell of chloroform and pulled it away from his nose quickly. "I think she was drugged. Chloroform is my best guess."

"They wanted her alive. Otherwise, they would have shot her and been done with it. They'll be back. We need to increase security on her. Bring her in. I'll have our medical team look at her. We can't trust anyone," he responded.

The beagle circled Allison, his body shaking. From the glass on the floor to the risk someone would return to shoot the little guy, Noah made a decision.

"I need to bring in Allison's dog too," he told Jason. The dog had also been sort of a hero, slowing the attackers down, and he was currently licking Allison's face. They probably needed each other.

"A dog?"

"Protecting the person includes protecting everyone they love."

Jason exhaled loud enough to send Noah's stomach to the floor. "Fine."

After he hung up, Noah searched around for the dog's leash. Instead of a leash, he found the body of an older woman. He braced himself for the fallout and then called Jason back.

Because they were being paid by someone deep in the government to look into corruption, the team had to handle this fiasco with finesse. Two team members arrived to help transport an unconscious Allison to their medical center so her name would not be listed on a hackable hospital databank. The dog accompanied Noah to headquarters. He preferred to ride on Noah's lap, which was not going to happen, so he created an area in the back seat where he could fasten the harness. As Noah drove, the dog got into his M&M's. He called his sister, a longtime dog owner, to confirm that the dog would not, in fact, die after ingesting three candies and then he met with Jason.

The minute he saw Jason's expression, he knew he was in trouble. The beagle did not pick up on the same cues and rushed over to the man who could make or break Noah's career, tail wagging and whining in an excited manner. Jason rubbed his head, but then stood up out of the dog's reach and focused on Noah.

Before Jason had a chance to criticize him, Noah said, "We would have been better off if I'd followed Allison into her apartment immediately."

"Except we were hired to watch over things, and now we've taken custody of the person we were supposed to be watching, never mind having to place an untraceable call to 9-1-1 to get local law enforcement to investigate a scream from Goodwyn's apartment so they can locate the body." He shook his head.

"Is she okay? Not the neighbor, but Allison."

"Dr. Morgan thinks she'll be fine after she sleeps off the chloroform. Good job figuring out what drugged her. It saved Allison a whole battery of blood tests."

"Do you want me back at the apartment?"

"Not right now. The place is crawling with a whole department of forensics ready to get out of the office for the day. Just stay here and help Calvin do some analysis. Maybe talk to Allison when she wakes. You have the friendliest face of all of us, including Meaghan. She's beautiful, but damn she could stare a person into an early grave. I'll have her step in to watch over her when she gets back."

Noah frowned. He'd just fought off two armed men and stopped a kidnapping and was still deemed a second stringer.

Chapter 3

Zoe woke with a bear of a headache. Used to living in a resort town where drunk tourists caused most of the problems, she hadn't expected to find both an unconscious woman and a burglar in her sister's apartment. But she did. The sensation of large hands wrapped around her neck crept over her sanity and made her stomach twist. She blinked her eyes open and looked around the unfamiliar room. Marlowe slept at the foot of her bed curled up tight like a doughnut. He was the only thing that looked familiar. The beige-painted room seemed sterile, hospital like, but not exactly. Maybe more of a hotel room with a small sitting area and a table, but there were no windows. *No windows?* That one fact unnerved her. The only things in the room that could be considered comforting were three paintings of a rocky coastline with pathways bordered by rosebushes. While they provided some color and interest, they couldn't transform the blandness of the room into an inviting space.

The door swung open and a woman dressed in a pink designer pantsuit and crisp white blouse entered. She was stalled by a visit from Marlowe, who had jumped off the bed to sniff the woman's legs. She greeted him with a rub under his chin, then turned her attention back to Zoe. "You're awake. Good. I'm Dr. Morgan." More fashionable than anyone Zoe knew in the medical field, the woman, no older than forty, wore her hair up in a messy bun and tortoiseshell glasses perched on her head. "How are you feeling?"

"Like I'm hungover." Her body had few actual aches and pains. Instead, she felt off internally, both physically and psychologically. Her attacker haunted her waking thoughts. Just the idea of a stranger putting his hands on her sent shivers down her spine.

The doctor nodded. "That's expected with chloroform."

The memory of a cloth covering her mouth before she passed out added to her queasiness. "Chloroform? How? Why?"

"Lots of questions that need answers. It seems you were drugged, but I did an exam and from what I saw, you're otherwise in good shape. Do you have any pain anywhere?"

"A smashing headache."

"Also expected. Drinking water will help."

Zoe stared at the person who called herself a doctor and paused. At present, Zoe didn't know whether she was a captive or in the basement room of a hospital, although not many hospitals allowed pets. "Where am I and when can I leave?" she asked.

The alleged doctor's lips pressed into a thin line. "Let me tell Jason you're finally conscious. He'll be able to explain more to you." With that, she moved toward the door.

Zoe needed answers. Who did this to her? What happened to Allison? Where was she? Then another question came to mind. "Wait. What about Mrs. Peterson? Is she okay?"

Dr. Morgan's dramatic pause said too much. "I'll let Jason talk to you about that too."

Zoe leaned back into the bed. So much had happened. She wanted to call her father. A retired chief of police, he'd be able to give her that calm reassuring voice that had been her backbone whenever life had become too much, but her phone wasn't anywhere near her. Several possible scenarios filled her mind. Was this a random act of violence? Had someone targeted Allison? If the man had been after Allison, was she still in danger? Where the heck was Allison? Where the heck had Zoe ended up? It felt like living through a true crime story, except this time, she was at the heart of the drama, without the protective screen of a television. Unlike Allison, who loved adventure and challenges, Zoe preferred tranquility and comfort. This was all way too much for her.

Adding to her confusion, a man with beachy brown hair casually tousled like a swimwear model entered her room, leaving the door open. His sun-kissed skin and relaxed demeanor suggested he spent plenty of time by the sea.

"Jason?" she asked, her voice tinged with hope and confusion.

He shook his head, his frown steady, or perhaps it was concern. Dressed in an untucked blue button-down and khakis, he looked more like one of the guys who weekended on Nantucket during the summer crush than someone who could assist with her current predicament. The fabric of his shirt hinted at a lean, athletic build.

He pulled up a chair beside her bed and sat down,

his whole aura more compassionate than critical. "I'm Noah. Noah Montgomery."

She stared at him, trying to place his face. Her silence must have prodded him to explain himself.

"We met at your apartment. I guess *met* isn't the right word. I found you unconscious and being dragged out by two men. I made enough of a fuss to scare them off. Luckily, they left you behind." He shrugged modestly. "I wish I'd been able to stop them. It would make figuring out who they are easier. Unless you have any idea who targeted you. From the circumstances, they wanted you alive." He spoke as though her everyday life came out of a thriller novel, no shock or drama, just facts.

Marlowe jumped onto her visitor's lap, his tail wagging forcefully. Noah rubbed behind his ears and gave him a partial smile to calm him down. Marlowe settled.

Zoe felt comfortable in Noah Montgomery's presence as well, despite her unanswered questions. Yet something he said stuck out to her. She had assumed only one man had attacked her.

"They? I only remember one person in the apartment," she said, trying to make sense of it all. The memory of the man who had grabbed her from behind and tried to suffocate her sent a shiver through her again. She could feel him against her back and the large palm of his hand over her mouth. She couldn't remember anything after that. The knowledge she'd been violated washed over her, lifting her heart rate and shaking her well-being. Her current location, stuck in this cell of a room, offered no relief.

"I encountered two men when I arrived. They were carrying you toward the front door. I stopped them from

taking you, but couldn't prevent them from escaping."
He sounded annoyed with himself. Perhaps he was Allison's current boyfriend. She changed her partners the
way most people changed their sheets. Monthly. And he
was the right age. On second thought, this guy wasn't
Allison's type. She preferred muscular guys forced to
order bespoke suits because of their shoulder widths.
This guy seemed more like a tennis pro. Athletic, but
not in a hang-out-in-the-weight-room kind of way. He
also didn't seem as condescending as Allison's typical
man candy. Most of her exes looked down their noses
at Zoe as though she were the sale rack version of her
identical twin.

"Why were you in her apartment?"

He continued rubbing behind Marlowe's ears. "I'm
with Fresh Pond Security. You have a target on your
back, and we've been charged with keeping you safe.
It's best if you remain out of sight for the next few days,
at least until the threat can be minimized."

"Threat?" She tried to process everything, but her
brain wasn't functioning at 100 percent with the drug
clouding her thoughts.

"I interrupted whoever was in the apartment, but
they're still out there. Do you have any place you can go
until this dies down? If not, we have a secluded cabin in
Maine," he said. His demeanor stayed relaxed, but those
dark eyes held a seriousness that sent chills through Zoe.

Her heartbeat sped up as she processed his words.
This guy with his wind-tousled hair thought she was
Allison, and Allison was in trouble. Big trouble. And
Allison needed protection to keep from getting attacked
or worse. She'd always pushed for more and more dan-

gerous assignments. While still in college, she'd found proof of sexual misconduct by the dean at her university. Protests erupted on campus on both sides, and the dean, his back against the wall, threatened to shut the whole paper down. His threats didn't intimidate Allison. She fought him until the day she graduated. Her story brought him down. Reporting the truth was her calling. If her current assignment had even higher stakes, Zoe was terrified for her.

"You're not law enforcement?" she asked the stranger, unease growing in her voice.

"No, but we work closely with law enforcement," he responded.

"So I can call the police to verify all of this." She glanced around for her phone again, not finding it anywhere.

"I'd prefer you didn't. If your whereabouts get to the wrong people, protecting you will become nearly impossible."

Panic set in. For some reason, she'd thought she was being held at a police station, sort of, but not entirely. Instead, she was trapped in this protection agency's office? She sat up. She needed to contact Allison.

"I can't protect you if you run," he stated, his tone firm yet devoid of aggression. "There's a whole team working to protect you. We can decide on the next course of action when we all get together. There's been a lot of rumblings about what you've uncovered. People will go to great lengths to keep that information hidden."

The words seemed benign enough, but something dangerous threaded through every word he said. Someone was after Allison and currently, this man thought she was Allison. Whether he could help her or not, she couldn't risk lingering a moment longer.

On the other hand, if he'd wanted to hurt her, he would have. They were alone, minus a dog who seemed to prefer his company to hers. If Allison was out there somewhere, these people would turn their attention to finding her and letting Zoe go. But Zoe couldn't unleash the hounds after her only sibling. Perhaps if they thought they had Allison, Allison would be safe.

Chapter 4

Noah had put hours and hours into his job, assuring he earned every dollar of his generous salary and proving himself an asset to the team. Lately, however, after the gunshot wound, he felt an even stronger need to demonstrate his worth. His last field assignment had been protecting Jason's son, Matt. That had been the day Matt was kidnapped and Noah was shot in the hip. Despite the team getting Matt back to safety, Noah couldn't forgive himself. This new assignment was a chance to start over. How hard could it be to protect a woman who regularly took on criminal enterprises and challenged the status quo?

Taking a deep breath to ground himself in his current assignment, he observed the woman in front of him. She wasn't at all what he'd expected after watching her on the news over the past few years. On-screen, Allison was poised and confident, her hair and makeup perfectly done, drawing viewers in with her calm assuredness as she reported stories. But here, as she moaned and stretched, waking her muscles from a drug-induced slumber, she looked soft and sweet. Without makeup, her natural beauty exuded a girl next door quality, so different from her on-screen persona. He'd expected confident, loud, and demanding. Instead, she seemed more reserved, although that could also be the chloroform wearing off.

Taking him by surprise, she stood, causing her dog to hop off his lap and stand at her feet.

"What are you doing?" he asked, prepared to catch her if her body hadn't regained its strength.

She grabbed a Black Dog sweatshirt from the end of the bed and pulled it over her head. "I need to get going. Thanks for everything."

She'd never get out of the locked facility, and trying would only cause her more distress than necessary, so he stood back and tried to act nonconfrontational. He wasn't her enemy and didn't want to act like one. She needed to trust him and the whole team.

"You aren't ready to get up and around. Why don't you wait for the doctor?" he suggested, hoping it might persuade her to stay.

"The doctor said all I needed was water. I think that means I can go as long as I hydrate when I get home." She sat on the edge of the bed and pulled on her shoes.

Noah couldn't allow her to leave, so he called Jason. "Our guest would like to leave. I was hoping you'd have the opportunity to meet her first. Can I escort her into the conference room?"

"Anything wrong?" Jason asked clearly sensing trouble.

"It would be easier to explain in person." Noah's eyes stayed on Allison, who had stood again and seemed ready to bolt.

"Sure. I'm in conference room three."

Despite being knocked out for almost an hour, their guest appeared stable enough. Until she wasn't. Her body swayed too far to the left and he dived several feet in order to stop her from crashing onto the floor.

Wrapping his arms around her, he curved into her fall and cushioned her impact with the floor. They landed together with a thud. Marlowe raced to them, barking. Allison didn't move. Her body pressed against his, her elbow digging into his side. Noah gently slid her arm from his rib cage and let out a deep breath. The pain from the hard impact made any potential meet-cute feel more like corporal punishment.

As the pain subsided, they both stayed still for a moment. Their faces inches apart, Noah became acutely aware of every detail—the softness of her lips, the amber flecks in her eyes, the way her hair framed her face. Then Marlowe pushed his way in and licked her cheek.

"Um…thanks," she whispered, maybe to him or maybe to Marlowe. "I should probably stay seated for a while longer. You don't mind waiting here for a few minutes, do you?"

He couldn't suppress the smile. "I have nothing else to do but be your personal cushion."

The floral scent of her hair was intoxicating, her proximity overwhelming, and the feel of her in his arms relaxing and painfully heavy.

"Can I help you up?" he asked.

"Probably not, since I'm sitting on you," she said, her tone light.

"Perhaps I should rephrase. You're killing me. Can you get up?" he quipped, trying to keep their connection lighthearted.

She laughed and nodded, carefully shifting her weight. "I think I can manage that." With a bit of effort, she moved off him and sat down on the side of the bed.

Noah sat up, rubbing his side. "I think staying seated is a good idea. I don't know if I have it in me to catch you again."

"I don't have it in me to fall again," she said, her eyes meeting his with a grateful smile. "Thanks for catching me."

"Anytime," he replied. His heart raced at the memory of her in his arms.

They sat for a few moments in silence until the quiet became the largest presence in the room. Before he could break the awkwardness, she was back on her feet, but not steady at all.

"What are you doing?"

"I really need to leave," she insisted. "No offense, but this place feels more like a jail cell than a safe house. I'm highly claustrophobic and need windows. If you can offer me an arm, I'm sure I can walk out of here fine."

Against his better judgment, since she needed rest, not a stroll down the hall, he wrapped an arm around her and helped her balance as they strode the forty yards to the conference room. It was better than explaining to Jason why the person they were supposed to look after was struggling to escape. Marlowe, his leash dragging behind him, trotted next to them.

The hallway to the conference room was quiet, save for the soft hum of the air-conditioning. When they arrived, Jason looked up from a map on the table. With his black hair pulled back in a ponytail, Jason seemed more like a motorcycle gang leader than a former military officer and business owner. Despite the ribbing he caught from the rest of the team, he insisted his wife, Fiona, preferred it that way.

Dr. Morgan came from behind them and rushed to Allison's side. "You look dizzy." She glared at Noah as though he'd dragged her out of bed.

"I'm a bit shaky on my feet, but I insisted on moving around." She surveyed the room, her eyes scanning every door, every screen, every person in the area.

"Understood, but let's not overdo it." Dr. Morgan pulled out a chair. "Take a seat. Noah, why would you let her walk around?"

"It was not my choice."

The doctor shook her head, then turned to Allison. "If you need anything, have someone call me. I'll be down the hall."

After she left, Noah and Jason's attention turned toward their guest. Despite her lack of makeup or camera-perfect hair, Allison's appearance commanded attention, altering the room's dynamics.

"Are you Jason?" she asked.

"I am. You must be Allison," he said as he bent down to pet Marlowe. "I've already met this furry fellow. Not the best trained dog in the world, but his friendliness makes up for it."

She nodded. "He's only trained to live in an apartment and curl up on the bed at night."

"I'm sure he does a great job at that." Jason's phone rang. He acknowledged the room and then stepped out to answer it. When he returned only minutes later, his demeanor had changed. "That was Meaghan. She's held up for a bit."

He walked around to Allison and sized her up, as though she were now a criminal defendant. "Do you feel okay, Ms. Goodwyn?"

"Yes, but I'm ready to go home."

"I'm sure you are. Before you go, I'd love it if you could answer a few questions."

"Um. I'll try."

"Good. Have you spoken to Brendan Quinn about what you're accusing him of?"

She stared back at Jason frozen in silence as though she had no idea what he was speaking about. But she'd been the person who had stirred up this controversy after chasing down a tip from one of the clerks at City Hall.

"Yes or no?" Jason demanded.

She looked at Noah, but he had no idea if she'd seen the city council member. Part of him wanted to step in and comfort her, but Jason was never mean to anyone he was protecting. Something was wrong.

After an uncomfortably long time, she shook her head. "No."

"That's interesting. We received information that you cornered him in City Hall Plaza in front of a crowd of tourists, made wild accusations with no evidence, and left. That doesn't sound like a sound investigative technique. Do you have any idea how fast evidence can be buried?"

"I…um…no."

"No, you didn't confront him or you didn't know how fast evidence could be buried?"

"Both." She took a few deep breaths and stayed silent.

Jason leaned in, his gaze as dangerous as a crowbar. "People want you dead. Do you know that?"

She swallowed hard, then nodded.

"And you're prepared for attempts on your own life?"

"Absolutely." Her voice grew more confident.

Jason's expression remained intense. "What about someone in your family's life?"

The question hit her like a physical blow. She recoiled, as though struck squarely by that imaginary crowbar.

Chapter 5

Zoe had never been so scared in her life. This gangster of a man seemed to want her head on a platter. Not hers, but her sister's.

Noah, the one person who seemed trustworthy, stepped forward. "What are you doing? She's not the enemy. She was almost killed."

His boss completely ignored him and stared Zoe down. "Do you think they'll leave your family alone? They'll hunt down everyone you love and destroy them."

"I'll do whatever it takes to protect them." She meant every word, although she wasn't entirely sure what that would entail.

"I believe you, but I won't protect a liar. Until you come clean, you're on your own and so is your family." He crossed his arms over his chest and glared at her.

Zoe could feel the weight of Jason's stare boring into her. Noah stood beside him, his expression confused. He had no idea that she wasn't Allison, but Jason certainly did. She should never have lied. Lies were always discovered, as she said to her third graders all the time. She couldn't argue with Jason, because he had the truth on his side, so she chose to defuse the bomb in the only way she knew how, with the truth.

Defeat weighed her down as she sank back into her chair. "I'm not Allison. I'm Zoe, her twin sister," she confessed in barely a whisper.

"Right." Noah's expression turned skeptical.

She had hoped for understanding from him, maybe even some empathy. Instead, she received suspicion and doubt. He'd believed she was Allison and she'd lied to him. For some reason, losing the trust of this stranger bothered her as much as all the events of the past few hours…this was all too much. A tear fell down her cheek. She dropped her head to hide the mountain of emotions threatening to erupt.

"I like my privacy, and she likes her fame," she said.

Noah's brows lifted. "That's convenient. A sister who just happened to be in her apartment?"

"Yes. She asked me to watch Marlowe." Her shame turned to annoyance.

"And why should we believe you?"

"I have nothing to lie about. Someone attacked me in her apartment, and I thought Allison would be safer if I took on her identity." She always took care of Allison. She turned to Jason. "I'm telling you, I'm not Allison. I'm her sister, Zoe."

Noah maintained his stance. "We can't just take your word for it. For all we know, you want to play the hero and dig up more dirt, but that's only angering your enemies and people will die because of it. If they don't silence you, they'll end up silencing everyone involved in the scheme and that's a lot of deaths in Boston we intend to prevent."

"Check my driver's license. It'll prove my identity."

Zoe spun around, forgetting she didn't have her phone or the attached wallet.

Jason, however, took a phone off the table—her phone—and handed it to her. He seemed to be the control center of the entire place. Her wallet was still attached to the back. She gave it to Noah, who took out her license. He examined it closely, comparing the photo and details with the person standing before him.

In the photo, she was smiling. A huge smile that generally wasn't allowed in government identifications, but the photographer had been a friend from high school and was making faces at her.

"Look at the name, the birth date. It's all there. I'm Zoe, not Allison," she said.

"It seems legitimate," he conceded, handing the wallet to Jason, who was calmly scratching Marlowe behind his ears. Marlowe's tail thumped in pleasure.

Noah studied the wallpaper on the phone. Zoe caught a glimpse of it and held her breath. The picture was of two high school– or college-aged women, unmistakably identical in their shared laughter. Both in graduation gowns and both seeming so young.

Grief flooded her eyes. "My mother took this photo. It was the last photo she ever took of us. She died a few weeks later."

"I'm sorry."

She shrugged. "It feels like a lifetime ago. My father and I live with her memory every day in the house she'd put her heart into."

He put the license back into its compartment and handed the phone to Jason.

"Incredible," Jason murmured, the word hanging in the air. "You look just like your twin. Identical?"

She nodded.

"You knew?" Noah asked Jason.

"Meaghan's with Allison right now." Jason handed the wallet back to her.

"Is she okay?" Zoe asked.

His interrogator demeanor had disappeared and his expression softened. "Meaghan found her in a small hospital ER in Rhode Island. She was hit by a car. Nothing life ending, but I think she'll be holed up in the hospital for a week or two."

Zoe nearly fell from her seat, but Noah shot out toward her and wrapped an arm around her to keep her steady. Jason looked as though he'd run in to help too if needed.

"Did someone target her?" Zoe asked, her expression falling.

"We don't know," Jason said. "Probably. A group of high schoolers who arrived to party in the parking lot for the last day of school must have scared away the car that hit her. It allowed her time to drag herself away from the area, which saved her life. Our team is already at the hospital. They blocked her name from reaching the computer so she is hidden for now. I'll have Calvin Ross, our chief of technology, scrub the medical records and Meaghan will remain with her."

"What about me?" Noah asked.

"Carry on watching over Zoe. With her looks, she could be easily misidentified as her sister. Since they'd targeted Allison in Rhode Island, the people in Allison's apartment wouldn't have been after her, so they must have been there looking for something. Maybe her evidence that linked Brendan Quinn to the person bribing him? Your appearance must have confused them. Even so, it's best you remained here."

Remain? Zoe recoiled from Noah as she realized that they intended to keep her in this basement. "I'm not staying here. I have to see Allison."

"Too risky," Jason replied. "I don't want anyone seeing you around there or you'll tip them off to your sister's location."

Zoe wasn't having it. "I have to be with her. She needs me. You can't keep me here. That's kidnapping."

Noah nodded. "Fine, I'll drive you."

A very chic woman, about five feet nothing, her blond hair in a ponytail, entered the room and pointed at Zoe as though she had heard the whole conversation. "We can hide her appearance. I think it's a good idea for her to see Allison. For both of them. Her presence will keep also Allison from bolting." She turned to Zoe and put out her hand. "I'm Fiona. I hope everyone is treating you well."

The more Zoe stared at the woman, the more familiar she seemed. Fiona? "Fiona Stirling, the author?"

"I try to keep my work with Fresh Pond Security quiet."

Noah stepped in. "She's more of a ghost employee."

"You're a security guard too?" Zoe couldn't believe such a successful author had to have a part-time gig to make ends meet.

Fiona laughed. "I like to think of myself as a consultant."

"You're one of my favorite writers," Zoe gushed. Fiona wrote amazing romantic thrillers that took place all over the world. Her presence increased her trust in Fresh Pond Security, despite having no other knowledge of her.

"Thank you. It's nice meeting you."

As people stood to leave, Zoe called out to stop everyone. "Wait. What about Mrs. Peterson? Is she here?"

Jason shook his head. "She's in the morgue."

The whole room stopped, all sight and sound frozen on those words. Her face fell and words failed her as she realized she too could have ended up in the morgue.

Chapter 6

Zoe remained silent as Noah drove to a small hospital in the southernmost part of Rhode Island. So many things had happened to her in the past twelve hours—almost kidnapped, assaulted, drugged. The frightening blur of chloroform and the terror of finding Mrs. Peterson's lifeless body haunted her. She stared out at the highway, trying to avoid the image of Mrs. Peterson's bloodstained hair. She was not cut out for all of this. She needed Allison.

"How long until we get there?" she asked, observing traffic crawling along the highway.

Noah continued watching the road. "Ten minutes."

Zoe couldn't wait. They'd been driving almost two hours. She tapped her fingers together until Noah turned and looked at her.

"It's rush hour. I can only go so fast without getting us killed."

"I know. It's just with everything going on, I want to see her with my own eyes to know she's safe."

He nodded. "We've got her under a false name, tucked away in a secluded room. We need to keep a low profile when we go in."

Touching the blond wig on her head, she mumbled, "I've never looked good as a blonde."

"It's not a beauty contest. You need to be unrecognizable, forgettable." He glanced over at her and nodded as though she'd achieved their goal.

"I'm perfect then." Dressed in a baggy URI sweatshirt, ill-fitting jeans, and oversize sneakers, she felt far from herself—let alone beautiful like Allison.

When they arrived, they slipped through the hospital's back service entrance and down sterile corridors to a small room where Allison lay.

The sight of her sister knocked her back. Allison looked like hell. Her face appeared pale and sickly with dark circles under her eyes. Her legs were immobilized, one in a full cast, and a bandage encircled her ribs. IVs and tubing appeared to anchor her to the bed. Zoe swallowed back the horror of seeing her sister so broken and banged up. Her fingers trembled as she took Allison's hand.

"How are you feeling, Ally?" Zoe's voice faltered as she took her sister's hand.

"Like I've been hit by a truck." Her usual flair for the dramatic was now a grim and sober reality.

"I was so worried about you." Zoe squeezed her hand. "I don't know whether to be thankful for you being alive or breaking down because of your injuries."

Allison closed her eyes for a moment. "Let's be thankful I'm not dead, although before they gave me the pain meds, I might not have minded."

"Don't say that." Zoe held back the tears forming in her eyes, as a lump formed in her throat. The idea of losing her sister left a huge hole inside her.

Noah introduced Meaghan, the person in charge of protecting Allison, to Zoe. She stood off to the side, a gorgeous tall sentinel in black cargo pants and a gray T-shirt. Although she seemed very beautiful, her demeanor remained calm, yet alert, seemingly ready to battle at a moment's notice. Her and Noah's presence made the room feel safer, protected.

As Zoe sat with Allison, she caught some of Meaghan and Noah's conversation.

"Nice seeing you back in action," Meaghan said, punching Noah on the arm.

"I'm just watching over Zoe for now." He sounded resigned in his role as chauffeur and guardian to Allison's sister. Not that Zoe blamed him. She wasn't in danger like Allison, and that's where all the resources should be placed.

"That's a step up."

"It is. Keeps me off of surveillance and more in the field. I honestly thought she was Allison when I met her."

Meaghan looked toward both sisters. "She does look similar, but you should be able to notice the difference. There are markers in each person and even twins carry themselves in different ways. Understanding people is a skill set you need to develop."

"I have years of analysis at my fingertips."

"Logic is only one tool in your belt, instinct is arguably the more powerful weapon." Meaghan spoke with a self-confidence that appeared earned through experience.

Noah frowned at her comment, then took a step back toward the wall and blended into the room, looking more like a boyfriend than a bodyguard. Bodyguards in Zoe's mind wore suits and earpieces, and never smiled, although she might be confusing them with Secret Service agents.

Zoe wondered about Meaghan's comments. Was she so dissimilar from Allison that their differences were visible? Probably. Allison stood taller, carried herself with more confidence, and could walk in high heels.

She stared at her sister's broken leg. She couldn't fathom the amount of pain Allison had been in. Their differences didn't matter when one of them was hurting. "Who would do such a thing to you?"

Allison shook her head, her expression falling further. "I have no idea," she whispered, pain evident in her voice. "I was meeting a source at the Enchanted Forest—an abandoned amusement park. I was supposed to meet someone with information on the bribes. Then everything went wrong."

Meaghan interrupted them. "I sent your statement to my boss, but he had some follow-up questions. Do you mind another round of questions?"

"Go ahead." Allison tried to sit up, but after wincing and letting out a moan that broke Zoe's heart, she remained in her current position.

"What we know so far is that you were found unconscious on the road about ten miles from here by a woman in an SUV. She called the police and they transported you here. No identification, no phone." Meaghan spoke methodically, like a police officer questioning a victim at a crime scene.

Allison tried to sit up again, the effort leaving her breathless. "I should never have gone alone."

"Why would the news station send you alone?" Noah asked.

"I'm pretty gutsy, but even I wouldn't subject myself to the ghosts of evil clowns without backup," Meaghan added.

"I've looked into stories alone before. Not in such isolated locations, but Glenn, my producer, sent me, insisting I go without the cameraman so I don't scare them off. I've always trusted him," Allison murmured, a hint of betrayal in her tone. "Now? I don't know."

"Do you know who you were supposed to meet?" Noah asked without the directness of Meaghan, less interrogation and more a conversation with a friend.

"I was supposed to meet someone who had information for me, but I received no name or description of the person. There was a source inside City Hall, a staffer who had sent invoices and a few other strange zoning requests. The papers are in my office. From what Glenn had said, I'd assumed the person I was meeting was a new source. But I should never have gone alone. I get that now." Her voice was filled with regret, something Zoe had never seen in her sister.

While Zoe sat beside her, the gravity of the situation sank in. Allison, the fearless journalist, seemed so vulnerable.

"I'm here for you," Zoe said. She squeezed her sister's hand and received a squeeze back.

"I know you are. Where's Marlowe? He needs to eat every four hours or he's a grouch." Allison looked around the room now completely consumed by the whereabouts of her dog.

"He stayed back with the team at headquarters. Just

tell me what he eats and I'll have someone get it for him. He seems to have adopted Calvin, our chief of technology. He'll be spoiled," Noah replied.

"Thank you. He has raw hamburger mixed with peas for breakfast and a cup of his salmon kibble for dinner." Allison's demands probably came off as spoiled to Meaghan and Noah, but that was how Allison did everything—perfection or not at all.

Zoe never had the money to spoil her cat Dory the way Allison spoiled Marlowe. "I'm sure he'll be okay with some regular kibble tonight."

Allison, hating to compromise on anything, conceded with a sigh. "I suppose so. Do you know when I can go home?"

Zoe looked at Meaghan, who stared at Allison with a frown. And at that moment, Zoe realized Allison had no idea what had happened at the apartment. And Zoe wasn't going to tell her. Not right now.

"The doctor thinks you need to stay on bed rest for at least two weeks," Meaghan said.

"Two weeks? How can I continue my investigation?" She'd never been able to relax when there was work to be done. Zoe doubted Allison would be able to stay locked away without someone tying her to the bed.

"Is it that important? You were almost killed." Zoe had almost been killed as well, and Mrs. Peterson, well, Zoe didn't want to think about that memory at the moment.

"Yes. It makes a difference. If a bunch of thugs can run the city and bribe the government, then the city I love is going to spiral into someplace I don't want to live. I'm willing to risk my life for it."

Chapter 7

With both side by side, Noah now saw the unmistakable resemblance of Allison and Zoe, despite the blond wig and baggy clothes Zoe sported. They shared the same long brown hair, same tawny eyes, same high cheek-bones, and perfect lips. Not that he was focused on Zoe's lips, but they seemed as though someone had drawn them as a perfect Cupid's bow. He shook his head to refocus. There were also significant differences between them that Meaghan had already hinted at. Meaghan, with her years on a police force, read people with decent accuracy. Allison spoke in a crisp, confident manner, while Zoe had a softer tone. Allison demanded. Zoe preferred to ask, even if she'd already made up her mind. Overall, however, they could switch places and be damn convincing.

Their resemblance meant Zoe was in as much danger as Allison if she walked out of here without protection. Whatever story Allison had found, it had tentacles. An internal investigation arm of the government wanted to have the whole story before people or evidence disap-peared. They, whoever they were, had paid Fresh Pond Security to handle the investigation. After years of un-covering money laundering crimes by criminal organizations, Noah could sense the depth of the corruption. In addition to whatever was going on at City Hall, the atmosphere at Allison's newsroom reeked of a cover-up. No responsible producer would send a young reporter on their own to an abandoned place unless they had ill intent or were an idiot. Which meant her producer had just become a person of interest, and maybe more people in the newsroom were associated with this. Payoffs for ignoring or shifting stories were not so unusual in parts of the news media.

Noah finally spoke his thoughts aloud, breaking the silence in the room. "How much do you trust your producer?"

"Glenn? He hired me years ago for my first job. I owe my whole career to him," Allison replied.

"Then why would he send you alone to such a vulnerable spot?"

"He told me something was brewing, and I wanted to break the story. I volunteered myself for the assignment."

Noah swallowed a curt reply to her obvious death wish. He didn't need to voice his annoyance that she disregarded all the warnings that had to have been going off in her head, because Zoe did.

"You volunteered to meet people in a secluded location? What were you thinking? I know your career is important to you, but you're important to me. You could have been killed." Zoe stared at her twin with her mouth open.

Allison, despite her injuries, seemed defiant. "I wasn't though."

"No, but Mrs. Peterson was," Zoe blurted out. "Someone has rummaged through all your papers at your apartment, and Mrs. Pederson was an innocent victim. And I almost was too. Don't you care about the bigger implications of this?"

Damn it. Zoe should have kept her mouth shut. Allison did not need to know about the murder of her neighbor. Not at this instant. But it was too late.

Allison flinched as though someone had struck her. "What? When? Why? Oh my God. I had no idea."

The alarms on one of her monitors screeched out what had to be her internal distress, and a nurse rushed in. "What's going on?"

Allison, now in tears, started choking.

"You'll all have to leave. She needs rest." The nurse did not seem at all impressed by her visitors' collective ability to rile her patient.

Zoe, now in tears as well, held on to her hand. "I'll be back as soon as things calm down. I promise." She reached over and hugged her, but was dragged away by the nurse.

"You too," the nurse said to Meaghan.

"I'm staying put." Meaghan remained leaning against the wall in the precise spot she was at when they entered the room. She was blessed with the ability to remain on her feet all day and show zero signs of wear.

The nurse scowled. Meaghan scowled back, but didn't move a fraction of an inch. Noah waited for a stand-off, but the nurse must have known from the look on Meaghan's face, she wasn't leaving Allison's side.

Noah and Zoe walked past an abandoned nursing desk and a few medical staff pushing mobile workstations, allowing for staff to work more with less backup. A boom for the bottom line, but not for employee morale. Noah thought of his sister Elise slaving away in a hospital near San Francisco. A NICU nurse, she cared for the most fragile of newborns. She didn't make nearly enough to compensate her for her work ethic. Noah's salary was almost four times hers. Granted, he had bullets to avoid, but she fought infections and birth defects and cardiac issues. And her success rate was much higher than his.

Perhaps it was thoughts of his sister, but an emptiness followed him into the cafeteria. There were too many days when he had no idea how he could give any more of himself to this career. The men and women around him had far more experience than him, so he made up for it by working more hours. Yet, until he could be assigned to something that involved more people interaction, he wasn't going to get better. So far, his two big chances at showing his skills involved failing to protect Jason's son when he was kidnapped and foiling two kidnappers going after Zoe, but failing to stop the men from escaping.

He followed Zoe, looking down halls, listening for anything unusual, and making sure she was protected at all times. He dreaded the thought of letting someone else down. The cafeteria had a few medical staff lingering around, but not many other people. They both grabbed some coffee, he opted for a blueberry muffin, and she chose a cup of strawberry yogurt, courtesy of Fresh Pond Security.

He pointed Zoe to a table in the quiet corner away from the windows. She sat in a rigid plastic chair, her eyes red rimmed, her hands clasped tight around her coffee cup. He sat in a way that blocked her from prying eyes. Even with her disguise, she was at risk being out in the open. She had the kind of demeanor that caused people to take notice. Or maybe it was just him noticing her, feeling bad that she'd been dragged into such a mess because of the dangerous decisions of her sister.

Breaking the silence, Noah leaned forward and offered Zoe a piece of his muffin. "It's not great, but it's warm." His voice came through as a low rumble in the sterile coldness of the hospital.

Zoe managed a faint, grateful smile as she accepted the piece, the warmth from her coffee cup jumping from her fingers to his.

"Thank you," she murmured, her gaze meeting his long enough that he noticed the deep brown of her eyes, like polished wood, rich and inviting. Eyes a man could easily get lost in.

He nodded, his fingers lingering on hers for a moment longer than necessary. He felt gratitude from the slight smile she gifted him and the way she sighed as she swallowed the muffin as if thanking him for being there while her world crumbled around her. At least that was his interpretation. She could just be tired and her defenses had long since collapsed.

Leaning back in her chair, she closed her eyes and took a slow, deliberate sip of the coffee. He was staring. Uncomfortably. When her eyes opened, he looked down at his own cup while battling with the conflicting sides of his professional duty and the personal sentiments that had unexpectedly taken root over the last few hours.

Zoe shivered in the cold air-conditioned room, and he reacted without thought. He removed his jacket and gently draped it over her shoulders. As the fabric settled around her, some of the tension melted from her neck and jaw. She glanced up at him, and for a moment, the hustle of the hospital faded away. They stared at each other, not a word said between them, but a thousand emotions, an acknowledgment of the danger, a concern for Allison, and something more that he refused to define because it would break protocol. Her appreciation for his gesture did nothing to send him back to a more neutral professional attitude toward her.

Zoe fiddled with the lid to her coffee cup, her mind probably down the hall where Allison lay recuperating. She'd seen a dead body, been attacked and drugged, effectively kidnapped by Fresh Pond Security, and seen her sister, not only injured, but in traction. Yet, Zoe wasn't crying in a ball on the floor or begging to be hidden away. She had guts.

Based on everything he'd gathered so far, this involved people willing to do whatever it took to stop the story and silence anyone who had information about the bribes. Allison had identified a key player: City Councillor Brendan Quinn. Noah's mind raced through a labyrinth of possibilities and scenarios. If only they could sneak into the news studio and uncover why the producer had sent Allison out alone. He could simply be a moron or be tied to something more sinister.

A plan formed in Noah's head. It seemed like a desperate shot in the dark at first, but the more he thought about it, the more the pieces fit together. Zoe, with her resemblance to Allison, could keep the investigation alive. Though dangerous, learning the bigger players now was better than hiding Zoe and Allison away indefinitely.

The clatter of trays handled by the kitchen staff and the distant call of a code from another part of the hospital created a disjointed soundtrack to his internal deliberations. It was risky, but so was allowing Allison's investigation to remain in limbo while she healed from her injuries.

"Did you ever switch places with your sister when growing up?" he asked, trying to sound conversational.

"Once when we were about five. Our mother knew instantly, so we never tried again. Allison walks and talks in a different way from me. Our looks are about the only thing we have in common." She shrugged, and Noah saw a woman who had lost out on a lot of fun. If he were a twin, he'd be in his brother's shoes all the time. How could she not take advantage of such a cool ability? It was a superpower.

"You don't think you could walk into that news station dressed as Allison and fool everyone?"

She clasped her coffee cup with her hands, considering the idea. "Not in a million years. I don't have a clue what she does at work. I teach elementary school, for Pete's sake, and I'm very camera shy. I've met her coworkers maybe twice at the most, and certainly not everyone at the station. I can't just step into her world. Those are big stilettos to fill, and I'm more of a Converse kind of girl." She paused as she realized the full extent of what he was asking. "No. I am not going to trade places with my sister."

"I get it," he said. "It was just an interesting thought, a way to find the people who want to hurt your sister. But you're right. It's a lot to ask. You don't even have the training for such an assignment." As he pondered it further, he knew she would have no idea what to do undercover. Too bad he couldn't transfer her looks to

Meaghan, who would be more than competent in a den of wolves.

Zoe's gaze dropped to the cup she was holding. "I want her to be okay," she whispered. "But I'm not the hero of this or any story, Noah. That's always been Allison."

Guilt tightened Noah's chest as he nodded and squeezed her hand in understanding. "We'll find another way to help Allison, a way that doesn't ask you to be anyone but yourself." He helped her up and they walked slowly down the hall.

"No matter what happens, I want you to know that I'm here for you," he said gently as they paused outside Allison's room. "Not just as an assignment, but as a friend. We'll get through this together in whatever way works best for you."

"I'm an assignment, I get it. You don't have to placate me," she replied, but also offered him a weary but genuine smile. "But I appreciate it just the same."

A few hours ago, he'd have agreed that he was placating the woman who had been assigned to him, but now his feelings had changed. He genuinely wanted her to get through this in the safest manner possible. Not out of some duty, but because he had come to care for her. His feelings were not only ill-advised and impractical, but could be downright dangerous.

As they entered Allison's room, he cast a final glance down the hallway, sensing an impending threat. The distant rumbling of staff and various others approached. "Get inside. I'll wait here until the coast is clear."

She nodded and slipped inside, sitting next to her sister. The commotion grew louder, and Noah held his breath, braced for a fight.

Chapter 8

Zoe sat with Allison in the now quiet hospital room. The rhythmic beeping of the heart monitor played a soft, persistent backdrop compared to the alarms going off only an hour before. Her sister seemed so vulnerable on the hospital bed with a tangle of IV lines and hospital sheets as pale as Allison's current complexion. Her lack of vigor, beaten out of her by a black sedan, made Zoe ignore everything Noah had said in the cafeteria. Instead of pushing Allison to continue her investigation, Zoe tried to convince her sister to hide out in Nantucket while she healed.

"Come on, Ally. It's not giving up, it's just…regrouping," Zoe implored, her voice a blend of concern and reason. "Nantucket would be perfect for you to recover, away from all this chaos. You could take a moment, breathe in some sea air, and—"

Allison cut her off with a resolute shake of her head. "I can't do that. This story is bigger than us. The moment I'm able to stand on my own, I'm finding out who bribed Brendan Quinn. No detours."

Zoe sighed. Allison's tenacity, her relentless pursuit of truth, made her an exceptional journalist, but it also painted a perpetual target on her back. "Please consider it. I'm worried about you." Zoe knew even as she spoke that Allison's mind was made up.

Her sister's expression softened momentarily. "We can plan a vacation just as soon as I finish this assignment." She was lying. She hadn't had a vacation for three years. There was always one more story to chase, one more opportunity she couldn't miss. But then she showed her true colors…"If you're going back to my apartment at any point, could you grab my laptop? It's in my office. I need to check a few things and send out some emails."

Before Zoe could respond, Meaghan interjected from her post standing by the wall. "That's not a good idea. You're off-grid right now, and that's the safest place for you. Any digital footprint, any hint of activity, and whoever's behind this will trace your location to this room number."

Allison's jaw set stubbornly, a look that didn't bode well for Meaghan. "I appreciate the concern, but I can't just lie here and watch TV. Someone tried to kill me. That's one hell of a story."

Meaghan crossed the room in a few decisive strides, her height impressive, her intimidation factor for someone so beautiful even more so. "I get it, I do. But your safety's my priority. My job. My paycheck. I have to insist you keep it low-tech for now. Notebooks, the back of napkins, anything that doesn't leave a trace. I won't have you adding risk to the hospital staff because you have a death wish."

"And if I fire you?" Diva Allison reared her ugly head.

Meaghan literally smiled at her. Not one of those mocking smiles that contained a threat. Nope. Meaghan wore a soft, pretty smile way more nerve-racking than one that challenged. "You're not my boss, so that would be difficult."

Allison wouldn't back down. "Who hired you?"

"A government agency that is looking for the same information you are. They tend to prefer other people do their dirty work, so they wanted you to finish the investigation, but obviously that won't happen. Instead, I'm here to protect you from whoever is trying to bury the story."

"And I can't investigate the story without my computer, so you'll never catch who made the bribe," Allison said as though she'd won the argument.

Zoe looked between the two women, and chose sides. Meaghan. While Allison was an unstoppable force at work, Meaghan made more sense. A computer would be a homing beacon to the bad guys.

"Meaghan's right." Zoe's voice was soft but firm, as though trying to convince a child that he did have to share the new markers in the classroom. "I can help you do some groundwork off-grid. I have nothing else to do for a few weeks before I start at the summer camp."

"Not a chance. I won't have you running amok and scaring away all of my potential sources."

"I don't run amok with anything." She reached for Allison's hand, holding it gently. She didn't want anything to do with this investigation, but she had no choice if she wanted to protect her sister.

A huge commotion came from outside the door. Meaghan reached for a gun, which made this whole ordeal feel much more dangerous. The door swung open and Marlowe rushed inside with Jason trying to control his leash. Noah stood beside him and quickly shut the door after they entered. Marlowe jumped on top of the bed.

"Marlowe!" Allison's face lit up. The dog landed far more gently than expected. He remained by her side and sniffed around her casts before settling down at the foot of her bed as though he had one job to do and he accomplished said job.

Meaghan broke out into laughter.

"Why is the dog in the hospital?" Noah asked Jason.

"If I did that, you'd place me on probation," Meaghan said with a grin.

"Good thing I'm me then," Jason replied with more confidence than the whole room combined. "I thought Allison could use the company, and honestly, Marlowe was driving Calvin and everyone else crazy." Jason's brows furrowed. His tense expression seemed to make Meaghan laugh louder.

"I never would have believed you'd be taken down by a beagle." She walked over to Marlowe and patted his back.

"Marlowe's too smart to be an apartment dweller. He needs a job or time with his owner." He looked between Zoe and Allison and paused. "You two couldn't avoid being recognized as sisters, even with your disguise and Allison's black eyes."

The mention of a flaw in Allison's appearance had her grasping for the mirror on her table tray.

"But we have bigger issues to worry about. I noticed two thugs circling the hospital on my way inside. Calvin's running the plates, but in the meantime, we all have to leave."

"Leave?" Meaghan said, glancing down at Allison's casts.

"Yes. Before they can confirm Allison's location. I estimate that we have less than four minutes. Wait here." Jason turned and walked out of the room.

Zoe stared at the back of the man who had just told them they were all in danger before casually strolling away. From the look on Meaghan's and Noah's faces, their focus had sharpened, yet they remained calm and stayed in the room.

Just over a minute later, Jason returned. He tossed a pair of scrubs at Zoe. "Put these on," he instructed before leaving again. Moments later, he returned with what looked like a large gurney with walls, resembling a mobile casket… Zoe stared at the contraption, realizing with a chill that they would be placing Allison in it.

"No. I will not be carried in that dead body box," Allison protested, a squeamish look overtaking her features.

"You're not in a position to negotiate," Meaghan replied firmly. "You can be treated like a corpse, or you can become one for real. Since I'm not in the mood to fight our way out of here, I've decided for you." Meaghan positioned everyone around Allison to help lift.

Jason ceded authority seamlessly, allowing Meaghan to take charge. Zoe watched as they transitioned from a group of individuals to a cohesive team. Seeing them work together with such confidence reassured her that they had some control of the situation, which made her feel a bit less nervous.

The four of them pulled Allison's sheet tight and shifted her, sheet and all, onto the gurney. When Allison found some semblance of comfort, Meaghan lifted the walls and covered her. Allison was completely hidden, leg cast and all.

Jason assured Allison he'd get the dog to her when she'd settled in to her new location. Then he glanced down the hall. "It's clear," he whispered. "Good luck." With a casual stride, he departed down the hall with Marlowe walking at his side and disappeared.

"Are you ready?" Noah asked Zoe. He seemed concerned, but he stayed back, holding Meaghan's hand as though they were a couple. She was a bit tall for him, although that was probably the three-inch boots she wore. Something bordering on jealousy went through Zoe. She wasn't sure if it was the hand-holding or the fact that they were able to remain dressed in the same clothes.

The danger, however, propelled her forward. She nodded to her sister's bodyguards and maneuvered the gurney with surprising agility. As she began to turn to the right, Meaghan coughed from behind her. "Left." Zoe turned left.

A nurse walked down the hall past them, her face pressed into a phone with only the slightest glance in Zoe's direction. People don't tend to notice average, and Zoe felt about as average as one could get.

As they went through the Emergency Room exit, cool fresh air greeted them. She wasn't sure where to go until she saw the sleek gray hearse parked inconspicuously by the curb.

"Hearse?" she said as though to herself.

"Yep," came a voice from behind her.

Zoe pushed her sister up to the back of the vehicle and swung open the rear door. It held the lingering smell of lilies, probably the scent of a thousand flowers that journeyed with prior occupants to their graves. Zoe wouldn't mention that to Allison. This was already far too morbid.

She slid her sister and the gurney mattress into the back. And then heard alarms going off in the hospital. Her instinct was to run. Before she could react, Noah was at her side, helping her move her sister inside and closing the door.

"Where's Meaghan?" she asked.

"Driving." He stepped back and pulled Zoe with him as the hearse drove away.

A few seconds later, two men ran out the Emergency Room exit. They were definitely looking for someone. Zoe had no idea what to do, but Noah's proximity gave her an idea. She wrapped her arms around his neck, pressed him against the wall, and kissed him. It wasn't anything epic, mostly because her body was shaking from the fear of being caught, but there was comfort in holding a man who didn't seem nearly as scared as she was. He held her tight and absorbed her fears and worries until the footsteps faded toward the side parking lot. Even then, she remained with her lips on his, drawing support from his physical and mental strength.

"How are we getting out of here?" she asked, lips still touching, and body warmly wrapped within his arms.

"My car. We'll wait another few minutes and then stroll at a casual pace to the car, not a care in the world. Can you do that?" His arm held her so tight, she could probably lift her feet off the ground and he'd hold her up.

"Yes. Just tell me when to stop." And she kissed him again.

Chapter 9

As Noah drove away from the hospital, he replayed kissing Zoe over in his mind. Actually, she'd kissed him and he'd enjoyed the hell out of it, even while trying to focus on her safety. Although he'd never forget how good her lips felt on his, his thoughts kept traveling back to the two guys who had been searching for Allison. He wanted to know who they were and how the team could protect Allison and Zoe while learning enough to shut down whatever criminal organization was involved.

"Are you okay?" he asked Zoe.

She nodded. Her face seemed flushed and her eyes betrayed her fear, no doubt from being chased down like prey. He didn't push a conversation because he had no idea what to say to her. So many thoughts twisted through him. So many emotions that he didn't want to be feeling—protectiveness, frustration, and an undeniable attraction to the woman he'd been assigned to protect.

Once in the underground garage at headquarters, Zoe lingered in the car, removing her wig wearily. Noah remained by her side as she strode with heavy steps toward the entrance. Her face was a blank page, drained of expression, as though she didn't have the energy to display any emotion.

When Zoe retreated to her room, Jason summoned Noah to the conference room. The problems compounding in this assignment followed close behind Noah, taunting him and reminding him that his last case had been a disaster. He measured himself against the top performers of the team, all with years more experience than he had. He was not yet in their caliber.

"You look exhausted," Jason said.

"I'm good," Noah lied. He wanted a nap and a shower, but he couldn't show weakness. Not to Jason, a person who rarely skipped a day of work and always seemed ready for anything.

"How was Zoe while escaping the hospital?"

"She blended in as hospital staff and handled moving her sister into the hearse without a problem." Noah would not mention the kiss between them.

"Perfect." He gestured for Noah to take the seat across from him. "I need you to stay with Zoe for the next few days. Keep an eye on her until we can make sure whoever is behind this won't go after Allison's family"

No more surveillance. This assignment would set him up for something bigger. Maybe international travel. The only problem involved his attraction to Zoe. No matter what happened, he had to make his decisions based on what was best for the team. Not that he'd ever do something that would harm someone innocent in all of this. In fact, he could handle his assignment, care for Zoe, and maintain a wall of professional detachment. The stakes were too high, and Jason's trust too valuable to lose. "I can handle it."

"You don't need to be glued to her side 24/7. We'll rotate you out for rest, although right now we're limited in field crew, but Fiona and I are available to assist you if you need it." Which meant this was their biggest case if both Jason and Fiona, Jason's wife, were working on it. That made it even more important for Noah to handle it like the best of the best.

The door opened and Zoe entered, dressed in sweatpants and a T-shirt, her hair wet from a shower, her energy revived, and her appearance a most beautiful distraction.

"Can I come in?" she asked.

Jason nodded and pointed to the chair next to Noah. "I'm sorry you had to be placed in such a tricky situation, but Noah told me you handled it well."

She stared at Noah for an uncomfortable minute, probably wondering what Noah had told Jason.

"You have the making of a spy. You moved your sister through the hospital with a calm that was impressive. And then we drove back here without incident. That's as good as it gets in terms of success." Noah didn't mention the kiss to assure her that he had skipped that aspect of their flight from the hospital.

"Thanks." She visibly relaxed. "I hope I never go through anything quite so crazy again. I could barely breathe by the time we got into his car. I just want to make sure Allison is okay."

"I have Meaghan online now. She and Allison are safe and Allison is set up comfortably." Jason turned an iPad toward them. The video call showed Meaghan in a nice-looking bedroom that seemed far better than the hospital where Allison had been staying.

"We're all settled. I'll keep you updated. Dr. M is here too, and can check in on her every few hours." Meaghan turned the video toward a queen-size bed with Allison resting on one side of it. She appeared comfortable and fast asleep. Marlowe, as asleep as his master, stretched out, his head resting against Allison's arm. Dr. Morgan, wearing her pink pants and a soft cream-colored sweater, stood next to her with a stethoscope draped around her neck.

"Where are you?" Zoe asked.

"I can't tell you. Her location is unknown to everyone but me and the good doctor. No one can leak information they don't have," Meaghan answered.

The stillness of the new room with Allison's soft breathing and the occasional beep of a monitor should give Zoe confidence that Fresh Pond Security was taking good care of her sister. However, from what Noah knew about Allison, she wouldn't take her forced time off easily. Once awake, she'd return to being the intrepid reporter who had uncovered the bribe at City Hall, even though her life had been nearly cut short at far too young an age. The threats would persist as long as Allison continued to pursue the source of the bribe, placing her sister at risk as well.

On this side of the monitor, Zoe stared at the screen, her brown hair up in a loose ponytail. Without the wig, their resemblance was even more striking. Noah's plan for Zoe to impersonate Allison to retrieve the notes and evidence in her office seemed like their best option for handling the case. It was a risk, but so was keeping the women in protective custody for an indeterminate time.

Now was the best time to get this plan in motion. Before Allison's absence brought her too much scrutiny. If Jason disagreed, they'd need a different means of finding the source of the bribe.

Breaking the silence, Noah leaned forward in his chair. "We need to obtain the information Allison left in her office. Calvin and his team as well as all of us could find out information that would lead to an understanding of whoever is behind the bribes and the attacks. We could break in, but I think there's a less risky plan. Zoe, dressed as Allison, walking in and out in under an hour." He turned to Zoe. "I know this is a lot to ask, but stepping into Allison's shoes might be our only chance to expose the corruption she uncovered."

Zoe's frown deepened, her annoyance at him bringing the idea up again visible. She responded before he could say anything else. Her frown making him almost regret his suggestion...almost. "What you're suggesting is insane. I'm a teacher, not an undercover agent. You can't seriously expect me to fool anyone into believing I'm Allison."

Jason nodded in agreement, his words a blow to Noah's confidence. "Zoe has a point. This plan is too high-risk. If there is a leak in the company, she would be at risk and so would our investigation. Without proper training, innocent people could get killed, and we could spook the very people we need to observe."

Noah felt Jason's words like a sucker punch. The complete rejection of his idea didn't bode well for his career goals. To be fair, Jason had watched Noah's failed attempt at saving Matt, Jason's son, from kidnappers.

Meaghan nodded in agreement with their boss. Her loyalty would always be with Jason, as he'd rescued her from a very bad situation at the police station where she'd worked, giving her more money and security than she'd ever received on the police force. "She's not trained for this kind of operation. This whole plan would be too much to ask of her."

"I'm not spy material," Zoe agreed. "I have a job and a life I love. Risking my life this afternoon was more than enough adventure for me for a whole lifetime."

Allison stirred and everyone fell into a charged silence. Even in her sleep, Allison commanded the room. Her bruised face wore a confident countenance and had the bone structure of a queen. Zoe did too, but she seemed afraid to step into her own power. She preferred a life on the sidelines, and he wasn't going to convince her otherwise.

She exchanged glances with Jason. "I'm sorry but I'm far more of a risk than I am a help."

Allison's wakening voice cut through the conversation. "Are you all out of your minds? Zoe, pretending to be me? She can barely stand in high heels, never mind speak in front of a camera."

Zoe's response came fast, as though a sibling rivalry reared its head in the middle of their debate. "Allison, I…"

"She could never be confused for me. Ever." Allison made a face that was as much an insult to Zoe as the words she spoke. "Zoe is… Zoe. She's not me. She's kind, gentle, not cut out for anything that involves bravery. No offense, Zoe. You see the best in people, believe in the goodness of the world. How can you possibly navigate the backstabbing world I walk through every day?"

She had a point. And part of Noah couldn't help but

feel drawn to Zoe's inherent goodness, a quality too rare in his line of work. Yet, she'd also demonstrated nerves of steel when thrust into the middle of a crime drama. If she was falling apart, she did a great job hiding it.

"As much as I hate to say it, the more I think about it, the more I like the plan." Jason's deep voice rumbled across the room, taking back control of the situation. "As Noah mentioned, Zoe, you're rarely in Boston, and very few people know Allison has a twin. If we proceed, we need to meticulously plan every detail. The more I think about it, the more I agree with Noah. In and out quick and no one will be the wiser." He turned to Allison. "We know it's a risk. But Zoe's unique position could give us the leverage we need. And with more information, we can help break your story, handing you all the credit if you need credit. This isn't about throwing Zoe into the fire, it's about using the element of surprise to our advantage."

Zoe's eyes met Noah's. A storm of uncertainty clouded them. "But I'm not an investigator. I don't have Allison's instincts, her experience. How can I convincingly step into her life, her investigation?" She said it not so much as a rejection of the plan, but as an honest interest in the logistics of the assignment.

Noah paused and made sure to frame his next statement as perfectly as possible in order to keep her confidence up and not scare her away. "You're more than capable of handling an hour or so in a newsroom. I'm sure you paste on a happy face every day when you meet up with your students."

"I love teaching."

"Every day?"

She looked down. "Well, no, but…"

"Exactly. You have to pretend sometimes and the kids are none the wiser. You swallow down your emotions to provide for a solid classroom experience. And you do that for what, seven or eight hours at a time? That's not easy. You have an innate understanding of people and you have major problem-solving skills. What teacher doesn't? Trying to line up twenty kids when one goes rogue. How often have you handled something like that?"

He could see her mind racing. She knew how talented she was but in a different context. It wouldn't be hard to transfer those skills for a small portion of one day. Especially since she was pretending to be the person she was closest to in the world. "These aren't qualities you can teach or fake," he continued. "They're uniquely yours, and in this situation, they'll be a huge asset."

Allison tried to sit up, but was hindered by the weight of her leg cast. "That's a pretty picture you're painting. But be realistic. Zoe teaching third graders is not the same in any way as working at a cutthroat newsroom. She's not only never left her hometown, she never left the home where we were born."

"I stayed on the island, Allison, because someone had to remain with Dad after Mom died. You chose to leave and that left me with no choice at all. But I'm not complaining. I love my life and wouldn't trade it for all the fancy shoes in your enormous closet. That doesn't mean I'm some country bumpkin, and you're this international jet-setter. I'll have you know that school board meetings are vicious. Our new principal is set on dumbing down the curriculum in order to boost his class promotion

rates and obliterate the budget, a plan I have been fighting every chance I get. I battle a whole lot of assholes
every single day. A newsroom just might be a picnic
for me." Zoe's voice carried a newfound edge of defi-
ance. Allison's words must have stirred up a whole lot
of resentment that had remained unsaid over the years.

The room stilled, the weight of her words hanging in
the air. Noah's respect for Zoe lifted to new levels. She
wasn't some pushover. She had more of a backbone than
anyone had given her credit for, which made Noah's plan
all the more plausible now. "Zoe, listen to yourself. This
passion you have, it's exactly what we need. You're more
like Allison than you realize."

Zoe hesitated, her retort wavering as she processed
his words. She'd probably been told Allison was the
golden child her whole life and moving out of that role
into her own sunshine was a huge step.

"I have to admit, she's got spirit. Perhaps we were
too quick to judge her capabilities earlier." Jason spoke
with a hint of newfound respect for Zoe. He'd recently
stopped judging people by their appearances after he
learned that his very short, very curvy wife, Fiona, had
been an operative for the government without Jason or
anyone outside the smallest of circles knowing. She had
been perfect for her job because many people looked her
over with her Marilyn Monroe demeanor and assumed
she had no idea what was going on around her. That allowed her to go places and do things without having
any suspicion landing on her. A whole team from Fresh
Pond Security had seen her in action and all agreed to
never let their guard down around her.

"It's not just about her resemblance to you, Allison,"

Meaghan said. "It's about having the courage to stand up when it counts. And Zoe is showing a lot of grit right now."

Meaghan also told Noah she did not like working for divas. They thought they deserved to call all the shots and could place everyone around them at risk. Her annoyance with Allison didn't bode well for their time together in the near future.

Zoe, on the other hand, seemed to have everyone's well-being at heart in her actions. Noah would have mentioned the kiss at the hospital, where she shielded herself from view by two men and whatever weapons they carried, but he didn't want to embarrass her. Not that what she'd done should cause embarrassment, instead it proved that she had great instincts, but she seemed the type to ignore her success.

As the debate continued, with the whole Fresh Pond team defending Zoe, Noah observed a transformation in her. Her eyes lit up with a fire that had, until then, been mostly hidden, except for when she pretended to be Allison back at headquarters. Her performance proved she was more than capable of acting as her sister with the right motivation. She'd have gotten away with it if Meaghan hadn't checked in with Jason about her and Allison's location.

He watched as Zoe handled their compliments and observations. He could be a real bastard and push her decision from a solid "no" to a half-hearted "yes," but he hesitated, remembering Jason's son feeling safe under his protection before being kidnapped by a drug cartel. While he cared about breaking cases that could make the world safer for everyone, he needed to minimize the risks toward innocent people caught up in the chaos of the criminal world. If Zoe got hurt, he might never forgive himself. And the thought of any harm coming to her made him fearful of how he'd be able to handle the inevitable danger around them without compromising the case.

"I'm not going to let anyone take my place. That's illegal, impersonating a reporter," Allison said, her anger focused on Zoe more than any of the other people in both spaces.

Although she had a point, this was sanctioned by some high-level law enforcement agencies. Fresh Pond Security had a certain amount of protection offered to them as part of their arrangement. No one in the conference room would be indicted in their attempt to capture the person who bribed City Hall.

"You'd really have me prosecuted? When I'd do it to keep you safe?" Zoe asked, her brows lifted.

Allison clenched her hand into a fist. "I don't need your protection."

"No. You're doing a bang-up job of keeping yourself safe. You went to an isolated area where someone could have just as easily shot you in the head and left your dead body to rot." Zoe shook her head as though clearing the picture out of her mind.

Interesting, Noah thought. She actually made a statement in favor of stepping into the ruse.

Noah didn't shine any light on her sudden burst of courage. Instead, he spoke to Meaghan and Jason. "She'd be far more protected than Allison was at the Enchanted Forest. It's not like we'd leave her alone. She'd have someone accompany her at all times for safety."

Meaghan stepped forward before Noah could volunteer. "If Noah can stay with Allison, I can go with Zoe." Meaghan never begged off a current assignment, but in this case, being locked away with a demanding, drama magnet, Noah understood.

Jason, however, disagreed. "You're assigned to Allison. I like the idea of Noah posing as Allison's new boyfriend and accompanying Zoe to the studio." He looked over at Noah. "Act curious about all the inner workings of the studio. I want you inside that producer's office to see if we can dig up something that would explain why he'd risk Allison for a story. Allison can create a map and help you and Zoe familiarize yourselves with the office layout, names, and positions of people to avoid arousing suspicion."

Meaghan nodded in agreement. "Of course. Are you okay with this plan, Zoe?" she asked, ignoring Allison's huff from the bed.

Zoe ignored her sister as well, focusing on Jason. "No, not entirely, but maybe..." And at that second, Noah knew they had her.

His gaze lingered on her, relieved he wasn't going to be sent over to babysit Allison. He didn't want to leave Zoe's side partly because the thought of Meaghan spending more time with her annoyed him. He also wanted to keep an eye on her while she was in a vulnerable position. And now he had his chance.

"Good," Jason declared. "It's settled. We're going to call you Allison from the moment we leave the hospital. You have to hear that name and react as though it's yours. It might take twenty-four to forty-eight hours to get you to a place where you'll feel more confident."

"More confident in Allison's really high shoes?" Zoe asked.

"More confident interacting with anyone who might know Allison. Noah and our team will handle the logistics. Just stay by Noah's side. Then when you're done, we'll relocate you for a week or so until we see what comes of this."

"What am I supposed to do?" Allison said, her annoyance growing.

"Help your sister get the information she needs and rest. No phone, no emails, unless we're in the room monitoring what you say. For the time Zoe's in the newsroom, we'll transfer your cell number to a temporary phone that can't be traced. Your phone is going to be shut down with the card removed until everything is ready to return to normal."

"You can't take my phone. I have rights."

Meaghan stood at the foot of her bed, her brows furrowed. "You would place your career and your own happiness over your sister's safety?"

"That's not fair."

"That's the reality. I'll be here with you," Meaghan said with a placating smile. "We can have lots of fun together. Do you play cribbage?"

Allison shook her head, completely shut down.

"Great." Meaghan clapped her hands together. "I'll teach you. It's a life skill worth having. Like golf, but for rainy nights with wine."

Jason interrupted Meaghan's pep rally. "Before you pull out your cribbage board and a deck of cards, Allison needs to call her producer and tell her she's still gathering information and will be back in the office soon,"

Jason said. "You need to make this call right now from Meaghan's burner phone. You've already been out of contact for far too long. It's vital to keep them thinking you're still investigating."

"And lie to my producer? No. What if he's innocent and I lose my job?" Allison said, as though her actions had no impact on anyone else in the room.

Jason's expression was unyielding, which meant he was one hundred percent on board with the plan. Allison's reluctance was understandable, yet the urgency of their situation left little room for debate. "It's the only way to buy us some time. To keep them off Zoe's back and give her a fighting chance to dig deeper. Make it happen, Meaghan."

Meaghan nodded, her personality hardened into someone who didn't play games. "She'll make the call."

With a shaky hand, Allison took the phone, her voice barely a whisper as she dialed the number. "Fine, but if this blows up, it's on all of you." A hint of her usual fiery spirit burned the air even in her weakened state.

The room fell silent when she spoke to whomever was on the other line. "Glenn? Hi, yes. I'm okay. It was crazy. The person showed up, but drove off in a huff as though they chickened out... No we never had contact and I didn't get the license plate, but I was looking over my notes and I have a few more leads. I've been following up on each one. I should be back in the office in a day or two... No, I don't want to come in before I'm ready. I promise to keep in contact... No, I can't say more right now. Just know that I'm on it." Despite her condition, Allison played her part convincingly, setting up a situation where Zoe would be able to walk into the newsroom without too much interest pointed at her. Unless the coroner leaked Mrs. Peterson's death. That would create a whole bigger issue. One that Noah couldn't worry about at the moment.

Once the call was over, Allison's hand dropped to her side, the annoyance remaining in her expression.

Jason and Noah exchanged a glance, an unspoken acknowledgment that they'd willingly placed themselves one step too close to the cliff's edge.

"Okay. Go get some rest and I'll meet you in a few hours in Conference Room two." Jason waved Noah and Zoe from the room. "I have a few questions for Allison."

Noah turned to Zoe, who had been a silent observer during this exchange. "Are you ready? We've got a lot of ground to cover and not much time."

She nodded and glanced back at the screen. "Take care of yourself, Ally."

"I don't have much of a choice, do I?"

Zoe took a deep breath. "Okay, let's do this."

With that, Noah and Zoe stepped toward the door.

"Wait," Allison called out to them.

Zoe and Noah turned around.

"Be careful," she called out.

Zoe nodded and something just short of a smile appeared on her face. "I'll do my best."

Chapter 10

Zoe stepped into the hallway with Noah, the tension from the discussions with Jason and Allison ringing in her ears. Despite the refreshing shower she'd taken earlier, her whole body felt like a plant that lacked water. Stepping into her sister's shoes presented an almost impossible task. Allison was right. Zoe had never mastered her sister's style and confidence. There was too much on the line for her to believe she could just wing it.

A short fashionable blonde wandered down the hallway. Jason's wife, Fiona. Dressed in jeans and a loose black blouse, she stood in heels without the slightest sign of distress. Fiona's self-assuredness unnerved Zoe.

"I heard about your harrowing day," Fiona said while holding Zoe's hands. "Jason asked me to stop by to see if you need anything."

Her voice faltered as she admitted, "I think I've made a huge mistake. I don't think I'm as capable as you all think I am."

"Nonsense. You'll be fine. Everyone starts somewhere, but let's not worry about that until tomorrow." Fiona handed her a business card. "You need a decent amount of sleep and a few moments to process everything. If you wake in the middle of the night and need to talk, don't hesitate to contact me. I like to be disturbed."

"Thank you."

"No worries. There's wine in the kitchen and herbal tea too if that will help you sleep. I'll see you first thing in the morning."

Zoe's nerves frayed. "You're leaving?"

"I need to get home to my son. You're safe here. There's not a safer place in the city, and Noah will be asleep in the next room. He's harmless toward people he likes."

Fiona didn't have to say anything for Zoe to trust Noah. She already did. He'd protected her, but he'd also volunteered her for the most dangerous job she'd ever held. "I don't know how I'll learn everything I need to know in a few days."

"Time is an advantage. We can make you into a replica of Allison with a month, but we need the information now," Fiona responded, her voice low and measured. "I agree with Noah about you giving us a tactical advantage. You know your sister, her mannerisms, her life. That's invaluable. But—" she paused, weighing her next words "—turning you into someone who can convincingly infiltrate a news station in a week will be a challenge."

Zoe's heart sank. The reality of Fiona's words hit hard. She was a third-grade teacher, not a spy. Her expertise lay in lesson plans, not espionage.

"I know. That's why I said I didn't want to do it," she murmured, glaring at Noah as her certainty faded. "I don't know why I agreed."

"You agreed, because it's the best way to keep you

and your sister safe in the future. As long as these guys want Allison silenced, they will keep going after her, and you too," Noah said.

Zoe studied him a moment, then bit her lip. "I'll just be getting you inside the news station, right?"

"More or less," Fiona replied. "Once Noah is on the inside, it's up to you to keep a level head. Even if someone accuses you of being a fake, you need to hold to your part. While the physical danger is there, it's the psychological game that you need to handle."

Noah nodded. "I'll have your back and we'll have a backup team behind us as well. Success is getting the information we're looking for and leaving before anyone notices anything out of the ordinary."

"But that's the problem. I have no idea what is ordinary in Allison's job."

"We'll figure it out together." He smiled, but his words weren't reassuring.

Fiona looked between them. "On second thought, it could only benefit us to give you some extra training. Tactical and physical defense is important, but more important is the ability to think under stressful circumstances. And thinking out of the box. Zoe, you can leverage your unique insights into your sister's life. You need to think like her, anticipate how she would react. That's your real advantage here. Noah, you need to convince yourself that even without the on-the-ground experience the others have, that you are just as able to handle whatever is thrown your way."

Noah frowned. "I believe in my abilities. It's Jason who doesn't."

"You are so wrong. He would never let you do anything he thought you couldn't handle." She put two closed fists in front of them. "Before I let you go to your rooms, here's your first challenge as a team. Which hand has a quarter in it?"

"Seriously?" Noah asked.

"Seriously. You can work it out together, but one answer."

It was as though Zoe had been sent into another dimension. One where she had to solve puzzles as the clock closed in on midnight. She could not believe life had brought her here.

Noah seemed to be rolling his eyes but Fiona stood with conviction, her hands offering no clues. Zoe shook her head, trying to wake up her brain after an impossibly long day. Fiona definitely did not have the look of a woman kidding, so Zoe stared at her hands. She hadn't noticed Fiona holding a coin or anything else for that matter, although maybe she should have. If Fiona pulled it from somewhere, there weren't a lot of options. She was wearing a long-sleeve shirt and jeans, but she'd never placed her hands in her pocket.

Zoe shrugged. "There isn't a quarter."

Fiona smiled. "You need to make that decision with Noah."

"This is ridiculous. She's exhausted," Noah said, but continued staring at Fiona's hands.

"So make a decision."

Something about Fiona's self-assurance woke Zoe up from her fatigue. She looked over at Noah, her former protector and new partner. "Well?" she asked him.

"Fiona is known to carry a pocketbook that doubles as Noah's Ark. It has everything in it. I've never known her to carry anything in her pockets, although I have seen her pull a knife out of a boot before."

Fiona laughed in that way a goddess laughed at the silly things mere mortals said. "A quarter. You don't have to analyze anything else I may have on my person."

Zoe didn't know whether she should laugh, because, although Fiona didn't look like the type who would harm anyone with a knife, the glint in her eyes said that she most certainly would. Noah wasn't laughing and that said a lot too.

"Can you turn your hands over?" Noah asked.

Fiona complied. They both looked identical.

This was such a silly test. She either had a quarter or didn't and it was in her left hand or her right hand. Two things to guess.

"Where did you come from?" Noah asked.

"Picking Matt up from the library and dropping him off at home."

"Where is the library?"

"Concord."

"And you can pay for parking with quarters there still, which you would, because you hate leaving any technological footprint." Noah grinned, as though he'd solved the whole problem. It would make sense she'd have a quarter if she planned on parking there.

"True, but there are cameras set up that can pick someone up on Main Street."

Zoe wasn't sure whether Fiona was incredibly paranoid or she truly had that level of awareness about everything around her. "How much is parking?" she asked.

"One dollar for on street parking."

"Did you pay to park?"

"Matt, in his infinite wisdom, chose to wait at the curb."

Noah went into his own pocket, pulled out his car keys, and without the slightest preamble, threw the keys at Fiona as hard as he could. Zoe's mouth dropped open at her inability to even warn Fiona. Without the slightest shift in her stance, Fiona caught the keys with her right hand.

"One quarter, the left hand," Noah said as though he'd tossed her the keys gently.

Fiona opened her left hand and there was the quarter. She turned toward Zoe as though she was the bellman of a swanky hotel. "Let me walk you to your room."

Zoe couldn't respond. As a teacher, that would never be the way to solve a situation. Yet, it got the job done. She had to really rethink so much about how she got through life.

"Zoe," Fiona said as she walked down the hall, her expression softening, "this isn't about turning you into a soldier. It's about expanding the skills you already have. You're not going into the studio alone. You'll have us backing you every step of the way."

Noah followed them and Zoe glanced back at him. He seemed to have his own shadows following him. Did he think he lacked the skills for this job? Because he sure as heck saved her life.

Zoe's resolve wavered under the weight. "I'm not sure I can…"

Fiona interrupted. "Noah thinks you can give us an edge. And Jason trusts his instincts. I do too. We'll give you some basic training—enough to keep you safe and make you useful."

"But in a few days?"

"It's not ideal," Noah answered. "But Fiona is no mere instructor. She'll give you a crash course in tactical thinking, observation, and evasion."

"Flattering, but you'll be just as involved. You both have to trust each other." She gave them a wave. "I'm off. Make sure you get at least a few hours of sleep."

Noah escorted Zoe the rest of the way. Her room now had a bottle of water and a glass on the bedside table as well as fresh flowers in a vase. Peonies.

"My favorites," she said, stepping to them and lightly brushing a finger over one of the petals.

"You had some on the kitchen island at Allison's," Noah said. "I thought they'd cheer up your space. It can get a bit sterile in here."

"They're perfect." Zoe relaxed further when she saw two pairs of sweats, some T-shirts, and a duffel bag where she hoped she would find some toiletries. She turned to him. He leaned against the doorframe, not stepping inside the room, a very respectful thing to do. "I hope I don't let you down. You seem to have far more faith in my ability than I do."

"That will change over the next few days. In the morning, we'll assess your skills, see where you stand. Then, we can tailor your training to maximize your strengths and mitigate your weaknesses. You probably have a lot more skills than you know."

Their eyes met, and Zoe stepped closer to him, mesmerized by everything about him. She didn't care that the door was open, nor did she care about whatever she was being asked to do. She only thought about how beautiful his eyes were. He took a stride forward, the heat of his body radiating toward her. His hand reached up, almost instinctively, to brush a strand of hair from her face. Her breath hitched, her heart pounded in her chest. But then Noah hesitated, his hand lingering near her cheek. He searched her eyes, as if seeking permission, and Zoe leaned in, drawn by a need for something solid to hold as her world swirled around in chaos. She closed her eyes and waited, but when she opened them, he'd pulled back from her.

"Good night, Zoe," he whispered, his voice husky and low.

"Good night," she choked out.

After a lingering glance, he walked away, leaving Zoe standing alone at the door with a racing heart and a hunger for a not-so-chaste good night kiss. As she got ready for bed, her thoughts stayed on Noah and what his lips would be like on hers. If he'd wanted to release the stress she'd been under, he achieved his goal. She was still nervous about tomorrow, but now all she could think about was what would have been an amazing good night kiss.

Chapter 11

Noah had come so close to crossing the line with Zoe. She had somehow claimed his heart. And he'd been only one inch from claiming her mouth, but self-preservation kicked in before Jason could turn the corner and see him kissing the person he was supposed to be protecting. In another world, where he wasn't assigned to protect her, he'd have taken her in his arms and held her all night. But he couldn't. Not to mention that she was the type of woman who probably wanted a husband and kids. His current job required him to travel and be away for weeks and months at a time. Even if he wanted to be with his family, the logistics of his schedule would make it difficult. In other words, they'd be better off not going there.

Now that the case was back on with Zoe playing a significant role, he had to make sure the plan went off without any problems. His mind kept drifting back to her smile, the way her eyes lit up when she talked about her students. He went into his office and shut the door. He regretted involving her in this. She'd stepped into the crosshairs of some very dangerous people and should have been sent away to a safe place until the risk dissipated. Tomorrow, Zoe, a third-grade teacher, would begin a two-day training exercise that would never prepare her for the risk she'd accepted. In fact, she was more likely to get overwhelmed by too much information and forget what they taught her. As much as he wanted to figure out who was behind the bribe and the murder of Allison's neighbor, he didn't want Zoe hurt in any way.

A text message pinged on his phone from Finn. Finn Maguire had been Noah's closest friend since he'd moved to Boston and joined Fresh Pond Security, but Finn quit after Jason admitted he'd lied to the team about his identity, pretending to be dead so a drug cartel would leave his family alone. He wouldn't stay where he didn't trust the leadership, because he'd already been stabbed in the back when Finn's superior officer lied about Finn's involvement in something he had nothing to do with. The betrayal resulted in Finn's dishonorable discharge. Noah missed working with him.

The text message had a picture of a nice black Ferrari.

Noah: New wheels?

Finn: Just arrived on the lot for someone with two hundred thousand to spare.

Noah: I doubt I'll ever have that much in spare change. And worse, my assignment is hammering me. Do you ever miss it?

The phone rang.

"I miss it all the time. I'm not a born salesman but will

manage until the next job comes along. What's wrong?" Finn asked.

Noah explained the situation without giving away the specifics. "Is it wrong to have someone so unprepared go into a deadly situation?"

"Does she want to do it?"

"She said she did, but it was after some arm-twisting." Even as Noah said the words, he could feel the hypocrisy. He'd pushed her into it, and her sister had helped provide the final jab. Zoe was the type of person who would sacrifice herself for everyone around her's benefit. Even if she was ultimately not acting in her own best interests.

"So you like her?"

"Wh-what?" Noah stammered. Finn's words lodged straight under his skin.

"I've always known you to place the good of an assignment over everything else. Not that you would go out of your way to hurt anyone, but the woman agreed to assist. Why the guilt?"

"I pushed her into it."

"Does it make sense for the assignment?"

"Yes, but…"

"And will you be with her to keep her safe?"

"Yes, but…"

"Seems to me that it's a no-brainer. And from what I know of Jason, despite the fact that he lied to us, he is a hard-core professional. He wouldn't send anyone into a dangerous situation without adequate backup."

"That's true."

"So put your energy into helping her get through the next few days, instead of stressing over what can't be undone. You're on this. I would trust you by my side any day." His words meant everything. Finn was the best of the best when it came to security and protection.

"Thanks. Any chance I can persuade you into coming back and standing by my side for a change?"

The pause was uncomfortable. Their friendship had meant everything and Noah could already anticipate his reply.

"Not this week. Catch you later, brother."

And then he was gone and Noah felt a bit more alone.

The next morning after little sleep, Noah ran into Zoe, dressed in jeans and a cable-knit sweater, in the kitchen. Her eyes sparkled with vitality, and her face glowed with a well-rested charm that accentuated her natural beauty. He felt overtired and grungy. He didn't have a bedroom at headquarters, so he slept uncomfortably on the couch. Not that he minded much. He was working in the field again. And he would prove that he could handle bigger and bigger assignments. He didn't need rest. If Jason asked him to fly over a small building, he'd figure out a way to do just that.

Zoe held a coffee mug between her hands as though it were a religious artifact. Noah's eyes lingered on her, drawn to the way her lips curved into a gentle smile.

"How are you feeling?" he asked, his voice softer than usual, betraying a hint of concern he couldn't fully mask.

Her eyes met his with a hint of a memory of the night before and what could have been if he'd moved one inch closer. "I just woke up, but I'm ready for a nap."

"Not until after the sparring," Fiona replied, walking in the door.

"Sparring? What happened to going in and out of the building?"

"You need some self-defense moves. Nothing dramatic, but I wouldn't feel right about sending you in there with no skills. I think you have some appropriate outfits in the closet in your room. There's a gym down the hall. See you in ten." Fiona grabbed an apple from a bowl of fruit and strolled out again.

Zoe refilled her mug and disappeared. When Noah saw her again, she was wearing a gray UMass T-shirt and black leggings.

"Are you ready?" Noah met her at her door after changing into a Salt Life T-shirt and board shorts. It wasn't the most appropriate gear for sparring, but he wanted her to feel comfortable with him.

"You look prepared to hit some waves," she said.

"I wish. I haven't had time in years to do anything other than a few miles of running."

"Where did you surf?"

"Long Beach. I grew up there." California was a totally different vibe from New England. Not better, not worse, just different.

"Why did you move to Massachusetts?"

"Jason offered me a job that I'd always wanted. So I picked up and moved." It was a chance to live outside the office. He only regretted it after being shot and sent to desk duty while healing.

"Do you miss the sun?"

"I miss my sister, otherwise, I'm happy here." He pointed down the hall, trying to get her to hurry—they were three minutes late. "Come on. Fiona, although new to the group, has the ability to make our lives miserable. We all fear her in a way."

"You fear Fiona? She's so tiny and doesn't appear the least bit athletic." Zoe, a woman who didn't seem that judgmental, was certainly judging.

"Underestimate her at your own risk."

Two hours later, Zoe would never underestimate Fiona again. She was on her back on the mat in the middle of the floor, panting as though she'd run a marathon while Fiona stood over her looking as though she'd just walked in from a hair appointment.

"Again," Fiona said to her.

"It's no use. I won't gain muscle memory in two days."

"Mind over matter. Besides, without any training, you'll be in a worse position."

Zoe stayed on the mat and shook her head.

"Let's see how you handle someone Noah's size." Fiona stepped back after throwing Zoe on the ground a hundred times, strangling her, and punching at her face and stopping millimeters short of breaking her nose.

Previously, Noah had been the attacker toward Fiona to show Zoe how to do the moves. Now he was stepping toward an exhausted and frustrated woman who had no energy to even feign a defense. He hesitated, not wanting to hurt her, but knowing she needed to be prepared. This was not the way to build trust with her, but Fiona told Zoe to get on her feet and for Noah to step behind her. He grabbed her ponytail, and instead of pulling away as she had on most of the previous attempts by Fiona, Zoe turned into him and slammed her fist right into his groin, then slammed her other arm into his back forcing him to the ground. The pain took Noah's breath away.

Although he caught himself before he hit the floor, he released his grip on her hair. Noah stepped back, his eyes tearing and his vision off.

"That was perfect," Fiona said to Zoe, with no thought to Noah's pain.

Zoe rushed over to him and placed her hand on his shoulder. "Are you okay?"

He nodded and forced a lame smile. "That's exactly how you need to protect yourself."

He glared at Fiona, but she merely shook her head. "If you wore the correct gear, you wouldn't be bowled over. I think we're done for the day."

"That's it?" Zoe replied, her hand still resting on Noah's shoulder. "How is this going to help me act like Allison in the newsroom?"

"Take a shower and come back after lunch. We're done with self-defense, but you have a lot to learn before you go to sleep."

Zoe turned one more time to Noah. "I'm sorry."

"Don't be. You did everything right." He meant it. If something happened, she'd have to know how to defend herself. And Fiona was right, he hadn't anticipated Zoe's strength when arriving in the gym, but she had to fight like she meant it. And she did.

The first part of the afternoon was spent on beauty treatments with Zoe getting a manicure and pedicure as well as her hair trimmed and colored to add the subtle highlights of her sister. Noah worked with Calvin during that time getting more of the security logistics of the assignment.

When he returned to see Zoe in action, he stalled at the door. The chill Zoe who wore sweatshirts and baggy jeans was now dressed in a tight black pencil skirt and pale green silk blouse with black high heels. Allison's twin in almost every way, until she took a few steps in her shoes. He leaned against the wall of the conference room, arms folded, trying not to look discouraging. Or to laugh. The main problem was that Zoe looked like her sister, but her mannerisms were low-key elementary school teacher, not überconfident television personality. The mission hinged on how convincingly she could impersonate Allison, an idea that seemed more far-fetched with each passing moment. Her facial expression beamed self-doubt. How could identical twins have such opposite personalities? He'd always had a great head for problem-solving but here he missed the mark.

At least Fiona had accepted the position of taskmaster. Her easygoing manner never once showed the frustration that even the stylist Eleni exhibited when Zoe almost toppled into a chair when trying on a pair of her sister's heels. Clothes, shoes, and makeup boxes were strewn about the floor and table, a chaotic attempt to transform Zoe from a third-grade teacher into a savvy and sophisticated news reporter.

Fiona held up a tablet, playing clips of Allison on air. Zoe copied whatever Allison said and tried to gesture with her hands and assume her stance in a similar manner. Whatever she was doing seemed awkward and out of place compared to her sister. Which was strange, because the day before, as she handled all sorts of big issues, she'd acted far stronger and more competent.

Fiona had brought in a full-length mirror so Zoe could mimic her sister's facial expressions. She was trying too hard. Draped in a sleek blazer right out of Allison's closet, she faced her reflection with pinched lips and furrowed brows.

"You look like you hate everyone in the world. Can you lift your chin and smile? See how she commands attention? It's all in the posture, the eye contact," Fiona directed, tapping the screen for emphasis.

"I see it, but..." Zoe's voice trailed off as she tried to mimic the stance.

Eleni pushed forward and adjusted Zoe's posture. "Darling, it's like you're apologizing for existing. Shoulders back, chin up. You're a lioness, not a mouse. Show us fierce."

Zoe, still staring at herself, lifted her brows, shifted her posture, but made such a forced expression, she almost looked like a caricature of herself. "This isn't working." She attempted to stride toward Noah in her new high heels, wobbling slightly. "I feel more like a circus performer," she joked, trying to lighten the mood, until she tripped and fell into Noah's arms.

He held her a moment, before feeling the heat of Fiona's stare and the wilting of Zoe's confidence. Lifting her back to a standing position, he thought about the circus performers he'd seen in his life. They walked on high wires with more ease than she walked on the floor.

"I want you to stay in heels until you go to bed tonight." Fiona pointed at Zoe's feet.

"All day? Then I really will be like Allison because I'll end up in the hospital with a broken leg just like her."

"Doubtful. After a few hours, you'll get your balance. It's like riding a bike. Once your body knows how to shift the weight to keep your balance, it will become one hundred times easier." Fiona turned to Eleni. "Thank you for your help. We could use your services tomorrow and the next day, before she goes into the newsroom."

"I thought Allison said her makeup gets done on the set."

"It does, but she always wears a base before heading into the newsroom. You have a simpler makeup style and you also need your hair blown out before you go." Fiona didn't seem to notice Zoe rolling her eyes. She'd endured an hour getting her hair styled. And tomorrow she'd do it again?

The long wavy hair that just yesterday had been pulled tight in a ponytail under a baseball hat looked good on her, but the maintenance wasn't worth it for most people. Noah was thankful for his shorter, low-maintenance style. A little gel, a quick minute under the hair dryer, and a swish of hair wax to keep his cowlick from running amok.

After Eleni left, their attention shifted to a mock newsroom setup. Each role and function appeared on a SMART Board with the current employees in each role at the studio. A Face Time video of Allison appeared to the right of the diagram, sitting at a table with a large window behind her. The background to the video seemed familiar. The cabin where Fresh Pond Security sent people who had to be removed from view for a while. Their other safe house, a very high-tech facility that seemed more like a dilapidated colonial farmhouse from the outside had been blown up at the time Jason and Fiona's son, Matt, was kidnapped. Allison, dressed in a sweatshirt with her hair put up in a ponytail seemed more like Zoe. It was as though they'd shifted bodies.

"I'm glad you could be here with us," Fiona said to the screen.

"It's no problem. I'm bored out of my mind." She turned her face toward Zoe. "You don't look anything like me," she said, causing Zoe's confidence to falter.

Noah wanted to strangle Allison. After spending all day trying to build her up, one comment from her sister could send her tumbling.

"Yes, you do look like Allison. Exactly like her," Meaghan said, appearing behind Allison. "Nice job. Love the highlights."

Zoe's expression brightened.

"I've been teaching your sister cribbage," Meaghan continued, deftly changing the subject. "She'll make a formidable opponent when she decides to focus." Marlowe barked in the background and she shook her head toward him. "I'll be back after I take this little monster outside." As Meaghan walked off-screen, everyone could hear her calling out to him, "Are you the bestest boy? Let's go outside for a minute and then we have to get back."

"How are you doing?" Zoe yelled toward the screen at Allison.

Her sister lifted her hands to cover her ears. "My ears work fine. My legs not so much. Let's get through this as I'm a bit dizzy from sitting up for so long."

Zoe nodded, but her energy seemed to have waned after Allison's attacks.

"The man with the dark brown comb-over is my producer, Glenn. He oversees the show, hands out assignments, and is generally my biggest advocate."

"But not your biggest protector," Noah added.

"That's not fair. He saw that I could get a big break from the meeting and I was more than willing to take that risk." Her defensiveness punched right back at Noah, not that her reaction changed how he felt about the guy. No reporter should go to such high-risk areas without a backup, especially a fairly young reporter whose biggest stories so far came from her university days.

Fiona gave him an icy glare, so he remained silent for the next few minutes as Allison went through the major players in the newsroom.

"Is Gretchen as off-putting as she seems or is that just her television persona?" Zoe asked about the morning anchor.

"At fifty-eight, she feels the daggers in her back. Her coanchor, Marty, is sixty-three, but he has no such pressure, despite both of them pulling in the same ratings. I'd put her name on a list of allies."

Zoe soaked up the information, her interest in the workings of the newsroom a thousand times higher than her interest in which color blue to wear with a black pencil skirt. Although her knowledge of the people was essential, she'd never get a chance to interact with anyone if she didn't succeed in mimicking her sister's mannerisms.

"And the camera and sound crew?" she asked.

"You should be familiar enough with each of them to be able to joke and smile. They're the unsung heroes of the place." Allison listed four camera operators and two sound techs who were particularly friendly with her.

Noah wrote down every person mentioned in a notebook. He'd memorize the details Allison listed about each part of the newsroom and the overall layout of the studios and then leave the notebook back at headquarters in order to have nothing on him that would implicate him.

They broke for dinner after Allison insisted she needed a nap.

"How are your feet?" Noah asked Zoe as she toddled to the kitchen. He wanted to keep their conversation on the trivial following the hours spent absorbing a mountain of data for this task.

"You put them on for even an hour and tell me how your feet feel." Her voice carried amusement laced with annoyance.

"I'm quite satisfied with my loafers." He strolled alongside her as she limped down the hall, now carrying her shoes.

"I bet."

They each grabbed some coffee and a sandwich from a tray someone had ordered for them. It was appreciated, as this assignment would take all of her concentration.

"Are you a fan of GDK news?" he asked about Allison's station.

"Not sure I'd say I'm a fan, but I find the station brings me the local news without a whole bunch of cooking segments and interviews with actors or writers. That's a huge time-saver," She shrugged. "So are you a fan of Allison and her station?"

"She's good at her job and the station is effective in their delivery," he conceded.

She smiled at that. "She *is* good at her job. I've always admired how natural she is in front of a camera."

From the sound of it, Zoe cared about Allison, but they didn't seem to share a bond. "How close are you?"

he asked in search of a better understanding of their relationship.

"We're siblings. We're going to have good moments and bad ones. We share much more of a past than we do a present. Perhaps that's the way it goes for all siblings. Once work obligations, families, and babies take over, there's little room for connection." She bit into her sandwich, a bit of mustard touched her chin, but Noah held back taking it off with his finger. Instead, he handed her a napkin and pointed to it. "What about you? Do you get along with your siblings?"

"I only have Elise, my sister." More than a sister, a confidante and a best friend. "And we get along great. It might help that we live by different oceans."

"I'm not sure. I think the distance between Boston and Nantucket might make us even more estranged. Perhaps being twins makes it different for Allison and I. The expectations to be married to twin brothers and each have two point five kids and puppies from the same litter came at us hard."

"Is that what you wanted?"

She paused. Her mind filing through a thousand memories. "I never wanted to be her next-door neighbor, but I wanted more contact than she was willing to give. The only times she calls me is when she needs something, like yesterday when she asked me to watch Marlowe. I grab at those chances, because I'm terrified that she'll let me go if I'm not useful to her in some way, and here I am again, being useful." Her eyes showed a whole mountain of hurt.

He couldn't imagine straining to hold on to his relationship with Elise. He always knew she'd have his back and he'd have hers. There was no secret tally keeping score of favors done or contact made.

"I'm sorry. I sound like a jealous child, but I'm not jealous. Not of her money and lifestyle. I am jealous that her work gets the best of her and I end up with only the scraps." She put the half-eaten sandwich on her plate and took a sip of coffee.

After lunch, Allison never came back on-screen. Instead, Fiona quizzed Zoe one hundred different ways about the people in the newsroom.

"Who loved the Red Sox more than the Patriots?" Fiona asked.

"Marty," Zoe answered after a moment of recalling all the information that had been thrown at her that morning. "Once Spring training began, he knew all the baseball scores and almost ignored football."

"Perfect."

As the day progressed, Zoe's transformation became more pronounced. She channeled some of Allison's confidence, her walk in high heels though not natural yet was definitely more assured, her questions were sharp and insightful, and her Allison expressions seemed more natural.

Despite his initial reservations, Noah found himself impressed by Zoe's progress. Leaning against the wall in the conference room, he analyzed each step she took and each word she spoke. Better. Much better. The physical transformation was striking, but it was the subtle changes in her behavior that truly surprised him.

"You're getting there," he said as they wrapped up for the day.

Zoe flashed a tired but grateful smile. "Thanks. While

I feel better than this morning, I couldn't walk into the studio in the morning and be anything near like Allison."

Noah pushed off from the wall, his skepticism waning. "I disagree. I have to admit, you're doing better than I expected. But remember, mimicking Allison is about more than looks and mannerisms. It's about mindset."

Zoe met his gaze. "If I could get into Allison's mind, I would be as successful as she is."

"Is that what you think? That she's more successful than you are? Tell that to the classroom full of children who were crying on the last day of school because you wouldn't be their teacher anymore."

"Only a handful of kids were upset. The rest raced off into the summer."

"You matter. Would you give up your life to have Allison's? Answer truthfully."

She tapped her fingers on the table and frowned. "I suppose not. I'd miss the stars at night and the sound of the ocean outside my window...and the children. So how does that help me turn into Allison?"

"You don't have to transform into Allison completely. Be as confident in your decisions as she is in hers. Be proud of who you are and what you've accomplished. Then take your own personal reservoir of confidence and act like Allison for one, maybe two days," Noah said, his doubts giving way to cautious optimism.

Chapter 12

Zoe fell asleep thinking about what Noah had said to her. She'd spent so long being jealous of her sister that she never thought of the wonderful life she'd made for herself on Nantucket. Instead of dreaming about being Allison, she dreamed of a simple coffee date with Noah, ending with a breathless kiss and a yearning for the one hole in her life to be filled.

At breakfast the next morning, she had a pop quiz on every part of the studio and the people there, including the security guards at the door to the building. Noah, seated across from her, his eyes occasionally meeting hers with a warmth that made her heart skip a beat, recited answers off the top of his head with an ease that only deepened her admiration of him. Although he would have to act ignorant of the workings of the news-room as her boyfriend, he understood the place and the people more than she did.

When she went to the training room again, Fiona pushed Zoe further. She threw her down three times and lifted Zoe off the ground, making her kick like a toddler getting moved around by her mother. The problem was that Fiona was shorter than Zoe. Much shorter.

When Noah came at her, Zoe hesitated. She felt bad about the day before, until he pulled back her ponytail and wrapped his other arm around and covered her mouth with his free hand. The action flooded back the fear and agony of having someone grab her from behind and drugging her in her sister's apartment. She stopped thinking and started thrashing her arms and legs, pulling away from Noah with every bit of strength she had. Her hair pulled even tighter until he let go.

Her breath came in short, ragged gasps, each one mirroring the frustration and doubt swirling inside her. The training room, with its huge blue mats and an entire weight area, felt like a prison. Fiona's instructions on self-defense were forgotten the second Zoe tried to put them into practice. Each attempt to replicate Fiona's and Noah's moves ended in bruises, falls, and a deeper sense of inadequacy.

"Focus. It's about anticipating your opponent's next move," Fiona reminded her, resetting her stance for what felt like the hundredth time.

"I'm trying, but my body and my brain aren't speaking the same language," Zoe confessed, her arms and legs aching.

"You did it perfectly yesterday," Noah said.

"But yesterday you didn't cover my mouth with chloroform."

He winced. The concern in his eyes tugged at her heart. Before he could say anything, the door to the training room opened, and Jason stepped in. He winked at Fiona, which might have been adorable had Fiona not spent so much time beating up Zoe prior to his arrival. His presence added to the pressure overwhelming her.

"How is our trainee?" he asked Fiona.

"I'm failing in every way." If she'd had even a speck of assurance in herself when she agreed to this, it was all lost with her poor defense skills and her inability to walk five feet in stilettos. "I don't think Noah and I can pull this off." She didn't want to throw him under the bus, but it had been his idea and it was a bad one.

"Would you feel more comfortable if I went inside with Zoe instead of Noah?" Fiona asked. "No offense, Noah."

Noah definitely took offense from the way his expression fell.

"That won't be necessary," Jason responded. "Noah will handle this fine and draw a lot less attention than you will." He strolled over to Noah's side. "Have you sparred with her?"

"A few times."

"Let me see how she's doing?" Jason pointed in Zoe's direction.

She almost fled the room. The thought of sparring with Noah again made her stomach twist, not wanting to hurt him, but needing to master everything she learned. Lose-Lose. She'd had a hard enough time with Fiona, knowing Fiona would throw her to the mat without any hesitation.

Noah approached her from the front, his face unreadable. Then he pulled a knife on her. An actual knife. What the heck? She stepped back, but he moved closer. Panic wrapped over her. Her foot slipped as she tried to execute a simple defensive move Fiona had made her practice twenty times, sending her crashing to the mat. The thud of her body hitting the floor echoed across the room. Noah, after putting the knife away, knelt down and put out a hand to help her up. "Are you okay?"

His touch, gentle and caring, sent a shiver down her spine. His pity, however, hit as hard as her fall onto the mat. She scrambled to her feet, her frustration burning her face. She turned to flee the room, but was blocked by Jason.

"You're not done. Show me what you've got," Jason said, more of a challenge rather than encouragement.

Fiona stood to the side, her perfectly curvy body and blond ponytail mocking her.

Zoe, wiping sweat from her brow, squared her shoulders, more to keep from crying than to build her own confidence. Jason approached her, no weapons, but his size alone intimidated her. Black hair pulled back in a ponytail, black T-shirt and jeans, he would be cast as a bad guy in any TV show or movie. As he stepped in to grab her shoulders, she went through her defensive motions again, every movement slow, predictable, and ineffective. Jason's expression remained impassive, but his disappointment was as palpable as the tension in the room.

Noah's eyes met hers. The flicker of concern he wore almost broke her resolve completely, yet something in his gaze, a silent encouragement made her ache with a myriad of unspoken emotions.

"I thought you said she was making progress," Jason remarked dryly, turning to Fiona.

Fiona defended her. "She is. These things take—"

"Time?" Jason finished for her, his skepticism clear. "We don't have the luxury of time. Brendan Quinn's chief of staff was murdered last night. It seems that whoever paid the bribe is sending a warning to Quinn to keep his mouth shut, no matter what. Quinn's family might be next. We need to cut the head off the beast or the morgue is going to end up with a waiting list."

Fiona shot him a look, as though he'd said too much, but Zoe caught the exchange. People were dying. And she was walking into the middle of this mess. Feeling the walls closing in, she excused herself, muttering something about needing a moment. She retreated to her room, her heart racing, her mind picturing a hundred ways to die by interfering with a criminal organization.

Alone, she sank onto her bed, head in her hands. The doubts that had been whispering at her now roared. Her life was literally on the line, including whoever came near her. This wasn't going to work. Even if she could figure out how to act like Allison, she was a liability.

She called her father. When she left to watch Marlowe, he'd told her to have fun. She'd since texted him a few times saying how great things were, at Jason's insistence. No need to force her father into the middle of everything, but she missed having his thoughts on her current situation. A former police chief in Nantucket, he was her biggest ally. Perhaps everyone else, including Allison, had been wrong about keeping him out of it. She didn't bother leaving a message when the call went to voicemail.

With a shaky breath, she dialed Allison next, but received her voicemail too. She left a message. "Hey there. They have me trying to act like you, but you are a one of a kind twin. And I doubt I'll ever be able to fill your shoes."

Hanging up, she sat in silence, the sense of isolation wrapping around her like an icy embrace.

Someone knocked on her door.

"Come in," she called out, because whoever it was, they'd barge in whether she wanted them to or not.

It was Noah. The sight of him freshly showered and dressed in navy khakis and a white button-down shirt, ignited something in her. He looked more put together, more striking than anyone else at Fresh Pond Security, besides Fiona, who dressed with a flair that outshone Allison.

"Are you okay?"

"No. I'm not prepared. And honestly, I'm not ready to die, and I'm not ready for my sister to die either."

Noah stared at her with an intensity she hadn't seen in him before. It spoke of pain, suffering, and a fortitude that seemed more like a brick wall than a ramming machine. And she knew he'd protect her to his last breath, whether she asked or not. "You're not going to die. And Meaghan is the best of the best. Your sister is safe." The silent promise in his eyes, a vow to protect her at all costs, suddenly had her fearing for his life. She didn't have him in any way but she didn't want to lose him either.

She stretched her arms overhead and winced. Even if she could remember the moves they'd drilled into her, she wouldn't be able to lift her arms to actually do the moves.

"You're using muscles you haven't used in a while, if ever. A hot bath tonight should ease the pain. You'll be fine tomorrow" He waved her to the door. "Ready for more training? I promise it won't involve being thrown to a mat."

"I don't think I'll ever be ready. I could get us both killed tomorrow." She needed to speak with Jason and convince him that she wasn't prepared. "Where's Jason?"

"He left for a meeting."

"Can you tell him I need him? Or even Fiona. I'm not ready to die."

"I'm not going to let that happen." Despite his appearance, all chill and casual, he did have an edge to him. And that should have made her feel more secure, but the only person in the newsroom she would be able to protect was her, and she didn't have an edge. She didn't even have a backbone, especially when murderers were involved.

"So many things could go wrong," she said on a sigh.

He stepped to her side. "Or we could pull it off beautifully and no one will be the wiser."

"That's a long shot."

His mouth lifted into a teasing smile. "I like betting on long shots."

By the end of the second day, Zoe was stronger and more of a mess. Jason's insistence on telling her about the murder at Boston City Hall destroyed her growing confidence. It didn't help that Allison had been on a phone call with her, whining about how Zoe had better not ruin her career while fishing for information that could help save Allison's life. Whenever Allison seemed bored, she entertained herself with bitter criticism of Zoe. According to her, Zoe had no ambition, no courage to go after her goals, no fashion sense, and an inability to attract the right kind of man, although Allison had yet to describe the type of man she should be attracting. To be fair, Zoe had committed herself to the wrong man back in college, someone smothering, who, in the course of three years of dating, had managed to strip Zoe of most of her self-esteem, but she'd found it again, most of it anyway. Besides, Allison had not been super successful with her string of boyfriends either. Once the men found themselves second to Allison's career, they tended to replace her with someone dedicated to inflating their egos.

Adding to Zoe's stress, she'd texted and called her father multiple times, but hadn't received a reply from him. Each unanswered call amplified her distress. When she called their neighbor to check on him, he didn't reply either. Noah found her sitting in the kitchen with Calvin, phone to her ear, a portrait of barely contained panic.

"I can't get through to him. What if something's happened? I need to go home." Her voice didn't waver on those last words. She'd decided on her next course of action and had fully committed to it.

Calvin shook his head. "The mission begins in the morning. We don't have time. I know Jason won't approve it. Can someone you know go over to the house? We need to be practical," insisted the most practical person at Fresh Pond Security.

Noah stepped closer to her, his eyes never leaving her. "Calvin's right. We can't afford to lose you now. But," he added, his voice softening, "we'll find a way to check on your father. Trust me." He reached out, gently squeezing her shoulder, the warmth of his touch a silent promise.

His touch provided enough reassurance to steady her beating heart. She nodded. "Okay," she replied. "I trust you."

As Noah turned to leave, his hand lingered on her shoulder. His hand on her at all wasn't necessary, but felt amazingly right. The overwhelming sense of dread steadied, still there, but grounded by a hero's touch. She wasn't in this alone, and that made all the difference.

Chapter 13

Noah, leaning against the doorway, crossed his arms. Zoe must be exhausted after all the training and the mental strain of the dangerous situation. The genuine concern etched on her face provided him a mountain of guilt, but this wasn't about making everything easy for Zoe. They had to get inside the news station soon. She wasn't as prepared as she could be, but prepared enough for the task at hand. "Calvin's right. We have a timeline. You know this isn't simply pretending to be your sister for a day. Every moment counts to find something that can help us."

Zoe spun to face him. "I'm not going anywhere until I hear my father's voice, or see his face. If I'm your only shot—which isn't true because you could break in, at some risk, but you could—then you need to go on my schedule. I'm not as ready as I want to be, and I'll be thinking of my father the entire time if I don't reach him soon. 'Trust me,' you said. Show me that I can trust you. If anything were to happen to him because I wasn't there—"

Her words gave Noah pause. He did want what was best for her well-being, and he'd told Jason about the situation with her father. They were already looking for him. If she didn't believe in herself, she'd never convince anyone else that she could handle this. Watching her struggle, Noah felt a twinge of empathy. He'd been in her shoes once, torn between his job and family. His mother had been in a car accident. He should have dropped everything and rushed to her side. Instead, he believed he could wait until the weekend to travel to see her. When he finally flew back to California, he'd been too late to say goodbye to his mother. She'd died from a head injury the moment he stepped on the plane. The memory still wrecked him, because at the time, he'd still been an analyst. He had no reason to stay at his desk and give more hours to his job. It wasn't as if anyone cared if he stepped away for a few days. There had been sufficient backups for him. He could have left. Zoe had even more reason to want to check on her father. If whoever had attacked Zoe at the apartment learned about the rest of Allison's family, they might harm them to stop her investigation. Besides, this wasn't Zoe's job—she'd volunteered to help. If she decided not to go through with it, there would be nothing they could do to keep her.

"I have been working on it, but let me get an update," he said and then stepped into the hall to call Jason.

"Is she ready?" Jason asked as soon as he answered the phone.

"Not really."

The silence on the other end of the line lasted decades. "What's her hang-up?" Jason finally asked.

"She wants to be sure her father is okay."

Jason was silent for a few seconds, then said, "Although I was hoping to keep her focus on the newsroom, no one on the team would be able to focus if they felt their family member was in harm's way. Go ahead and take the jet but be back in time for her to get some rest. There's a lot happening on that island and she should see it personally."

Noah couldn't believe his ears. They'd just acquired the Gulfstream after signing several more than lucrative government contracts. It made flying in and out of areas quicker and easier. Taking it for a quick flight to Nantucket seemed frivolous, but he accepted the offer anyway.

"Is there something I need to be prepared for over there?" he asked.

"You should be prepared for anything at all times."

"Not an answer." He'd worked with Jason enough to know that his boss held his cards tight as he manipulated everyone around him.

"Just keep her focused on the greater good. I'd prefer you to go in unaware. It will keep you honest with her." The big honesty line was a bit hypocritical, since Jason had hid his staged death from everyone around him for years. Noah had given him the benefit of the doubt and had chosen to stay with the team, while his best friend, Finn, had decided to leave because he'd lost faith in his boss. Although Noah had good relationships with Sam, Meaghan, Calvin, and the other members of the team, he missed Finn. They shared a comradery and friendship that was difficult to build in their field.

Noah returned to Zoe and Calvin. They were facing each other as though captains of rival debate teams. Calvin's fists were clenched together, while the color in Zoe's face was an alarming shade of red.

Calvin shook his head and stepped back as Noah arrived. "I can't believe you'd just quit after all you've already done. We don't have time for a Plan B. This could make Boston safer and keep your sister safe as well."

Zoe crossed her arms across her chest. "I said I would try. I never said for sure that I would do it. I can't believe you're bullying me. I'm not getting paid enough to have to deal with you. Oh, that's right. I'm not getting paid at all."

She did have a point, but Noah had high hopes that she'd help them anyway. Perhaps a quick trip to see her father would ease her fears.

Calvin appeared ready to challenge her again, but Noah stepped between them and cut him off. "Listen," he began, "what if I could get you to Nantucket and back quickly? We have a private plane. We fly out, check on your dad, and return right after. Would that put your mind at ease?"

Zoe blinked, the offer clearly catching her off guard. "You'd do that?"

Noah sighed, a decision made. "Ensuring your head is in the game by knowing your family is safe is just as important as a good night's sleep." Although they would hopefully be back in time for her to get some sleep too.

"Thank you, Noah. I... I appreciate this more than you know." There was relief in her words, and less strain than the one directed at Calvin, which had bordered on panic.

"No problem. Let's get you to your father, and then you can make your decision with a clearer understanding of everything going on around us." He turned to Calvin. "Can you contact Hanscom Field and make flight preparations?"

"For when?"

"Right now, and have them on standby on the island. This is a quick round trip. Jason's orders."

That last part took the thorns out of his request. It was Jason and Steve Wilson's company. What they said went, no arguments. Calvin nodded and turned toward his computer screen.

An hour later, Zoe stared wide-eyed at the sleek contours of the private jet at the small airport just outside of Boston. She tried calling her father a few more times until Noah asked her to put away her phone. She'd be there soon enough, and each unanswered call only made her more anxious.

Noah prepared himself for the worst. If Jason wanted them over there, something must have happened. He said a quick prayer that it didn't involve any harm to her father. She didn't deserve any more disasters happening to her. When the flight attendant offered them each champagne, he turned her away. Neither of them needed weakened reflexes both physically or mentally. The flight attendant returned with water for each of them and turkey sandwiches.

As the engines roared to life, Noah settled into his seat across from Zoe, who remained peering out the window, her gaze unfocused. Her tension eased slightly with the ascent, perhaps the physical distance from her problems on the ground lending a temporary reprieve. A very temporary reprieve. Before they were halfway through their sandwiches, the aircraft was preparing to land.

Noah allowed himself a moment to simply watch her,

appreciating the resilience she'd shown throughout this ordeal. The soft light filtering through the window gave her beauty an ethereal quality. He took a moment to appreciate the smooth contours of her cheeks and the way her eyes gave a glimpse into her thoughts. He imagined a world where they could live a simple life, but he didn't live a simple life. He wanted to make a difference. His work targeted ways to help the people who weren't able to help themselves. People like Zoe. He didn't want to give that up.

"Once we're on Nantucket," he said, breaking the silence, "we'll head straight to your house to check on your father."

Zoe turned from the window, offering him a small, grateful smile. Her eyes, though shadowed with worry, shone with a trust that made his heart ache. "Thanks, Noah. I can't tell you how much this means to me."

The words were simple, but the sincerity behind them struck a chord in Noah. He tried to keep his feelings locked behind his character, a person who had more confidence and bravado than Noah, the former analyst, but helping her had become more than just a means to boost him back into fieldwork. He cared about Zoe, deeply, and the lines between duty and affection were becoming increasingly blurred.

The late afternoon light cast a subtle glow over the clouds, bathing the sky in gold and orange hues that reflected on the ocean below. As the plane descended toward their destination, Noah forced his mind to focus on the positive. The constant pressure, the weight of responsibility lifted, if only briefly. This was more than just a flight to ensure Zoe's peace of mind; it was his way of demonstrating to her the lengths he would go to protect her, to prove that he was looking out for her no matter what.

"I've always liked flying," Noah found himself saying, his voice reflective. "There's something about being above it all that puts things into perspective. Makes the problems on the ground seem…smaller, somehow." He hadn't traveled by private jet since his father had left. Once he'd decided to stop being a parent to Elise and him, he held back all but the minimal support the court had ordered him to pay. In the blink of an eye, they lost access to their private school, the golf and tennis lessons, and lavish vacations to the most beautiful places in the world.

Zoe turned to Noah. The thoughtful expression on her face made him forget his bad memories. "Flying like this is beautiful in a way I didn't expect. I've only flown once on a school trip. We were all so exhausted, none of us stayed awake for the final descent. Except Allison. She had a collection of pictures she'd taken as the plane landed. She was always one step ahead of everyone. In intelligence, personality, and strength."

Zoe had truly defined her whole life as a comparison to her sister. Allison was the traveler; Zoe was the homebody. Allison wore the best clothes; Zoe dressed comfortably. Allison fought for her dreams; Zoe stayed complacent. Yet Noah didn't believe Zoe's own analysis of herself and her qualities. Zoe seemed protective of her sister. She nourished her relationships. She supported Allison's dreams, even putting herself at risk to protect her sister. Zoe would push her own needs aside to protect those she loved. And in that, Noah saw a strength and bravery she couldn't see in herself.

When the pilot announced their final descent, Noah felt a twinge of regret that the peaceful interlude had to end. Jason had a reason for letting Zoe visit her father as he wouldn't spend such a huge portion of their travel budget out of the sheer goodness of his heart. As the plane touched down, he reached over and took her hand in his, giving it a reassuring squeeze. "We'll get through this, Zoe. Together."

Her fingers tightened around his, the silent bond between them growing at the speed of an out-of-control freight train. "Thanks for doing this and everything for me," she whispered, her voice filled with gratitude and something deeper. "I don't know what I'd do without you."

His heart filled with something he didn't want, but craved all the same. As the plane came to a stop, he vowed silently that he would do everything in his power to keep her safe.

Not knowing what they'd find at her home, Noah braced himself for the worst, so he could stand with Zoe and support her no matter what they discovered on the island.

Chapter 14

The wheels of the private jet touched down on the tarmac of Nantucket's quaint airport. Zoe had never experienced such a luxurious flight. For most of her life, the ferry had been her main mode of transportation back and forth to the mainland. As the plane slowed, her tension returned. Enjoying the trip even the slightest bit sent waves of guilt through her. She called her father again, hoping he answered even if she'd feel foolish if he did after all the arrangements Fresh Pond Security had put in place for her. He didn't answer. After losing her mother to cancer, her father meant everything to her. Both her father and Allison did, although her father had been the far more supportive of the two. Allison had always found a way to compete over everything from the size of her waist to their relative incomes. Their father had done the opposite, supporting each of them for their own successes and not once pitting them against each other.

As they made their way through the tiny terminal, the salty breeze of Nantucket greeted them, a familiar scent that brought a fleeting smile to Zoe's lips. It was good to be home.

Noah was on his phone next to her. He glanced over

and gave her a subtle smile and a wink as they made their way to a waiting car. A black Jeep Rubicon. A man exited the car and handed Noah the keys. Noah acted as though this was no big deal, like anyone could snap their fingers and have a jet gassed up and waiting for them and then a car standing by when they arrived. She couldn't begin to calculate the cost of such extravagances. She wouldn't complain, however, because they'd offered. What she could feel guilty about was her decision to remain behind when the flight returned to Boston. She hadn't mentioned this to Noah, but if her father had any need for her, she would remain at his side. There was no way to be able to handle the complicated task she'd been given if her thoughts remained on her father's safety.

She still worried over Allison's safety as well but had faith in Meaghan's ability to protect her. Even though she had committed herself to stepping away from this charade, it was not because of Noah. She trusted he could keep her safe, although she wasn't prepared to mention that to him yet, in case he became overconfident. She wanted him crossing all his *t*'s and dotting all his *i*'s. The only person she didn't have any faith in was herself. In the past week, she'd been knocked out by someone in her sister's apartment and had pretty much failed her training despite Fiona's irrational confidence in her. She'd had all the excitement she could handle for a lifetime. Curling up for a good night's sleep in her bedroom as her father played the news on full volume in the living room would be a comfortable way to spend the evening and release the stress that had built up in her bones over the past few days. The only difficulty would be convincing Noah that their assignment was better off without her as the unknown variable. She had no desire to be the weak link in this plan to bring down some of the most dangerous men in Boston.

"Let's not waste any time." He guided Zoe toward the waiting car with a gentle hand at her back. His touch both comforting and something more, something she didn't want to think about, because what she was feeling for him couldn't be reciprocated. Her heart had stumbled right into him, and they had no future together. She lived on an island, he lived across the bay. Perhaps she was falling for him because he'd been her hero. A common affliction in romance novels. "Need help?" He held out a hand to help her climb into the passenger seat.

"I've got it." She smiled at him, appreciating his offer, but grabbed the handle and pulled herself up. A much taller ride than her MINI Cooper.

As Noah drove the Jeep, he surveyed everything around him except her. There was a seriousness to him, as though primed for a fight. His demeanor, combined with her father's lack of communication, made the trip excruciating. Fifteen minutes later they pulled into her neighborhood. Not the richest area on the island, not by any means, but it was charming and most of her neighbors lived on the island year round, forming a tight-knit community.

As they turned onto her street, a scene straight out of Zoe's nightmares unfolded. Her home, a white cozy cottage nestled among several beds of flowers and greenery, was besieged by police cars, their lights vandalizing the scene with their harsh, blue flashing.

Zoe's peace shattered, replaced by a rising tide of panic. "What's going on?" she said, her voice barely a whisper over the thudding of her heart. The garden, once a vibrant tribute to her mother's love for horticulture, was now a crime scene.

Before Noah could respond, she was out of the car and running toward the chaos, driven by her biggest fear—losing her father. Noah followed close behind, his footsteps staying close, but not overpowering her.

Her heart raced as that fear had come straight to her doorstep and threatened the person she loved the most. She scanned the officers, searching for someone in charge, someone who could give her answers.

The officers stomping over the pachysandra border carrying an empty body bag stopped Zoe in her tracks. Noah reached her side just in time to catch her as her knees buckled, her ability to hold herself together weakening by the second. His presence anchored her as a rush of emotions barreled over her.

"If he's hurt in any way, or worse—" Her voice faltered over the words.

"One step at a time. Let's see what's going on," Noah said, his voice steady and calm, grounding her amid the chaos.

She braced against him and looked around. Her confusion eased as most of the faces came into focus. This had been her father's world, her father's officers. One of her father's most accomplished mentees, Lieutenant Talia Coleman, seemed to be overseeing the scene. Talia's family had been on the island longer than most of the houses. Her dedication and service to her job earned her the respect of locals and high profile visitors. When she noticed Zoe, she ran over to her. "Zoe? Where have you been?"

"It's a long story. What…who?" She could barely get the words out. Her eyes locked on the body bag. It represented an answer she wasn't sure she could bear. "Who is it? Please, tell me it's not…" Zoe couldn't finish. Tears released as she anticipated the very worst.

The overwhelming trauma of the past week struck her like a bat to the head. Without Noah still holding her, she would have hit the ground. Her whole family was at risk, and she didn't have enough people in her life to ever be prepared to let any of them go.

Talia hesitated, then sighed. "It's not your father."

Zoe looked over the garden once more, the scene etched into her memory. Half the police force was there, she knew most of them. They didn't meet her gaze. Since they weren't talking to her, she became determined to find out the truth on her own. She rushed past Talia and ran into the garden. As she approached, the other officers turned, their faces a mask of professional detachment, yet their eyes betrayed a hint of sympathy. And then she saw the spot where someone in jeans lay, covered in blood. It wasn't her father, but someone she cared about nearly as much.

Mr. Noonan, Zoe's father's lifelong friend and neighbor, lay motionless, his body bloodied and limp. The vibrant life that had once sparkled in the elderly man's eyes had been extinguished, leaving behind a haunting emptiness. This wasn't a random act of violence, it couldn't be. The timing, the brutality of the act, spoke of a message, a warning. Could Allison's actions really have come across the bay and affected Nantucket, Zoe's home, and family?

She gasped at this fresh horror washing over her. "Mr.

Noonan," she whispered, her hand flying to her mouth. "But…why? Where's my father?"

Noah's arm came around her again, not holding her up as much as backing her up. A stone wall blocking out a tsunami of loneliness and fear. She'd only known him a few short days, but his presence made everything easier somehow.

Talia arrived a moment later. "Let's step away. You don't need to see this. Mr. Noonan was a lovely man and this shouldn't be your last memory of him."

Zoe turned away, closing her eyes and trying to imagine the last time she'd seen him, only a few days before, before she'd been pulled into her sister's mess of a life. They'd been on the porch playing poker. Mr. Noonan, her father, Chief Bishop, and herself. She always lost, but this time, she'd turned over the queen of hearts to the shock of all the men at the table. As she pulled the chips she'd won with her flush toward her, Mr. Noonan said, "It's about time you took us all down. I knew you had it in you." That faith in her had supported her through the death of her mother, applying to college, and applying to work at the local elementary school. He'd been more than a neighbor. He'd been family.

"Do you have any suspects?" Noah asked Talia, pulling Zoe out of the past.

One of the drawbacks of living her entire life in the same small town was the constant surveillance of her life by everyone, and the assumption that they knew every part of her personal life. As visual proof of that, Talia eyed Noah up and down as though he was far too bougie to be Zoe's boyfriend, as everyone assumed she'd settle for some low-maintenance local guy, like her mother had.

"This is Noah Montgomery," Zoe said. "He works for Fresh Pond Security and is sort of my bodyguard."

Talia's gaze returned to Zoe, as though it all made sense why the preppy guy was standing with her. "Why do you have a bodyguard?"

"Long story, but it might have to do with Mr. Noonan's murder."

Noah did not appear too pleased that she'd said anything about him. Perhaps he'd wanted them to stay undercover even here.

Talia didn't seem to notice and answered his question. "We're still piecing it together. It seems Mr. Noonan was tending the garden."

Zoe placed a hand over her chest. He always tended their garden, because neither Zoe nor her father had a green thumb and what did he get for his kindness? She bent over, losing the contents of her stomach.

Noah wrapped an arm around her, offering her his strength to keep her upright. "Go ahead, let everything out," he murmured.

She turned into his embrace, burying her face into the crook of his shoulder. Her sobs echoed across the area, the overwhelming feeling that she was losing everyone she loved. Noah never let go, he continued to hold her, rubbing her back and easing her into the present.

"Who did this?" she managed to utter through slowing waves of sobs.

Talia placed a hand on her arm. "So far, we have no witnesses and no motive. I promise, we'll get the bastard who did this."

Zoe's mind held a tempest of emotions. Relief mingled with pain, fear mixed with terror. Mr. Noonan's murder wasn't a random act. It was a direct consequence of Allison's investigation bleeding over from the mainland. Nantucket, once the most peaceful place on earth, had pools of blood that Zoe might never wash away.

"Do you have a time of death?" Noah asked, leaving one arm around her. He was in investigation mode. Zoe appreciated it. Fresh Pond Security had been hired to figure out who had targeted Allison and find a way to stop them.

"A jogger found Noonan about five hours ago. The Crime Scene Unit just finished, so they're now moving his body to the morgue."

"Oh my God. Where's my father?" Zoe said, her anger rising. This was a crime at her home. Her father was missing. Someone was dead.

"To be honest, we don't know. His boat was out since early this morning, but we've had no radio contact. Someone had seen you on the ferry a few days ago, and no one saw you since then. We assumed you were safe with Allison." Before Talia added to what she'd said, the lieutenant's phone rang. She stepped aside to take the call.

"Let's get you somewhere safe," Noah said to Zoe, guiding her back to the car. "I'm so sorry."

Zoe didn't want platitudes, she wanted her father. After retiring from the police force about five years earlier, he'd bought a boat and would spend hours out fishing with friends or occasionally by himself. The vibrant blue hull of her father's boat caught people's attention, but what really made the boat stand out was the image of a large sperm whale on each side, seemingly cresting out of the water. The boat's absence from the marina was always noticed.

Talia strolled back to them. "Where are you going?"

"To find my father." She also wanted to go into the house, but with police swarming all over the yard, she thought a visit to the marina would be the most useful thing to do.

"No need."

"You have him?" Zoe asked.

"His boat came in fifteen minutes ago. Seems he lost his radar and had no way to contact anyone. He's at the police station speaking with Chief Bishop. The chief wants to speak to you as well."

Zoe didn't care about the circumstances, she only cared that he was alive and well. She clenched her fists together, feeling a twinge of guilt for being so relieved about her father's safety while Mr. Noonan was being taken to the morgue.

"Perfect timing. Let's go see your dad," Noah said, holding the Jeep door open for her.

Talia shook her head. "Give it about an hour. He still needs to speak to the Chief."

"Why? He was gone all day."

"You know the drill. Everyone has to be questioned. You'll be next." Talia sighed. "Why don't you grab yourself some coffee and maybe even a sandwich. It might be a long night."

Unlike most places, they wouldn't have to keep tabs on her here. She couldn't go through the airport or the ferry lines without someone minding her business and tattling. And by now, the movements of the black Jeep would grab residents' attention as well.

As they drove away from her home, Zoe sat in stunned silence, her thoughts focused on seeing her father. Noah reached out and took her hand, a gesture that made her feel less alone.

Chapter 15

Neither Zoe nor Noah were hungry, so they went straight to the police station, a colonial-looking brick building that could easily have passed for the town hall. Noah observed every person around him while Zoe greeted half the building, not with any enthusiasm, but more subdued as though they'd all seen each other only a few days ago and making a dramatic greeting was overkill. Most everyone she spoke to had little focus on him, except to size up whether he deserved to be standing with her. Overall, he felt most of them didn't approve, especially the men. He could imagine Zoe breaking the hearts of half the island, not that she'd even notice. Her self-esteem was rock-bottom, she couldn't see her own sparkle.

Growing up in a large city, he'd never known the claustrophobia of life in a very, very small area. In ways, it seemed comforting and in other ways, smothering. He walked beside Zoe, but kept his hands to himself. No use giving any more gossip to her neighbors. If she needed him, she just had to say the word. Otherwise, his job was to observe and make sure she was safe.

After chatting with the woman at the reception desk,

Zoe was asked to wait on a set of benches. "Do you need anything? I could run out for some coffee or something?"

"No thank you, Helen. We'll be fine."

The woman waved her arm at Noah. "Can you show some identification before going back into the offices?"

He looked at Zoe, who gave him a half smile. "Protocol," she said.

He provided his license and put his name on a sign-in sheet, then stepped away for a moment to call Jason. The second he answered, Noah grilled him. "You could have warned me."

"I gave you a heads-up. I didn't specify what, but I had Calvin monitoring police scanners for the locations where we have people of interest on the ground. This came up a few hours ago. I wanted you there to find out what you can. You can also look Zoe in the eye and tell her you had no idea."

"I'd prefer to have all the details instead of a sliver of an understanding. And I will be bringing that up at the next team meeting," he replied, his annoyance so high, he didn't care that he'd just chewed out his boss. What he did wasn't fair to Zoe or him.

"Point taken." Jason said, his voice not perturbed in the least. "Let's get her father back here so Zoe doesn't have to worry about him while she's working tomorrow morning."

Noah forgot all about the early setup time. This was going to be a disaster. They'd both be off after a long night of travel and stress. Perhaps he could call it off or at least delay by a day. "What if she waits to go in, so she has more time to prepare and rest?"

"No." Jason's response did not leave an opening for a debate.

"But…"

"The threats are ramping up, and I do not want any more deaths while we're on the case. It could jeopardize our standing with our client. I have a whole team narrowing down the source of the bribe to Quinn. Now I need the insider at the news station willing to take down his own reporter. My guess is on the producer, but we need to be sure." Their client was an organization in charge of a large segment of U.S. intelligence. They used Fresh Pond Security like a small splinter group, except Noah wouldn't receive a lucrative government pension when he retired. He did, however, have a higher salary than anything on a government pay scale.

He bit back his reply and told Jason he'd have them both back on the plane tonight. When he returned to Zoe, she was being escorted into the back offices. Noah followed. Helen gave Zoe a look that told her Noah would be stopped if she said the word, but Zoe didn't say a word. So he followed her.

In the chief of police's office, two men sat at a table on one side of the office, both with mugs of coffee in front of them. The men seemed of an age, but one was in a uniform and the other wore jeans and an old flannel shirt. The chief seemed to be sharing memories with Zoe's father more than he was interrogating him. When Zoe caught sight of her father, a formidable figure with a heavy-set frame and a gruff expression that seemed to have been etched from years on the police force, she rushed forward. Despite his imposing stature, his overall demeanor exuded warmth, especially when he saw Zoe and enveloped her in his arms.

"Dad!" she exclaimed, her voice mixing relief and excitement. She clung to him and he hugged her back in a grip no person would be able to break.

"I'm so glad you're safe. I worried so much about you after they told me what happened at the house. I still can't imagine life without George." Her father was most likely talking about Mr. Noonan. His relief in seeing Zoe faded as they held each other, knowing someone they cared about had died on their property. He gently stroked her hair.

"Why didn't you call me? I couldn't get in touch with you since last night."

"I left my phone at home when I went out on the boat, then had a mishap with the satellite radio. I will never be on the water again without a backup."

Zoe nodded, her head resting on his shoulder as he rubbed her back. "I may put a tracking device on you."

"I probably deserve that." His expression turned serious. "Were you at the house?"

She nodded. "It's a mess. And Mr. Noonan. I can't believe it." She held her tongue on all that had happened to her and Allison, not knowing what was able to be discussed openly and what should remain confidential to protect Allison.

Noah, however, had a different agenda. After several minutes of discussion about what happened at their home, Noah broke the news of the threats on Allison's life and that Zoe was under their protection and now Mr. Goodwyn, her father, should be under their protection as well.

"Allison is chasing a story that hasn't broken and she's being threatened?" her father asked.

"Yes. Her apartment was broken into and her neighbor killed."

Chief Bishop looked over at Zoe. "Is this true?"

"I was there. They almost killed me too," Zoe said, holding herself together under the most stressful of circumstances.

"Who are the suspects?"

"We don't have any leads yet, but it's most likely tied to one of the bigger criminal organizations in the city," Noah replied.

He gave them as much information as possible without revealing which groups they suspected. He'd started to narrow down his own list of suspects, one group linked to the Russian mob, and another with deep ties to the Irish mafia, but these organizations worked through secret trusts and corporate entities, making it hard to pinpoint the people controlling it all. He also kept out the part where Zoe was bait in this dangerous investigation. If her father learned about that, there was no way he'd let her go with Noah. "I don't want to cut this gathering short, but we need to catch our flight back."

Zoe visibly stiffened at his pronouncement. "I don't think I can go back. It's safer here. Besides, someone needs to watch my father."

Noah stood his ground. "He should come with us. He'll be safer off the island."

Her father did not acquiesce. "Not happening. I have everything I need here to remain safe."

"I have to agree," added his ally, Chief Bishop. "I have more than enough resources to protect both of them."

The argument heated up when the chief's phone rang, cutting through the escalating voices. He answered with a curt, "Chief Bishop speaking."

The room fell into a tense silence, everyone's attention now on Bishop as his expression turned from annoyance to surprise, and then to reluctant acceptance.

He ended the call. "You're not going to believe this," he said to Mr. Goodwyn. "That was Homeland Security. They've just taken jurisdiction over this...situation. And according to them—" he paused, his eyes narrowed, as he looked at Noah "—we need to listen to Mr. Montgomery."

Zoe's eyes widened in disbelief, and her father leaned forward, his interest piqued.

Noah, for his part, remained calm, feeling a rush of vindication, although he didn't want to overstep because he had no official law enforcement role. He wasn't going to fake it either and risk arrest for impersonating an officer. "I work for Fresh Pond Security, as a consultant to Homeland Security. I'm not going to force anyone to do anything they don't want—" he stared directly at Zoe "—but the people who want to stop this story from being published will not rest until the story and everyone associated with it are buried. I recommend coming with me. As the call indicates, I'm not making any of this up. The danger is real, and staying here puts everyone at risk. We need to leave."

Chief Bishop sighed, rubbing the bridge of his nose. "All right. Homeland Security trumps local police. But—" he pointed a stern finger at Noah "—you better make sure nothing happens to them. We'll be coordinating with the federal authorities, but if one hair on the head of anyone in the Goodwyn family is knocked out of place, I will gladly resign my position and hunt you down." He pointed a chubby finger directly in Noah's face.

Noah knew when to accept a gift when he received one, so he merely nodded and stood. Zoe remained seated, as though about to stage a strike, despite what the chief said.

Her father reached over to her, squeezing her hand, offering silent support. "I need to stop at the house and pick up an overnight bag."

"No, we should stay here," she insisted. Noah could see all the anxiety over doubling for her sister rushing back into her thoughts.

"This might take a few days. Once we know the players, we should be able to take them out one at a time. If we don't find them all, this situation could put everyone in danger." Noah's words shot out at Zoe, trying to make it clear that she was a necessary piece in all of this.

She didn't appear too happy about it but did stand and head to the door.

Noah nodded, the tension in his back releasing a bit. "Thank you for your assistance," he said to the chief. "I'll arrange everything and keep them safe." He stopped short of promising, because this situation could go sideways at any moment, and he didn't want to promise anything he didn't have control over.

Chapter 16

After a whirlwind of packing their things and heading out to the airport, Zoe fell asleep on the flight back across Nantucket Sound. When she woke, her father and Noah were speaking together in hushed voices. Noah using his hands to highlight something he was saying, while her father had his undivided attention. She didn't know how Noah did it, but he'd effectively neutralized two of the most hardheaded individuals she knew. Her father and Chief Bishop.

Her father sat up when he saw she was awake. "How are you feeling?"

"Tired."

"Nervous?" he asked.

"About?"

"Noah told me about where you're headed tomorrow. I have to say, I'm proud of you."

She looked over at Noah, who was wearing a neutral expression, though it was evident that something he said to her father resonated. But his response was not what she expected. "Proud? I'm going to be a disaster. I can't carry myself as Allison."

He placed his hand over hers, the familiar contact more

soothing that a bottle of wine. "You aren't Allison, but you make a pretty amazing Zoe. And Zoe can handle anything that she puts her mind to. She's pretty similar to her sister, except for the high heels. You never could walk in anything higher than sneakers."

It was the same thing Noah had told her, that she didn't have to be Allison exactly and that some of her own qualities would be more than enough to complete this task. Her father had supported everything she did, but this was beyond her usual risk level. He'd never pushed her to be more or to take chances, even when encouraging Allison to try for bigger and better everything. "Why now? Why do you want me to do this dangerous thing when you've never even encouraged my surfing lessons, telling me that fishing is more than enough of a thrill?"

"Because you can do it and help stop some really bad characters. I believe in you and I think you'd regret it if you didn't make an effort."

She didn't know how to respond, so she just nodded. "I love you, Dad."

"Ditto, darling."

After they touched down, Noah drove them to headquarters. He'd decided they should sleep there for simplicity's sake. It was late and moving to a new location would take too much effort. Zoe glanced at her phone. It was 2:00 a.m. and they wanted her at the studio by ten, coiffed, made up, and dressed to kill. It was going to be a very difficult morning.

She anticipated an argument from her father about where they were going, but he went along with everything, although he took in every bit of their surroundings, and she wouldn't be surprised if he had a handgun packed away with him. Old habits die hard.

They each went to different rooms and Zoe made sure her dad had his cell phone and a charger so she could reach him if needed. Noah was more of a shadow around her. He never stepped between her and her father. A nice gesture. Her father had always watched her back and it was an old habit to rely on him, but she also liked having Noah close by. He seemed to believe in her as much as her father, which felt like a first for someone outside of their family.

She woke at eight to Fiona knocking on her door. "Ready?"

"Ready? For a shower, yes. To leave? Not even close."

Fiona opened the door and carried in two cups of coffee. "For coffee. It's important to fuel up."

Zoe sat up and took the steaming mug. "You're an angel."

"Some days I am. How are you feeling after yesterday?"

"Scared." She needed more time and more preparation, but she also realized her family would be at risk if they didn't take down whoever wanted to stop the investigation.

Fiona nodded. "That makes sense. After years of training and experience in this field, I thought I was prepared for anything. Seeing my house attacked and my family at risk, however, nearly knocked me to the ground."

"Really?"

"Well. I'm not a fall-to-the-ground-in-a-panic type of person, but I was upset."

Zoe couldn't see Fiona falling apart over anything.

She'd probably just become really pissed off and transform into someone even more deadly.

She showered and then followed Fiona to a conference room, which had transformed into a beauty salon and pop-up designer store.

Upon entering, she was greeted by Eleni, the stylist, and more coffee. "Hurry in. We only have about an hour to fix you up." She gestured toward three suits hanging on a clothes rack. "I found several outfits that should be perfect for today's undertaking. Pick the one you feel most confident in."

Every suit appeared exactly like the style Allison had curated during her news career. Brighter colors, and the high heels made more for Allison than Zoe.

Zoe, feeling out of her element but intrigued, replied, "Can I try them all on?"

The stylist chuckled, "Absolutely. After we get your hair done."

As the stylist turned on the blow-dryer, warmth spread around Zoe. Dressed in the sweatpants and T-shirt she'd slept in, she sipped on coffee as Eleni worked her magic brushing out Zoe's long hair, section by section. It was a soothing process. By the time her hair was done, she was down to fifteen minutes. At least she'd received a mani-pedi the day before to save time.

Fiona helped her change into a red suit with a skirt, then a bright blue dress, and then a navy pantsuit.

Slipping into the navy suit, Zoe couldn't help but feel transformed. The fabric became a second skin, molding her into a version of herself she barely recognized. "I... I look like someone who knows what they're doing," Zoe admitted, examining her reflection.

"That's the point," the stylist replied, continuing to fix Zoe's hair. "You're not just dressing for today. You're preparing yourself for every challenge that comes your way."

"Do you think I'll look the part?" she asked, loving how she felt, but doubting herself again.

Fiona clapped her hands together. "You look amazing. How do you feel?"

"Honestly? Pretty unstoppable."

"Then my job is done," Eleni said. "The right outfit is more than just fabric. It's armor for today's battle. Elegant, commanding, and absolutely you."

Dressed meticulously and with her hair styled to perfection, Zoe faced the stylist, "Thank you. I feel like an imposter in my own skin, but strangely, it's a good thing today."

The stylist smiled knowingly.

Stepping out to meet Noah, Zoe was a carefully curated version of herself. She was ready. Until she saw Noah. He had transformed into someone else. His posture, upright and relaxed, revealed a sense of authority and control that seemed to come naturally to him. His normally tousled hair had been neatly styled. He stood with assurance clad in a meticulously tailored blue button-down shirt and tan khakis. A portrait of success. He didn't appear to be acting a part. Unlike Zoe.

He smiled when he saw her—his expression glowed with admiration, making her feel wanted, truly wanted. "You look amazing."

"Thanks, so do you." She waved her hand up and down in front of him, emphasizing his fashion choices. An overwhelming urge to hug him nearly got the best of her, but she held back, trying to maintain an air of professionalism.

"It's just an outfit from my life a long, long time ago." His answer had her thinking about his past, and his family, and what he saw as a successful life. She found herself wanting to know more, to peel back the layers he'd hidden from everyone. So far, she'd seen him outsmart most of the people around him, and try to please Jason as though he were the father he'd never had. In addition, he had the utmost respect for women. An intriguing combination.

For a moment, the world faded away. The air crackled with unspoken words and possibilities. Her heart fluttered as though she were falling in love, but that was impossible. They were a team for an assignment. He was paid to look after her. That was all this could be.

He stepped closer, his eyes searching hers. "You really do look incredible, Zoe. It's...different, but in a good way. It suits you."

She felt a flush rise to her cheeks, and looked away for a moment to gather her composure. "I feel like I'm playing a part," she admitted. "But seeing you like this... I'm glad to have you as my partner."

When they arrived out front, Noah pointed to a white BMW. "Jason thought your boyfriend should look well-off but not too ostentatious."

"My boyfriend?"

"We're partners. And I want access to you at all times. Being your boyfriend will draw much less scrutiny than having your manager, agent, or lawyer shadowing your movements. They don't want you bringing in people who want to negotiate a higher salary or a promotion

without a heads-up. Boyfriends are generally harmless."
He reached out, gently lifting her chin with his fingers,
forcing her to meet his gaze. "Generally."

As they drove into the city, she imagined a life where
her boyfriend drove a fancy car and had ambition. The
daydreaming gave her a reprieve from obsessing over
her next few hours acting as Allison. In reality, however,
she couldn't imagine having a boyfriend like Noah. He
was too polished, too self-assured, too everything. Her
former boyfriends had all been down-to-earth guys who
wanted a down-to-earth girlfriend who would eventually
become a wife and then mother. None of them had ambition or any desire to give her anything but their bare
minimum. The way Noah cared for her, although it was
his job, made her want something more. She wasn't able
to articulate it exactly, but it was definitely more than
she'd received in the past.

Before they left the car, he handed her Allison's name
badge and her phone. "These are the final pieces. If you
are unsure of something, give me a hug and whisper your
thoughts in my ear, as quietly as possible. I can help."

His proximity encouraged her and made her want to
curl up in his arms and remain hidden for the rest of the
day. Everything was so real now.

As they approached the towering glass facade of the
news station, Zoe's heart pounded against her chest, adding to her indecisiveness. Noah offered her a reassuring
wink. His confidence never wavered, as hers plummeted
by the second.

"You look great, Allison," he whispered as they entered the lobby, his breath warm against her ear. The way
he looked at her, with such unwavering trust and subtle

affection, made her wonder if he felt the same pull she did. She dared to glance up at him and received a lightning bolt of connection between them. The boyfriend ruse certainly felt real.

At the security desk, the familiar face of the guard Allison had often spoken of offered a semblance of normalcy. "Morning, Allison. How's Marlowe? Still chasing his tail?" he joked, his casual demeanor a balm to Zoe's frayed nerves.

"He's doing well, thanks. Keeps life interesting," Zoe replied while Noah signed in and received a guest pass. The small victory bolstered her confidence.

Once in the elevator, she tried to keep her eyes on the door. Noah stood beside her rambling on about the Red Sox. She nodded and smiled, but wasn't listening at all.

When the doors slid open, they both focused on the newsroom and everyone there. Zoe's entrance didn't go unnoticed, with a few of Allison's colleagues offering friendly waves and smiles. She returned their greetings, her smile tight, her mind scrambling to remember any details Allison had shared about them.

"Morning, Allison," Dominique called out as they passed each other. That woman was Zoe's idol and Allison's biggest competitor. The sight of her rendered Zoe starstruck.

After an uncomfortable silence, she managed to say, "Good morning," a bit too enthusiastically. Noah's slight nudge reminded her to temper her responses. She straightened up, acted a bit colder toward the world as she assumed Allison would do, and led Noah to her office.

Once inside, she closed the door and took a deep breath. A Boston University coffee mug waited on the desk for Allison's return while three news reporting awards lined up like military guards to interrogate anyone questioning her abilities.

"So far, so good?" she asked Noah.

He sat down on the wooden chair in front of her desk. "Take your time and breathe, you'll feel more in your body."

Someone knocked. When Zoe opened the door, a woman, dressed head to toe in black with her long dark hair pulled back in an elegant twist of braids, rushed up to her and gave her a hug. Zoe hugged her back and tried to but failed to remember this woman's name.

"Hi, what's up?" Something Allison would never say, but Zoe's nerves blocked out her two days of practice.

"You're on the air in ten. We need you ready pronto." She stood back and stared at her. "Your hair looks great, so let's just touch up your face."

So this was the makeup artist, except her name became lost in the hundreds of other names they'd tried to force down her throat. She made a face at Noah, begging for him to help.

Noah, leaning against the wall, his hands in his pockets stepped toward the woman as a response. Zoe hoped he knew what he was doing, because this would be humiliating if they didn't know the makeup artist. Then he took the woman's hand, clasping it between his hands. "Tansy?" When the woman nodded, he added, "Allison has spoken so highly of you. No one holds a candle to the magic you create."

Zoe wanted to hug him for remembering the name, but bit her lip and tried to appear as though she had known Tansy a long time.

"Thank you," Tansy said to Noah. "Allison is one of my favorites, because it's easy making that girl gorgeous. And who are you?"

"I'm Noah. Don't let me bother you. I'm going to stand back and enjoy."

"You can bother me anytime." Tansy placed a hand on his arm and something twisted in Zoe's gut. She couldn't be jealous. She'd only just met Noah, but she liked that he'd dedicated all of his time and attention to her. He gave her more attention than her past three boyfriends combined had provided, which said a lot about her dating life.

He stepped back, his hands in the air. "Don't get me in trouble. Allison is as possessive of me as I am of her."

His words didn't make Tansy mad, instead she let out a laugh. "Smart woman. Okay, Allison, let's get you ready." She pointed to a chair in front of the mirror.

Only then did Zoe realize what Tansy had said.

You're on the air in ten.

"I think there's a mistake. I came in today to look over a few things and meet with Glenn."

"And Glenn is the person who wants you on the air. You have a new story, something about the baby lion at the zoo. So cute. Now, sit yourself down so I can keep my job."

"No. No. No. I am not ready."

Noah walked over to her and placed his hands on her shoulders to ease her anxiety. It didn't work. "This is perfect. I always wanted to see the news as it happens." He turned to Tansy. "Does she read cue cards, or just speak from the top of her head?"

"There's a teleprompter. It's pretty cool to watch."

"Fantastic," he said, squeezing her shoulders in a sign of encouragement.

She glared at him in the mirror. He responded with a mouthwatering grin, the jerk. So she did what she assumed Allison would do, and allowed Tansy to prepare her for the camera.

Over the next eight minutes, Tansy transformed Allison from what she'd assumed was a working professional into a television star. Zoe stared at herself in the mirror. The woman had amazing skills, polishing Zoe's skin until not a pore could be found.

The door banged again, this time with some heft behind it.

"Come in," Zoe called out as Tansy brushed highlighter over Zoe's cheekbones.

Glenn, a person Zoe had never met, came at her with a smile that the vice principal at her school often used with parents who had demands that would never be met, but he had to keep them on his good side. Except Zoe had assumed Glenn had always been on Allison's side, until he nearly sent Allison to her death.

"Ready?" he asked.

"Let me fix her lipstick and then she's good to go," Tansy responded and then left.

"I thought I should talk about my investigation so far."

"No. We discussed this. You need a complete story to break something like that or we'll be sued for every penny. I handed you the lion cub story. You can head to the zoo tomorrow for some up close and personal time."

"What about my investigation?"

"Dominique is on it."

"Isn't she busy enough?" Zoe said, trying to reflect her sister's opinion.

"Jealousy isn't a good look on you," he said with an oily patronizing tone that made Zoe want to slam down on his foot with her stiletto. "You have the makings of a great reporter, but you need to follow orders and know when you're in over your head. You disappear for a few days and come back with nothing. I shouldn't have sent someone so inexperienced to do a professional's job. When she has the time, she'll continue where you left off." The pitting of one reporter against another and the insulting way he spoke to her provided a whole new look at Allison's job. She'd always said positive things about her work, minus her desire to move up and past other colleagues, but she'd never spoken about the demoralizing treatment she'd had to endure. And now he was effectively cutting her out of a story that she'd discovered herself. "You have two minutes." And then he was gone.

Allison would be furious, not that Zoe had any way of getting her sister's leg healed in under two days. Yet, here she was, trying to protect Allison and drowning in the process. She turned to Noah. This whole charade was his fault. "Now what?"

"You go on camera, and I sneak around. If he's taking Allison off the case, perhaps it's for the best. She'll be safer for the time being until we find evidence linking Glenn to Councilman Brendan Quinn and to some other player, someone with a lot of money and muscle on their side."

"Did I ever tell you I have stage fright? I stand in front of a group of my peers and I freeze. What if I stare blankly into the camera the second the green light goes on, if I can even find the green light. Is it on the camera? Is it just a thing people say on newsroom dramas? I can't do this, Noah," she said. She looked the part, but in this situation didn't have even the slightest bit of experience.

"You have more experience speaking in front of a captive audience than anyone in this studio," he responded. "Third graders are people too. You're beautiful, you're poised, and you have something to say. You're going to tell a story to the audience that you don't even have to memorize because you'll have the teleprompter, and you'll do it with a smile. The same smile you have on your face when some snotty kid forgets his lunch and wants to go home. Nothing to worry about. I'll be right with you every step of the way."

"Except you won't be on camera."

"I like my anonymity. If you don't do it for the good of the city, do it for your family."

His words did little to ease her stress. Yet, she thought of her father, hidden away for his safety, and of Allison, recuperating from an attack meant to silence her. Their courage and sacrifices made Zoe appreciate how much she could help if only by allowing Noah time to search Glenn's office.

"Fine, I'll do it, but do not offer any judgment or positive or negative comments on my performance. I don't want to hear a word of praise or criticism from you from the moment I step away from the camera," Zoe said.

Noah nodded his agreement, so she straightened her spine and left her sister's small office and proceeded to wobble on her heels and nearly fall to the ground. She saved herself and merely shook her head as though she'd just tripped over something. She tried to remember Fiona's advice and strode forward again with a more solid step.

The walk to the studio was a blur, every step added another reason for her to run as far away as possible. When she entered the hustle of the space, no one noticed her presence. Camera crews, lighting crews, and a whole slew of other people rushed around pointing to the two anchors at the desk. Zoe took a deep breath. She was not Zoe Goodwyn, elementary school teacher from Nantucket; she was Allison Goodwyn, investigative reporter. And she would be speaking about a lion cub. She then smiled to herself. Noah was right. That story would be something she could tell her students. And they'd give her their full attention.

During a commercial break, Fred Scott, one of the anchors left. Someone pulled Zoe to his spot at the main desk, next to Natalie Johnson, the longtime anchor, who didn't so much as look up to acknowledge her. Zoe sat up straight and forced a smile as she waited, her stomach wrapped up in knots. There was a countdown down with fingers, not spoken words. Three, two, one... The camera operator pointed at her. The red light on the camera lit up. Everyone went silent.

Natalie's face went from frowning to hyperenthusiastic. The change was incredible, as though she were an actor and the camera shifted her personality immediately into her role.

"In today's Afternoon Smile Segment, we're taking you to the best place in the city, the zoo." Natalie read off her lines with polished perfection. "Take it away, Allison."

Chapter 17

The studio lights blazed down on Zoe, casting her in the spotlight. The red recording light telling her anything she did was being beamed to the whole city. She should have frozen, terrified of the attention, but she remained in her seat, poised and ready to go. With Noah's words whispering in her mind, she found herself not channeling her sister, but rather herself. She was standing before her classroom of eager third graders rather than an entire television viewing audience.

"Good afternoon," Zoe began, her voice steady and infused with a warmth she hoped was convincing. "In today's segment, I'm so excited to announce that Dakari, the beautiful African lioness gave birth this morning to a female cub. Mom and her baby are doing great. Dakari's pregnancy has captured the hearts of everyone as this will be the first birth of a lion at the zoo in twenty years. From what the zookeeper has told us, the cub is very healthy and will be introduced to the public in six weeks. But we have a treat for you. We'll be sneaking back into the veterinary center for a peek at the newest member of the zoo family. When mother and baby are comfortable, a webcam will allow the public to watch mother and baby bond.

"A team of sixteen veterinarians and veterinary technicians helped to deliver the cub. Although they were hoping Dakari would carry three to five cubs, they discovered that she carried only one when they gave her an ultrasound, which is a very tricky thing to do with a full grown lion." Zoe's confidence grew as she described the birth, the details flowing easily since they were typed in front of her.

"Dakari, and now her daughter, will be able to educate people about the importance of wildlife conservation as lions are classified as vulnerable in the wild. With habitat loss, poaching, and conflicts with humans, they face many threats.

"So stay tuned tomorrow to meet our newest resident. Back to you, Natalie."

Natalie asked Allison something quippy, and Zoe responded with a hand to her heart and the look of someone caught up in an adorable lovefest. "I'm looking forward to tomorrow."

As the segment wrapped up and the cameras turned away, Zoe let out a breath she didn't realize she'd been holding. She'd presented a report on live TV without faltering. And then she was literally pulled from her seat, the microphone unclipped and yanked from under her shirt and she was sent on her way while the next segment began.

As she walked off the set, Noah was there to meet her, a huge smile on his face. "You were fantastic," he whispered, guiding her away.

Zoe felt a mix of relief and exhilaration at what she'd

done. She'd stepped into Allison's shoes and, for a brief moment, lived her sister's life. It was an experience she would never forget, and in some ways, although she'd never admit it to Allison, she really enjoyed it. She had to thank Noah for that. He'd reminded her of her own set of strengths and, stepping back to her classroom, she could see the skill set required to educate and entertain children for hours at a time.

As they left the studio behind, Zoe walked with a bit more steadiness in the heels. She'd always thought she would be incapable of handling Allison's job because Allison had so much more poise and confidence, and that had been the barrier for Zoe. But it wasn't a barrier. She possessed her own poise and confidence, her own voice, her own personality. No, she didn't want to permanently change lives with her sister, but she could now appreciate the benefits and drawbacks of each of their careers.

Chapter 18

While Zoe was speaking on camera, Noah had seized the moment to sneak into the producer's office. Glenn was caught up in a heated argument with one of the camera operators, which left Noah a few minutes, he hoped. Remembering the map of the building, provided by Allison, he left the studio, turned back to the hallway, and found the third door to the right of the elevator. Noah slipped through the partially open door and returned it to its previous position, about three inches from closing. Three large screens adorned the walls. One had the news show on it with Zoe looking every bit the professional in front of a screen showing a lioness at the zoo. He almost paused to watch her, but refocused on his task. Any delay could get both of them in trouble.

Noah's movements were swift, his senses heightened for any sign of Glenn's return. The desk was a mix of organized chaos, awards mingling with stacks of scripts and production notes. But Noah's target was the computer sitting on the mahogany desk. Regrettably, he couldn't outright steal it, so he had to do the next best thing. Allow Calvin, back at Fresh Pond Security, to scan and store the contents.

"Calvin, you there?" he whispered into his earpiece.

"Ready when you are," Calvin's voice crackled back. "I just need remote access, and I can start digging."

Noah slid the thumb drive into the computer, a way to minimize their fingerprints, both physically and digitally on the target computer. "We're in. Tell me when you've downloaded everything." As Calvin worked his magic, Noah skimmed through the producer's drawers and files, looking for any physical evidence to complement their digital haul. The tension in the air was palpable, a silent countdown ticking away in Noah's mind.

The seconds stretched into eternity as Noah kept one eye on the door, the other on the screen, watching as folders and files flitted across it. He flipped through a few stacks of papers, and located a note for Glenn to contact POR Development. He wasn't sure if it had relevance, but he snapped a photo anyway and waited for Calvin. "You good? Because we don't have much more time."

"One more minute," Calvin said, his voice tense.

"We don't have the time. I need to get back." Noah glanced up at the screen and saw the anchor speaking to Zoe. Not good. "Gotta go." Noah disconnected the thumb drive and reset the computer, erasing any trace of their intrusion. His heart pounded, not just from the thrill of the covert operation, but from the realization that he wasn't sure if he'd be back in the studio before Zoe got off the air.

"I don't know if we have everything," Calvin replied.

"Not my problem. It's enough for now. We'll analyze it when I get back and if we need more, maybe I can make a return," Noah replied, aware that each moment spent in the lion's den increased their risk of discovery.

"We have about 80 percent," Calvin confirmed, a sigh of relief audible even through the digital connection. "It should be enough."

Exiting the office, Noah strolled back to the studio, his expression neutral. Zoe was being manhandled by a hyper sound tech and if his hand slipped any closer to her more sensitive areas, Noah would wrap the cord around the guy's neck.

When she was free, she turned to him. Her excitement beamed across her face. From what he'd seen, she had been brilliant.

"You were amazing out there," Noah said as she walked up to him.

She nodded and then gave him a huge hug, squeezing him tight with a sense of accomplishment and a sense of relief. To play the part, he kissed her cheek and nearly went to her lips but that would be overkill for the assignment.

"I can't believe I did that," she whispered to him.

"Let's get you back to your office." He kept an arm around her and led her inside. His own excitement for successfully getting in and out of the producer's office had him on cloud nine as well.

Zoe slumped into her chair, the tension slowly leaving her shoulders. "That was the most exhilarating thing I've ever done in my life," she admitted, a tired laugh escaping her. "What did you think?"

"You were amazing. And I think we should celebrate by heading out for lunch." He wanted to lean over and give her a hug, but they had to stay focused. The longer they remained in the area, the higher the chance they could be discovered or Allison could be dragged on air again. Either way, they had to leave.

She grabbed the stack of notes on the back of Allison's bookcase and placed them in a tote bag from under her desk. Then she held on to Noah's arm with all the strength she had left.

In the car, Zoe leaned her head back and shut her eyes for a moment. "I can't believe I took over Allison's life and actually handled it."

"Don't tell your sister, she'll be furious."

"She probably would be, but I give her a lot of credit. She not only has to look amazing and sound great, but she also puts in hours and hours into researching her assignments on her own. She's not a reader at a desk, she's an on-the-ground hard-core investigator. I wouldn't choose that for my life, and I have a new respect for all she does."

"I agree. Although to be fair, would she be able to manage your classroom for more than a few hours?"

"Not at all. She can barely handle Marlowe. Although they do love each other. I'm not sure Allison would be able to function if she didn't have her little buddy there every night to keep her company." Zoe would never badmouth her sister or anyone she'd met so far, except of course any person who threatened her family. Noah loved this quality about her. A whole mountain of positivity, like his mother, a stark contrast to the competitiveness, materialism, and jealousy he'd seen consume his father.

Perhaps that was why he and his sister had always preferred helping others like their mother rather than focusing their whole lives on bettering themselves. His father's focus had never been on their well-being, it had been on them being more attractive, educated, athletic, and talented than the rest of the community. Parenthood as a means to boost his own ego.

"So where is lunch?" she asked.

"Headquarters. We downloaded Glenn's computer and while you get a refresher course in self-defense, Calvin and I are going fishing."

From the frown on her face, she had probably envisioned something with a better menu. "Can we stop at Allison's apartment? I was hoping to get something more comfortable to wear, like her sweatpants and sneakers." Zoe looked fantastic, but more comfortable clothes would make the rest of the day easier.

"Let me call in to Jason and get permission." Noah pushed the button to have the call go through the car system.

"How did it go?" Jason asked with no preamble.

"Zoe took the folder from Allison's office and Calvin has the download from Glenn's office."

"Fantastic. And great job on the news today, Zoe. Not many people could step into such a public role so easily."

Zoe looked up at Noah, trying to bite back her smile. "Thank you."

"We're stopping at Allison's apartment, unless you've seen anything unusual there," Noah said.

"It's been quiet all day, so go ahead, but get in and out quickly in case you have a tail."

Noah placed a hand over Zoe's, feeling utterly invincible. "We will."

"And don't let your guard down. You're both running off a high. That's the most dangerous time of an assignment." With that, Jason hung up.

Chapter 19

The journey to Allison's apartment in Beacon Hill felt like traveling years back in time, but Zoe had been there only a few days ago. It was a memory Zoe would prefer to forget. The memory of the neighbor's tragic death and her own brush with danger within these walls followed her inside. Although she needed to gather a few of her sister's things to wear, she regretted her impulsive request as they opened the door.

Exhaustion had caught up to her and created all kinds of worst-case scenarios running through her head. Maybe someone was hiding out in the apartment. She paused before entering.

"Are you okay?" Noah waited for her, with no pressure to enter.

"I'm not sure."

"I understand. I'll check the place first. Wait here," he said, disappearing inside.

Zoe took a few deep breaths while waiting in the hallway. Her heart pounded against her rib cage—perhaps she didn't have to enter the place at all. Noah could grab a few things and then they could leave. Before she turned and left the apartment building altogether, Noah reappeared, his posture relaxed, a re-assuring smile on his face.

"It's safe," he said, holding the door open for her.

Stepping inside, Zoe had an immediate visceral reaction. One of her sister's vases was smashed on the floor, a chair overturned, and the peonies she'd brought to give her sister sat wilted on the counter, having never made their way to a vase. That Noah had observed the peonies in the middle of the chaotic scene and had decided to bring her some to cheer up her room comforted her. His focus on details helped him to excel in his job and impress the women in his life.

"No one cleaned up the mess?" she asked.

"The police came in and investigated, taking photos and video, but it's the responsibility of the resident to clean up."

"That's unacceptable. Allison's broken apart and when she finally gets home, she does not need to walk into this." She headed to the pantry and grabbed the broom and dustpan from the door.

"What are you doing?"

"I'm cleaning."

Noah walked over to her as she started to sweep. "We can send a service over."

"No one knows where everything in her house goes. I do. I can do it." She swept up the broken vase and threw the pieces into the trash. She also tossed the flowers. They had no chance of recovery at this point.

She cleaned up the countertop and turned on the dishwasher as it had started to smell with the dirty dishes inside. The floor still had tiny shards of glass, so she walked into the back room to grab the vacuum and ran right into yellow police tape and a large bloodstain. The visual of Mrs. Peterson came rushing back to her. Her ignorant assumption that the woman had fallen, when in reality someone had murdered her and then gone after Zoe.

She turned and rushed into the bathroom, retching. Noah appeared immediately, his hand supporting her. She ignored him as she bent over the toilet and sobbed.

"Come on. Let's get you cleaned up." He led her to the sink and then into the living room and sat her on the couch. "I'll be right back."

Returning with two glasses and a bottle of some amber liquid that appeared stronger than anything she normally drank, he poured two generous portions. "This might help," he offered, handing her a glass.

She accepted it, allowing the sting of the alcohol to warm her from the inside out. They sat in silence. She wiped a few more tears from her cheek. "This whole situation is embarrassing. I trained to protect myself, and I fall apart at the sight of blood."

"That's not embarrassing at all. You give a damn. It means you're human. And training for two days doesn't inoculate you from your humanity. People who have no reaction either have lived in such trauma they have no more emotion to give, or they have a psychological disorder that doesn't allow them to feel. Contrary to everything you see on social media, there aren't many people like that." He sat next to her. "We're going to get through this."

Zoe looked at him, really looked. He didn't seem upset over the blood on the floor. It seemed like nothing fractured his composure. She wasn't like him. "I'm scared. After someone tried to kill Allison, attacked me, and went after our dad, I'm terrified that one of us is going to be killed before the end of this," she confessed, her voice barely above a whisper.

Noah reached out, his hand finding hers. "I understand. But you're not alone in this. You have the team. We're stronger together. And I'm not leaving your side."

His support made her feel better. She leaned into him, resting her head on his shoulder. The moment stretched, some calm in the storm, until a deafening crash destroyed the aura of safety. An explosion of sound and glass had Zoe diving to the floor. Noah dropped to the floor over her, a human shield, as another bullet embedded into the wall just inches above where they'd sat.

"Stay down!" he ordered, his body covering hers as he scanned the room.

The silence that followed was deafening, broken only by the sound of their ragged breathing. Her heart raced, and her whole body shivered as she tried to stay as small as possible on the floor. Noah had crawled over to the window and was peering through a corner, a gun in his hand.

"We have to leave. Now," Noah said, as he returned to her side. His arm wrapped around her was the only thing that anchored her to reality.

Zoe struggled to escape. She relied one hundred percent on Noah to help her scramble onto her feet and lead her out of the room. His body protected her from the debris coming from the window. He picked a few of the larger pieces of glass off her back and shoulders. One near her elbow had caused a small laceration. She didn't care—that small cut wasn't as dangerous as the bullets flying at them.

"The police should be here soon," Noah said. "That sound echoed through five other buildings at least. Someone is going to notice the shattered window if they haven't already. Having the whole neighborhood looking at us as we leave will not provide more security, it will create a social media moment and could possibly place a spotlight on your location."

He glanced around the apartment. "I need a view of the back alley. The location of the dumpsters."

She thought about it for a moment and pointed to the back rooms. He grabbed his drink, a paper bag from the counter, and some matches next to a candle on a side table.

"Come on." He waved at her to follow him. One of the back rooms was an office with a huge built-in bookcase and windows overlooking another building, parking, and three dumpsters. With a bit of effort, he opened the window as wide as it would go, a whole five inches, while hiding himself behind the heavy brocade curtains.

Placing the glass and alcohol in the paper bag, he lit a match and set the bag on fire. And then, to Zoe's shock, he sent the flaming package into the dumpster. His throw was perfectly aimed as it sank down between plastic trash bags and cardboard boxes. There was no explosion or other dramatic event. Instead, smoke rose up and then a small flame and then...the contents of the dumpster were burning. With little wind in the area, the fire stayed contained inside the large metal container. As smoke billowed up, people came running.

He pulled Zoe away from the spectacle behind the

building and into her sister's bedroom. "Take off the suit and put on some jeans and a T-shirt. Quickly. And cover as much of your figure as possible, then tuck your hair all the way up into that Red Sox hat on your sister's dresser." As he spoke, he unbuttoned and took off his own shirt.

"But you can't go out shirtless." He'd draw too much attention with his abs alone.

"I'll be fine." He went into her sister's closet and rummaged through a drawer of lingerie and pajamas. From the third drawer, in a sea of primary colors, he pulled out a black cotton tank top, two sizes too small. After wetting down his hair in the bathroom, he appeared completely different from the person who had walked into the building only fifteen minutes before.

"Okay, let's go. Keep an eye out for anything." His calm helped Zoe refocus and not panic, although she was a gunshot away from completely falling apart. There was no way out of the apartment except the way they'd entered. If one of the bad guys came inside, he could take out both Zoe and himself before they had a chance to save themselves. The thought scared Zoe to her core.

"We're going out the door?" she asked.

"Unless you want to jump out the window." Taking the gun back out of the concealed holster, he led her to the foyer and turned back to her. "Stay right behind me. If someone's shooting, put me between the bullet and yourself."

"You're not serious," she said, as the continued threat of violence had not yet punctured her everyday reality.

He stared at her, gun in hand, until she nodded. He was very serious.

Pushing open the door with a cautious hand, he paused, allowing it to swing forward until it met the wall with a muted thud. The hallway contained a stillness that made the turmoil churning within her intensify. With a measured breath, he stepped out, leading Zoe. Together, they moved toward the stairway, his gun tucked into his side away from her. They descended the stairs with as much speed as possible. She listened for the presence of anyone else near them, but silence surrounded them.

As they turned at the landing, she caught a glimpse of a man positioned on the first floor. Jeans and work boots were his only identification. He lifted his hand up and pointed a gun at them.

"Over there." She pointed toward him, but Noah had already aimed his weapon over her shoulder and shot him. The man appeared as though he'd been struck in the chest with a two-by-four. Blood splattered on the back wall as he slumped to the ground. Zoe's scream echoed up the stairwell, a sound that shuddered through the walls around them. Then she froze, staring at the blood. More blood. She was not made for this.

"Shhhhh," Noah said, his voice a low, urgent whisper. "We can't risk the extra exposure." She turned to run back upstairs, but Noah's free arm circled around her waist and held her with him as he continued to descend the stairs. His body now blocking anyone in front of them.

"Can we escape by the fire escape?" she asked.

"Not unless you want to be dangling over the back parking lot like a tin can ready for target practice."

"Where are we going?"

"The front door is no longer an option, not with the risk of drawing more attention. We need to go in a different direction."

Several people had opened their doors, and she could hear their footsteps on the floors above them. Noah veered away from the front entrance, dragging her with him, toward an alternative escape, heading to the back of the building, where tenants typically brought their trash.

"How do you know where you're going?" She had been in this building a hundred times and had only gone out the front door.

"It's how I carried you out a few days ago."

The reminder that he'd already saved her life and now he'd done it again added a whole mountain of conflicting feelings that swirled inside of her. His hand tightened on her waist and she trusted him enough to let him lead her through the back exit.

"When we get outside, stare at the fire as though you're a tenant who is concerned for the building. Don't look at anyone directly in case they think you're your sister. Trust me to guide you to the right place." He handed her his sunglasses as they stepped outside.

She nodded in reply, put the glasses on, and accepted the arm he draped over her shoulder, shielding her from too much attention. They joined a group of residents lingering outside and Noah pushed his way around the mob until they blended in. She had her doubts that they'd make it, convinced she'd be recognized as Allison, but so far so good. He edged them closer to the back of the crowd and then swerved her away from everyone by walking with another couple and making it appear that they were together.

When they got to the corner, an old Jetta pulled up next to them. The window was down and Fiona sat in the driver's seat.

"Get in," she ordered.

Zoe didn't question her, she slid into the back seat with Noah as though they'd called an Uber.

Chapter 20

The adrenaline surging through Noah's veins was not a familiar sensation for a guy who had spent years at a desk job at the NSA in Washington. The bullets that had shattered the window back at Allison's apartment were a stark reminder of the danger Zoe and her entire family faced, a danger he'd sworn to protect her from. And that didn't include the collateral damage like neighbors in the wrong place at the wrong time. As they drove away from the chaos, his mind raced. How well could he actually protect her against an unknown opponent who seemingly had unlimited resources? If Allison's investigation was important enough, wouldn't the FBI step in and assist? Or was she one small piece of a larger investigation?

"Nice timing," he said to Fiona, who appeared perfectly calm and collected as the fire raged behind them.

"Calvin had alerts for any 911 calls coming in from that area. He sent a call out and I was nearby. Your text giving us a pickup location helped."

Zoe stared at him. "You had time to text her?"

"Alexa contacted Jason while I was in the bathroom wetting down my hair." He'd always been better at strategy and logistics than most people. When the window smashed, his order of thinking became: protect Zoe, secure area, locate source, pull attention from building, contact headquarters, escape in disguise, make sure no one kills either of them while getting to the meeting point. A lot of luck helped his plan succeed.

Fiona focused on the road, but called back to Noah. "Very impressive, Montgomery. I don't know anyone who would have turned everyone's focus toward a controlled fire instead of gunshots. Your plan worked beautifully." He accepted the praise from a veteran of an unknown number of difficult situations.

"It wasn't as successful in keeping the idiot in the hallway from dying," he admitted.

"He pointed a gun at us. I can't even count how many times you've saved my life." Zoe didn't sound as though she were fawning, she appeared exhausted.

All the confidence she'd gained by going on the air as her sister had been wiped away by their visit to Allison's apartment. Jason had warned him to get in and get out. Instead, Noah decided to comfort her with a shot of whiskey. They could have been killed. He had to get his head more on his job and less on his crush on Zoe.

Zoe stared out the window as they drove on a highway to the north of Boston. "Is Allison okay?"

"She's good. Fairly demanding and driving Meaghan crazy, but her leg is healing," Fiona said from the driver's seat.

"And my dad?"

"He's been questioning Jason about his credentials and those of Meaghan and Noah."

"Oh no. I'm sorry. He's very protective of Allison and me."

"Don't apologize for a dad being a dad," Fiona responded. "Jason is confident enough in his team's abilities. At this point, he's probably brought out news articles about our more recent public projects."

"Dad's not easily impressed, but I appreciate your efforts to keep him not only safe, but comfortable as well." Then her expression tensed. "Where are we going?"

Noah was fairly curious too, but when Fiona made a decision, he just followed it to the end, not bothering to argue.

"Noah's place," Fiona said with such definitiveness that Noah hadn't realized she'd said *his* place.

"My place?" He glanced out the window, and sure enough they were headed to Cape Ann, located about forty miles north of Boston. His small two-bedroom apartment in the town of Rockport had been his sanctuary when he moved to New England. The rocky shoreline, the quaint village that had accepted him as a local after mere months, the smell of the ocean waking him up in the morning, and the sparkling stars sending him to sleep combined to make this place home.

Rockport, with its serene ocean views and the charm of his small place looking over the pier, seemed worlds away from the violence they had just escaped. Here, amidst the calming sound of the waves crashing against the shore, Noah thought Zoe could find a moment's peace. Fiona definitely knew what she was doing.

"No one will look for her there. You rarely crash there yourself."

"How do you know?" Noah knew Fiona had amazing instincts, but did she also have someone following him?

"Because you spend more time sleeping on the couch

in your office than you do having a social life. You need more balance in your life. Believe it or not, that balance will actually make you better at your job."

Okay, she didn't exactly have to spy on him to know that. For the past few months, he'd been trying to make up for his inability to be in the field by adding some type of value to every case assigned to him, whether a more detailed analysis than requested or finding and monitoring live stream cameras in areas they were curious about. His extra work paid off a few times when he located information that assisted the people in the field. Yet, his hyper work ethic had led to fatigue and some weaker judgment calls. But there was no balance with Zoe as he tried to watch over her. If he thought too much about his feelings for her, he'd put her at risk, and he wasn't willing to do that.

"You'll be safe here," Fiona assured Zoe as they entered his modest apartment, a stark contrast to the opulence of Allison's place in Beacon Hill, but rich in warmth and security. Sandy Bay appeared like a huge blue watercolor through the window, an endless expanse that made one feel powerful and powerless at the same time.

Zoe, still shaken from the threat against them, managed a weak smile. "Thank you, Fiona. For everything. I… I don't know how to repay you."

All five feet of Fiona walked over to Zoe and gave her a hug. "Take the night off and we'll meet in the morning at headquarters to discuss if you're headed to the zoo."

"Um, the zoo?" Her face paled as she spoke.

Fiona nodded, without a hint of apology for making Zoe uncomfortable. "You said you were reporting from the zoo tomorrow."

"Yes, but that was what the teleprompter told me to say."

"The audience doesn't know that. You should go. It's supposed to be a beautiful day. Noah will be beside you, although he has a thing for giraffes, so don't let him wander off." She winked at them and said goodbye.

After she was gone, Noah and Zoe headed to his kitchen. The room embodied cheerfulness with pale yellow walls, large windows, and white cabinets. He tended to keep the gray granite counters as clean as possible, preferring a more minimal appearance.

"Giraffes?" Zoe asked.

He laughed. "Have you ever seen a giraffe run? It's a thing of beauty. Seriously, one of the coolest animals on earth, but I've already seen them at least three times this year. I'll be able to control myself. Tea?" he asked to change the subject.

She nodded. "Let me help. I need something to do to keep my mind from stress overload."

"The tea is there." He pointed to a cabinet next to the window. "And the mugs are on the opposite side." He realized she'd had a muffin for breakfast and nothing except a sip of whiskey for lunch—no wonder she was feeling off.

"You heat the water and I'll prepare us some lunch. Grilled cheese okay?"

"Perfect. Thanks."

As Zoe moved around his kitchen, Noah stepped away to contact Jason. The weight of their situation, the news station's desire for her to be outside in public, pressed heavily on him.

"Jason, it's Noah. Zoe's safe, for now. Has Fiona spoken to you?"

"She has. Thinks an evening away from this place will help Zoe get her head back in the game."

"That's the problem. She isn't in the game, she never was. She's a teacher and although she did a damn good job today, she was almost scalped by a projectile through her sister's window. We can't keep putting her in danger. It's too risky," Noah began, his voice tense with barely contained frustration.

Jason's reply was immediate. "I understand your concern, but we need her. She has to head back to the television studio so we can access more of Glenn's data. The information you sent in from Glenn's office that listed POR Development? It was exactly what we needed to get us a focus. Patrick O'Reilly. He runs a real estate development firm in the city, but has many other shadier dealings. He's applied for a few permits in Brendan Quinn's district. All of them turned down. Without the permits, the residential property lots are worth only a fraction of what they would be with commercial rights for much larger buildings. A relatively new LLC purchased the development rights from a title holding trust. Layer upon layer of bureaucracy covering up the actual owner, but Calvin found a way to follow some money and sure enough, they're linked to O'Reilly. The LLC has applied for new permits on the same sites."

"Then you have what you need." The more he thought about sending Zoe into harm's way, the more he wanted her as far away from Boston as possible.

"Not even close. We need more to implicate him directly, and Zoe's our best shot."

Noah clenched his jaw, the protective instinct that had surged to the forefront clashing with his assignment. "I am one person. I need backup if she has a target on her back. We can't afford any mistakes. Not with her life on the line."

"I understand more than you know. You may have a handle on the back workings of criminal organizations, but the actual structures are like spiderwebs. Unless you get rid of the spider, the web will be rebuilt in a day. We're doing this to protect her, to protect all of them," Jason reasoned. "At least we know our enemy now. That keeps things more focused."

Jason told him to report to headquarters in the morning and they'd walk through the logistics of the day. The conversation ended with no resolution. They were fighting an enemy that had massive resources and no morals.

Noah returned to the kitchen, his mind going over everything that could go wrong. Zoe was leaning against the counter in front of the sink with a steaming mug in her hands. The warmth of the room, the sound of the ocean, the sight of Zoe finally relaxing took some of the strain from Noah.

She looked up at him, her eyes searching his. "Any updates?" she asked with a vulnerability in her voice that tugged at his heart.

Noah took a deep breath, choosing his words carefully. "Based on what you and I did this morning, we found a connection between Patrick O'Reilly, who has his fingers in many criminal activities, and Brendan Quinn. It's not 100 percent linked, but all the evidence points to O'Reilly being the person who bribed Quinn.

He has a hundred million reasons to make sure certain permits are granted in a timely manner."

She stared at him, her lips pursed. "How is Allison's producer, Glenn, involved in all of this?"

"That's something we don't know. But he did send her out to a highly dangerous situation with no protection, which is not any industry standard I know of, as well as pulling her off the investigation with no regard for what she found." He pulled the frying pan out from under the counter and gathered the ingredients for the grilled cheese. He lifted a large tomato out of the refrigerator. "Tomato?"

"That would be great, thanks." She sat at the island and continued to sip her tea.

"Maybe he put her on the zoo story because he already knew the answers to the bribery investigation and wanted to bury it. She was getting closer to an answer."

Zoe paused, her fingers tracing the rim of her mug. "Or maybe he was trying to protect her by pulling her from the investigation and putting her on something less risky."

Her optimism and seeing the best in others changed the charge in the air from negative to positive. Noah made the decision to leave it there, a hopeful outlook instead of considering the malice and evil that people could carry with them and use to lash out at anyone in their way. He doubted Glenn had any redeeming qualities, he seemed more dirtbag than do-gooder. As they shared a quiet moment, he found himself relaxing in Zoe's presence, something that rarely happened to him. Granted, he hadn't put a priority on dating these last years, because he'd struggled to feel comfortable enough to open himself up to people around him. Those types of connections left him feeling even more alone than if he'd never made an effort to meet someone. Zoe seemed different. They kind of skipped over the awkward and superficial stage of getting to know each other and ended up in something that had more depth. But in reality they weren't a match. Zoe was a woman from another world, a small island, spending her days teaching and caring for children and her nights keeping her father company. No future existed for them, and why he'd even circled around to those thoughts was a mystery.

He stared at the woman who appeared almost exactly like Allison Montgomery, except she didn't have that cutting-edge reporter instinct to ask two hundred questions and grab a laptop and work all night. She had only one question that she repeated over and over again— would her family be okay?

She returned to the electric kettle with her mug. "Do you want anything to drink?" Her hand shook as she poured the hot water.

"Something a bit stronger than tea. Maybe some scotch." He pointed to a liquor cabinet close to the dining room table. He then buttered the bread and placed a slice of tomato between two slices of cheese and put it on the pan. "I can get it."

"It's not a problem, it's good for me to move a bit." As a new tea bag steeped in the hot water, she poured him a tall glass of Macallan as though she were pouring soda.

"I think that's more than enough," he said in mock alarm. About four times too much.

After he finished cooking, they sat across from each other at the table and devoured their sandwiches.

"Want another or should we move to ice cream?" he asked.

"What kind?" The question added a lightness to her mood and the hint of a smile looked good on her.

"Chocolate Fudge Brownie, Cherry Garcia, or Phish Food."

"Hmm. I'm kind of a chocoholic," she confessed.

"So Chocolate Fudge Brownie it is." He scooped them both the same flavor and filled two large mugs of ice cream to the brim. She'd moved to the couch and he so wanted to sit next to her, but starting something would be a disaster.

"For you." He handed her a mug with a spoon.

He sat across from her on a love seat.

She leaned back and moaned as she took a bite of brownie. "It's funny. If a guy invited me on a first date and fed me this meal, I'd be inclined to marry him."

He laughed, forcing back a completely inappropriate desire for a chance to take her on a real date. "I'll remember that."

His chest filled with a warm, romantic longing for Zoe, and he sensed the same from her. As she curled her legs beneath her on the couch, he thought he saw a similar yearning in her eyes. Was it bittersweet longing, the same feeling that kept him from crossing the boundaries that he wanted to cross more than anything? He couldn't deny the intense pull he had toward her. Yet, the trauma of the past few days made her vulnerable, and although she wasn't a paying client, she was as much a part of the team as anyone in Fresh Pond Security, willing to place herself on the line for the greater good.

He'd walled off his feelings for her, thinking it would

keep their relationship easier, but tonight felt different. Maybe the quiet intimacy of the moment or the way her eyes held his convinced him that it would be okay to cross the boundary just for tonight. After all, life was unpredictable and Fiona insisted he needed balance in his life. This would certainly balance it.

"Why did you choose to be a teacher?" he asked, curious about everything to do with her.

She tilted her head slightly, the swirl of her thoughts almost perceptible. "My mother taught at my elementary school. She loved all of her students and they seemed to love her as well. Yet, the second she arrived home, she poured all her attention toward Dad, Allison, and me. I wanted that. A career that changed lives and a schedule that would permit me to have time with my family. How about you? Did you follow your dad's footstep's into security?"

The question cast a shadow over him. Noah hoped he bore no resemblance to a man who had discarded his original family for an upgrade. "I wanted to change the world. My father prefers sucking everything good out of the things and people around him for his benefit. I think I'm more like my mother, who protected my sister, Elise, and me, after our father took off for greener pastures. She went back to school and became a social worker and truly saved lives. I hope I can do even a small bit of the good she's done for world." But so far, he'd had only minimal impact on any assignment.

She listened with undivided attention and never gave him pity. "You saved my life. Your mother would be so proud of the man you are." Her warmth and understanding struck him in the solar plexus, leaving him breathless.

It was too early for bed, but they couldn't just stare at each other with longing, at least longing on his side. "What kind of movies do you like?" he asked.

"I don't care. You pick."

He clicked on the television and turned on the one movie that always made him smile. *"The Princess Bride."* He hoped for the same reaction from Zoe.

"Good choice, Montgomery."

"Last names? Are we teammates now, Goodwyn?" Perhaps that was her way of keeping him at an arm's length. He stopped himself from stretching out next to her, allowing her some space.

"Maybe. I'll let you know in the morning. I can't think straight right now."

"Good enough." Picking up the cream-colored fleece blanket from the back of the love seat, he approached her with far too much contentment for a man who had to watch over a woman who had a price on her head. "Here," he said, draping the blanket over her shoulders, "it gets cold at night." His fingers brushed against her shoulder, a brief touch that mattered far too much and sent him rushing back to the love seat.

She looked up at him, a soft smile gracing her lips. "And Noah?"

"Yeah?"

"Thanks."

"Anytime, Zoe."

The sound of the waves was a constant reminder of the world beyond. Tomorrow was coming far too quickly. As he watched Zoe, her face lit by the soft glow from the television, he vowed to shield her from the darkness she'd willingly stepped into, no matter what it required.

Chapter 21

The relentless sound of the ocean waves crashing against the shore provided a soothing backdrop to an evening that had unfolded with unexpected intimacy. At the end of the movie, Noah brought her more tea. She shifted over so he could sit next to her. She wanted to sleep, but the idea of closing her eyes only scared her. Too much blood in her memories to promote anything less than a nightmare. Noah pulled the blanket over their laps. She leaned into his embrace.

"I always thought I'd miss the sunny days and cool nights of California," Noah said, his voice a whisper in the now dark room. "But the East Coast suits me. I traded the Pacific for the Atlantic, and warm weather for miserably cold winters, but it's home here now. A view of the ocean helps."

She turned her face toward him, her fascination with everything about him eased the strain of the day. "Do you visit your family at all?"

"My father blotted out his old life for an aspiring actress and a new family with her. My sister and I were casualties. I see my sister when I can, but my mother died a few years ago of a head injury in a car accident," he revealed, the weight of her passing pressing down in each word.

"That's horrible."

He nodded. "She'd been hospitalized. I didn't think there was a rush to see her, so I delayed. And she died a week later when I was on a plane home." Regret laced through his tone as he explained how he'd been too busy at work to justify an earlier flight to see her.

"That wasn't your fault. How could you know?"

"I'd been so focused on my work, and not on my family. I'll have to live with the regret for the rest of my life."

"This job seems all-consuming." Her fingers brushed over his, offering him comfort without pity.

"Depending on my assignment, it can be near impossible to leave, but I wasn't in this position when she'd died. I was at a cubicle farm in Washington, DC. I guess that was the point where I decided if I was going to work to the detriment of everything else in my life, I might as well be in a field that brings me satisfaction." He caught her fingers in his hand and held on, as though she were a lifeline preventing him from drowning.

She didn't ask any questions about that one memory he'd probably played over and over again in his mind. Instead, she brought them back to the present. "It seems you landed in a good place. The way everyone at Fresh Pond Security knows each other, looks out for each other. There's a sense of belonging there that's hard to find anywhere else." Her gaze drifted to the window and the moonlight dancing on the water's surface. There was something incredibly peaceful about his apartment. The turmoil of the day felt miles away, replaced by the quiet comfort she found in his presence.

Noah nodded, understanding. "I've never really had that. DC is a place where everyone fights to gain power and money. The friends made there were all looking for a leg up, some advantage to move them into a place. When I moved here, I found a sort of family, although there's a schism right now that has taken some of the enjoyment out of the job."

"Would you ever leave and find another firm to work for?"

He shook his head. "Not right now. I like what I do, and I'm hoping the team becomes a cohesive group again. We all have each other's backs and I trust them with my life, but there are a few missing pieces. One of my friends left the team last year. If he came back, my adopted family would be less fragmented."

"What are the chances?" Her voice was soft but curious.

He shook his head. "He and Jason need to have a heart-to-heart, but they're both stubborn."

She turned to look at him. The reflection of the moon shimmered in his eyes. "Your job must be lonely at times. I can see how the team becomes your support group, your friend group, and your family," she said, her heart aching at the thought. "Do you feel isolated living out here?"

"It can be. But it's also peaceful. After being hyper-aware of everything and everyone around me all day, it's nice to have solitude at the end of the day. It's where I come to think, to reset. It's my own form of community, I suppose. I can say hi to Debbie at the coffee bar, and Bob at the fish market. They welcome me by name but don't ask anything of me." Noah's smile was wistful.

Zoe could see a whole wall of emotions churning inside of him, but also a steadiness, a centeredness that allowed him to be intense and yet grounded at the same time.

Their conversation drifted then, from lighthearted tales of Zoe's childhood in Nantucket to Noah's travels around the world. Each story, each shared memory wove them closer together. The world outside faded away, leaving two hurt souls in the tranquil atmosphere of his apartment.

"Are you ready to sleep?" he asked her at a lull in their conversation.

Zoe, wrapped in a soft blanket, relaxed with her head resting on Noah, shook her head. "I don't want to close my eyes. I know I need sleep, but I'm scared."

He nodded, not once suggesting that she had to sleep to make it through tomorrow. "How about *Amélie*? It's a happy movie."

"I don't want happy. It seems artificial to me right now." Zoe wanted something to punch at her nerves and keep the queasy, heavy feeling that had lodged in her stomach occupied. She'd actually craved a different kind of escape, a physical one, where her body could rock against his, channeling the tensions of the day into sexual gratification. But she didn't want to overstep their current relationship, not that she had any idea what type of relationship it had become. So she said the only movie she could think of. *"John Wick?"* While Westley and Buttercup had eased her back into the present after having survived a series of bullets, John Wick, through his relentless need for revenge, might numb the vision of their attacker's death in the stairwell.

"A bit different from the French heartwarming and

whimsical film I suggested, but I can compromise. It'll be the perfect distraction."

So *John Wick* it was. He could kick and shoot and fight the bad guys and would find some resolution before the final credits. When the men came after the dog, Zoe turned into Noah and hid her face. "Maybe this was a bad idea."

He lifted her face to his and kissed her. "Let me keep your mind off everything bad in the world," he said, in a low murmur that rumbled through her heart.

His lips kissed the tip of her nose, then touched her closed eyelids before returning to her mouth and parting her lips. She couldn't help but moan and grip his arms. Her reaction seemed to spur him on, and he deepened their kiss with something urgent, something on fire, something burning down the memories of the day. There was gunfire in the background and instead of making her pull back, it pushed her closer to him. Her hands gripped his shirt, pulling it over his head. He gathered her into him, and somehow they were skin to skin, her shirt tossed to the floor next to his.

His embrace drew her closer, the heat of his body both burning and comforting. They kissed as though they'd never have another night together.

"I don't think…"

"Jason would…"

"…against the rules…" Noah struggled to speak because every time he opened his mouth, she kissed him into silence.

This was so wrong and so amazing. She didn't care if they were breaking rules because she was neither colleague nor client. She was a woman stuck in a crazy situation and as far as she was concerned, she had to earn something for all the trauma she'd been through. His attention was more than enough payment.

"To hell with it," he whispered to her, taking her mouth as fiercely as she'd just taken his.

For this moment in time, she felt in control and completely adored. His strength protected, but never hurt her, making her feel as though she were the most precious thing in the world. Her heart grabbed hold of a piece of him, cherishing every moment they had without regard to the future. The roar of gunfire made her yank away from him, staring at the flashes of light on the screen and the sound of bullets echoing across the room. Fear took over, and tears arrived. Instead of pushing her away, he hugged her into him, kissing her tears and murmuring that it would be okay, that tonight there was nothing to fear. She wrapped herself into his words, his arms, and stared up into eyes that told her everything would be okay, even though they both knew that guns would be out there, pointed on her again in the morning.

The movie ended, their feverish movements slowed, their breath labored, and neither of them moved. She didn't want to leave the safety of his arm wrapped around her or the touch of his cheek against the top of her head. Her head rested against his shoulder as her eyelids grew heavy. The warmth of his body, the steady rhythm of his heartbeat, lulled her into a sense of security she hadn't felt since she'd arrived to watch over Marlowe.

Still on the couch, she awoke as the first light of dawn burst through the window. The soft orange glow gave the room a magical appearance. Curled up against Noah with his arm around her and their bodies entangled in a comfortable but fairly awkward position. With the exhaustion of the day gone, their closeness brought a flush to her cheeks.

The growing daylight seemed to wake Noah as well. He curved his back in a stretch, his arm tightening for a moment across her arm and then loosening. As she met his gaze, any embarrassment dissolved into a warmth that spread through her chest.

"Good morning," he said, his voice deep and groggy.

"Morning. Did you get any sleep with me keeping you in such a strained position?" She sat up.

"I slept just fine." He straightened up as well and pulled his arm from over her shoulder to stretch it. "How about you?"

"I slept, so that's something. I might have a kinked neck all day though."

He rubbed his fingers into her neck and shoulder muscles. "I can help with that. Just tell me if it hurts."

"It feels amazing." She dropped her head back against the couch and allowed his fingers to press into her muscles and soothe away the ache from leaning into him in one position all night. If he never stopped, she'd be stuck there forever, because her whole body woke up with the massage.

They had so much to do, starting with her turning back into Allison. The idea of wearing another suit and more high heels, then acting like Allison, instantly shook the magic out of the morning.

His hands slowed and he looked at her. "I can feel you overthinking everything we're doing today. But you don't have to do anything. This is risky and it's not your job. Stepping back into Allison's life is your decision.

Why don't you go take a shower and I'll make us some breakfast? Something more substantial than the muffin you had yesterday."

She didn't want to leave his side, but the day had commenced. She stood, letting the blanket fall onto his lap. "What should I wear to headquarters?"

"I have some sweatpants and a sweatshirt here. No one will see you until we get to headquarters if you're self-conscious."

"That will be great, thanks. If we decide to cancel the whole plan, I have some jeans there I can I wear." She looked over at him, nodding to her statement. He wasn't pressuring her to go and she appreciated it. She appreciated everything about him. Before she disappeared into the bathroom, she wanted to tell him, "I've never felt this amazing waking up in someone's arms." Instead, she chickened out and said, "I haven't woken up next to someone in a long time." Which was probably the more awkward thing to say, but telling him how wonderful she felt with him would also be awkward.

Noah's response was a gentle squeeze of her hand, a silent acknowledgment of the shared sentiment. "Neither have I," he admitted, his honesty yet another lasso around her heart.

Chapter 22

When they arrived at headquarters, they headed straight to Jason's office. Jason was already there, coffee in hand, on the phone. He waved them in.

Noah pointed to a chair for Zoe, and he sat next to her. He hadn't asked her what she'd decided. The danger had come too close to hurting her, so he was on board with her stepping back. His own perspective had split between wanting to take down Patrick O'Reilly and his thugs and keeping Zoe safe. After the night before, he wanted her safe more than anything.

When Jason finished his call, he faced Zoe. "Rough night?"

"Noah made it easier." She glanced at Noah and a tenderness there tugged at his heart.

"In what way?" His question hinted at violations of every rule Fresh Pond had on fraternizing with clients.

Zoe didn't seem to pick up the warning coming from Jason toward Noah. "We watched *The Princess Bride*."

"Did you?" Jason's lips wavered on a laugh.

"We watched *John Wick* too," Noah said as though he needed to prove that they hadn't crossed any lines, although they most certainly had, and he didn't regret it one bit.

"I needed something with a bit of a punch," Zoe added.

"I've had many nights like that while I was in the military. I'm impressed how you're handling yourself without any experience and the most minimal training. I understand how dangerous it was at your sister's place yesterday. And it's my decision to pull you out," Jason said.

"What do you mean?" She looked between both men, her expression tensing.

"I mean that I'm sending you and your father to a safe location for the next few weeks as we complete the task we've been given."

Noah felt a weight off his chest. Zoe would be safe. He glanced over at her reaction, and saw a whole lot of apprehension. The exact opposite of how he'd expect her to react.

"No." She stood. "I want to do this."

Jason stood as well. "O'Reilly is not going to let anyone who has any connection with the bribery story live. I will not have blood on my hands when we can finish the job without you."

"I don't care. I'm ready to risk things. What will it look like if Allison doesn't show up for work today? I said on the air that we were going to the zoo. I don't want anything bad to happen to her, and if I'm on the camera, and that will protect her, I'm willing to do that."

Noah stared at her, as if she were someone he didn't recognize. "I understand what you want, but we can keep Allison and you and your father safe." Did she realize that any harm that came to her would hurt her family just as much as something happening to Allison would?

Probably not. Zoe tended to see herself as the fixer, the person who made everybody else's life easier. She never seemed to value herself.

"Do you need access to the studio today?" she asked.

"Maybe. We've figured out the link between O'Reilly and Quinn, but we still don't know Glenn Morrow's connection to either of them." Jason frowned. "While it would be nice to walk in with a personnel pass, I can find work-arounds."

"That's easily rectified. I can sneak in at night. That would give me far more time to locate something. If I don't find anything helpful through that, I can head to his house. Even easier, maybe I can swipe his phone, and Calvin can work his usual magic on it."

"Breaking and entering?" Jason had a thing about breaking the law. He tended to be against it unless it was necessary to save a life. "Barbara has a murder trial this month. I don't think she's going to want to bail you out of jail and handle an arraignment."

"Who is Barbara?" Zoe asked.

"Barbara Singer is our attorney. We spent far too much of our budget on legal fees this past year. She's not too pleased about our former actions, and I promised her that we would try to do everything by the book."

"Is sneaking into the newsroom and shuffling through Glenn's desk considered legal?" she asked, looking like she knew the answer.

"If Allison brings a guest into the newsroom, she has no control over what that guest does, and if he happens to sneak into Glenn's office, and no one finds out about it, all the better."

She looked over at Noah, her expression earnest. "So my presence would help protect you."

Jason stopped his standoff with her and sat down. "It would make our lives easier if you took her place for one more day, but I hesitate because it's dangerous and I do not want you to feel any pressure."

Zoe sat again too. She ignored Noah and focused on Jason. "I think I can do it. I want to see this through."

Jason turned his attention to Noah. "What do you think?"

Noah didn't know how to answer. So many things could go wrong. So many things almost went wrong the day before. Yet, taking down the scum of the city might make it worth it. "If she's willing, I've got her back."

"Are you certain?" Jason asked Zoe. "Because you can back out now or at any time."

She nodded without hesitation. "I want to do this."

"Well then, Goodwyn, the stylist is waiting in conference room three."

She nodded again, as though a good soldier responding to her superior officer. The image of her as a soldier didn't make Noah more certain about this, but he'd respect her decision.

Two hours later, they arrived at the news station. He'd always taken pride in his ability to remain unattached, to be more professional than the person next to him, regardless of the situation. Yet, as he stood on the edge of a bustling newsroom, he focused on Zoe and his detachment slipped away bit by bit.

Zoe, on the other hand, had transformed from a nervous imposter the day before to a confident, professional reporter. Dressed in black with a green blazer, she spoke to everyone around her with poise. She stood in heels as though she'd been walking in them for years. When someone asked her to return to camera, she agreed. She stood in front of the camera with grace and determination, and read a short preview of her visit to the zoo.

Glenn, arguing with half the staff around him, had become occupied with the position of a light on the green screen. That distraction was all Noah needed. He slipped back into Glenn's office on a more limited search without the worry of needing access to the computer. Calvin had pulled everything Noah had downloaded the day before. Nothing in his notes would tie him to Brendan Quinn. He spent a good three minutes riffling through any papers that weren't news related. And then paused.

On the credenza by the window stood a family portrait that included someone who looked exactly like O'Reilly's ex-wife. The O'Reilly divorce had been a headline in the news. One of the nastiest legal battles the city had seen in a long time. O'Reilly took custody of their daughter after proving neglect by the wife. Noah remembered shots of the wife breaking down on the steps of the courthouse when the decision had been handed down. He glanced around a bit further, saw two more photos of the woman, took a few shots on his camera, and then stepped back into the newsroom studio. As he walked, he texted the pictures to Calvin and asked for any connection between the two. Since they'd only tied Patrick O'Reilly to the bribes the day before, they hadn't looked in the right directions for Glenn's involvement. Now, however, they had a line from one man to the other.

Luckily, Zoe was still by the cameras when he returned. Glenn, finished with his inspection of the lighting, walked over to him. "Noah, isn't it? I see you're spending quite a bit of time with one of our reporters," he said his tone casual, but his eyes assessing.

"I'd like to think we have something special. I'm here to support her and hopefully take her to lunch."

"No time for that. The van is waiting to take her to the zoo." Glenn paused before walking away. "Whatever you're doing for her, keep it up. She seems more focused on what her actual job is and isn't out running around and making more work for herself."

After he left, Noah went to meet Zoe in her office.

When she spotted him, her face lit up with genuine happiness. She rushed over and hugged him, her excitement visible. "Did you see me? I think I handled it well."

"You were amazing." He held her in his arms until she was ready to let go. Logically, he did that to make them appear more like a couple. Emotionally, her hug gave him an overwhelming sense of joy. When she stepped back, still smiling, he asked, "Are you ready to leave? The van is waiting. I'll follow in my car."

Her smile slipped. "You're not going with me?"

He'd debated staying at her side, but the logistics would be difficult. He'd been told that only employees were permitted to ride in the van. "I'll be right behind you. Not to worry." He would have pushed for her to drive in his car, but too much conflict might make Glenn suspicious and make her more of a target.

It turned out that it wasn't difficult following them. The bright blue and white van had an enormous satellite dish attached to the roof. When they arrived at the zoo, the news van parked up front in a space reserved for buses. Before Noah could park, he saw her exit the van. She only had a cameraman with her, some young guy in his midtwenties jabbering nonstop.

He couldn't afford to drive around the parking area looking for a decent spot, so he parked illegally in order to catch up to them. If Jason's car received a ticket, Jason would probably deduct the cost as a job expense. At the entrance, Zoe and the cameraman walked past the front gate, but Noah was caught up at a ticket booth. No ticket, no entrance. If he'd been with her, he would have gone in as part of the news team.

The line for tickets had ten to fifteen people at each booth. He rushed over to the membership desk, bought an all access VIP pass for a few hundred dollars and hustled past an explosion of children, teachers, parents, and strollers. He saw her up ahead. A few of the visitors waved at her, no doubt recognizing her as Allison, in black pants, a black top, and a bright green blazer with perfectly styled hair. He had almost caught up to them when they disappeared behind a door into the birthing den behind the main big cat exhibit.

He attempted to navigate through the locked entrance, but a formidable barrier in the form of a stern-faced security guard halted his progress.

Noah tried to charm his way past the woman. "Hi, I'm part of the news crew that just went through. They seem to have gotten a bit ahead of me in the crowds." He smiled for good measure.

"May I see your pass?" The guard's gaze swept over him with a calculated assessment.

Noah didn't want to reveal that he was there to protect her, because in this case, it might put her more at risk, but he paused too long.

"I'll need some form of ID or a confirmation from your team to grant you access," she said.

Being her boyfriend wouldn't get him past the guard, and neither would his nonexistent press pass. He decided to play his only card. "Listen, I'm Noah Montgomery, assigned to ensure Allison Goodwyn's security. For her safety, we don't advertise our presence with her generally, but in this case, I need to be with her. She's inside, reporting on the cub," he explained, trying to keep the desperation from seeping into his voice.

Her expression softened marginally, yet her stance remained unwavering. "We've had numerous attempts to breach this point today. It happens all the time when babies are born," she admitted, her voice laced with a hint of regret. "Without proof of what you're saying, I can't let you pass."

"I understand your protocol, but this is critical."

His attempts to contact Zoe failed. She could be focused on the story and would have the phone turned off. "Could you please contact a superior? It's important I reconnect with her."

With a sigh, the guard keyed her radio, engaging in a brief, static-filled exchange with someone named Roy. After a tense wait, she finally motioned for Noah to provide some form of identification.

He presented a laminated card, a makeshift credential Jason had prepared for such predicaments. It was simple—no elaborate designs or security features—just his name, the emblem of Fresh Pond Security, and a photo.

The guard relayed the details to Roy, and after a moment that stretched into eternity, she received the go-ahead. She stepped aside and allowed Noah to enter. He darted through the door, his heart pounding with a mix of relief and annoyance.

He navigated the long hallway, his footsteps echoing off the walls, until he stumbled upon Zoe. There she was, radiant and poised in front of the camera. Behind her, the clear divider protecting her from the lioness sprawled out on a bed of hay with her new cub. Noah felt a surge of pride. Zoe appeared poised, calm, and professional on camera without any visible signs of the threats closing in on them.

While he could have felt foolish for demanding he accompany her, he didn't. If anything happened to her on his watch…no, he was only thinking of his job and her safety. He remained nearby, monitoring everyone in the area and assuring himself that he could keep her safe. One thing for certain, he wasn't leaving her side again.

Chapter 23

After the hell she'd gone through the day before, Zoe relaxed into the playful atmosphere of the zoo. Even though she'd been away from her bodyguard for a bit longer than she'd wanted, the zoo had a warm, welcoming atmosphere from the colorful banners to the friendly staff. And now that she'd already been on camera once, she thought she could handle this assignment. Allison's job always looked glamorous, but Zoe never thought it would be so much fun. She'd always pictured her job, down on a colorful rug with a bunch of children reading stories and playing with art and music and LEGO more fun. Yet, the glamor of dressing up and interviewing a zookeeper about a lion cub ranked right up there with the privilege of telling a parent just how wonderful their child was. She held the microphone in her hand and interviewed the zookeeper, who appeared a mere five feet tall, but ran the entire big cat area of the zoo. The woman loved her job and helped make the segment as entertaining and educational as Zoe would try to make each lesson in her class. Not that Zoe had been perfect. She'd never actually interviewed anyone, so she bobbled over some questions, but overall, it seemed successful enough to make anyone think it was Allison in front of the camera. She glanced over at Noah. He was leaning against the wall, one hand in his pocket, the embodiment of classy casual. And the warmth in his gaze sent a lightning bolt straight through her heart. It was fun to be in the presence of somebody who didn't hide his appreciation for her. In the past, the men in her life treated her as a potential wife and mother, or a potential fun Friday night—granted, she was the one who chose poorly. None of them actually spent the time to really look at her as an individual. They seemed far more interested in what she would do for them.

When she finished the interview, she walked over to Noah with a smile. "What did you think?"

He pushed off the wall and stepped toward her. "It's like you were made for this job, or at least some of your DNA was."

"It's been really fun. Have you met Tom?" She called over the cameraman who had been putting away his equipment in a backpack. He'd just graduated film school and was the backup cameraman but was allowed to film the zoo interview when the senior cameraperson called out sick.

"Nice to meet you." Tom shook Noah's hand. "How did you get past security? They're pretty strict when it comes to VIP access."

"It wasn't that hard—I said you forgot your battery pack in the van and I forgot my ID."

"Nice, man." Tom fist-bumped Noah.

When they walked out to the parking lot, Noah swore under his breath.

"What's wrong?" Zoe asked.

Noah pointed to Jason's car being towed away.

"There goes my yearly bonus," he said, although he didn't sound as stressed about it as Zoe would have been. "Do you mind if I grab a ride back to the station with you?" he asked Tom.

Tom waved his arm toward the van. "Sure, if you don't mind sitting in the back with all the equipment?"

"No problem. Feel free to treat me like any assistant."

Tom laughed. "Perfect, assistants are in charge of buying coffee on the way back to the studio."

Zoe enjoyed Noah and Tom's banter back and forth. They argued about the newest Red Sox pitcher and the best place in town for seafood. She sat in the front with Tom but glanced back at Noah. As he spoke to Tom, he scanned out the back window and when he could, through the front windshield.

As Tom turned right onto the highway on-ramp and Noah suggested a specific Dunkin' for coffee, Zoe thought over all she'd accomplished while helping her sister remain safe. It had been quite the adventure, one she never wanted to relive, but it had provided a perspective on her sister she'd never had before. Tom asked Zoe what she wanted in her coffee. Cream and sugar forever.

There was a lightness to the moment, as though she were in the middle of a romantic comedy, until blood sprayed across her face. A bullet had gone through the windshield and straight through Tom's forehead. His head slammed back and then slumped forward. Zoe swallowed her scream, terrified. She ducked to protect herself. Noah, on the other hand, jumped up next to her, taking control of the steering wheel as the van veered off the road.

"Stay down." He slid onto Tom's lap and slammed his leg toward the brake. The van came to a rough stop feet from a huge metal light pole.

Noah, as serious as he'd been casual only a minute before, secured the van, unbuckled Zoe, and made sure she was okay. She wasn't. Blood was everywhere. On her, on parts of Noah, and Tom, he was a mess.

"Is anything hurt?" Noah asked her.

She took a breath, but nearly vomited, and barely indicated she was fine. As she pulled on the door handle to get out, a police officer was already at her side. Another stood at the driver's seat, looking in the window.

"Ma'am, are you okay?" the officer closest to her asked. He took her by the arm and helped her out of the van, escorting her straight into the back of their police car.

"I'm fine." She turned back to see if Noah had followed, but she couldn't see him or the van from where she was sitting. When the second officer returned to the police car, they drove away.

"Wait. What about Noah?" she shouted.

Neither man answered.

Zoe stared out the back window of the police car as they moved away from the accident scene. No, it wasn't an accident scene. It was a murder scene. The blood had seared itself into her mind, an unwanted memory branded onto her soul. The police car with lights flashing cruised onto the highway and away from Noah. For a woman who had been dropped off at school in her father's police car, this car seemed uncomfortably silent, with no siren wailing nor the chatter of a police radio. The two men stared straight ahead, with not the slightest interest in Zoe's health and well-being in the back seat.

The driver, the police officer who had asked her to sit in the car in what she had felt was a protective move, turned his head slightly, his features hard, his expression jagged. "Just relax, we'll be there shortly," he said, his voice lacking empathy.

"Where are we going? We can't leave everyone back there." Tom, that young man who got his big break today, was now dead. Her whole body waved back and forth, trying to relieve the intensity of what she'd seen, to understand what it all meant.

Neither of the men answered. They had zero interest in anything she'd said. The most unprofessional police officers she'd ever met. They hadn't asked her one question about the accident, not one question about who she was, not one question about what she'd seen.

Something was unnervingly precise in the way the driver kept the car just about the speed limit on the highway. Taking her away from the protection Fresh Pond Security had offered to her. Her body understood the situation before her brain registered that her worst possible fear had occurred without her putting up even the slightest fight. She'd been kidnapped.

Her hands fumbled for her seat belt, her fingers trembled. A stupid gesture. She couldn't jump out at sixty miles an hour even if the door would open. Then the car turned off into a secluded area where buildings were sparse and no one would find her. Her mind raced.

They pulled into an abandoned lot and yanked her out of the car. One of the men held her and the other ripped off her necklace, stripped her out of her shoes, her jacket, and her watch. The watch had been given to her from the team as a way to locate her at all times. Without it, no one would be able to come to her rescue.

In no time, they'd stripped her bare and manipulated every part of her clothing. She stood exposed and terrified. Neither one of them, however, gave her a second glance. It was as though she had a force field around her body. She was thankful for that, even as her body shook from the breeze and the fear. When they had accomplished their task, they opened the back door and allowed her to get inside. They tossed her dress and panties inside with her, but nothing else.

As she sat in the back seat, she glanced onto the floor. Hidden by the front armrest was her cell phone. She put her clothes back on and, in the process, picked up her phone, turned the ringer off, and slipped it into her underwear. The car drove around in what felt like circles. Each lap adding another knot to her stomach, turning her insides into a tangled ball.

They stopped outside a large nondescript warehouse. One that could be anywhere. As they opened the door, she couldn't smell the tang of the sea or the lingering diesel of airplane fuel. Inside, the air tasted thick with the smell of oil and rust, a tangy scent that clung to her nostrils and made her stomach churn. As she was dragged deeper into the bowels of the building, past rows of pickup trucks, Honda Accords, and nothing as glamorous as a Ferrari or Lamborghini, she searched for any chance of escape.

The two men who had acted as saviors turned her over to a man she'd never cross. He had to be seven feet tall with hands that could squeeze the life out of her without much effort. He seemed maybe thirty, maybe forty, with his hair in a buzz cut, and his chin coated in stubble.

The man who had pulled her from the van pushed her toward him. "She's yours. Have fun."

The police pretenders laughed, her new captor merely grinned, but didn't put out his hand to grab her as she stumbled forward. He remained focused on the men behind her. "See Bobby for your fee minus the hassle for cleanup in the van. You're getting sloppy."

Zoe straightened herself out and looked around. She'd seen enough of *The Fast and the Furious* movies to recognize this as a chop shop. Her heart hammered in her chest, fear coursing through her veins. The sight of a gun in a holster at her captor's waist warned her just how dangerous a situation she'd found herself in. And how utterly powerless she was. The self-defense training she'd undergone, those futile few days she'd pretended to learn what she'd need to handle this, seemed laughable when faced with this reality.

Alone, without Noah or any hope of immediate rescue, Zoe was acutely aware of her vulnerability. She found some comfort in the knowledge that her father and sister had adequate protection and were in hiding. Despite knowing Allison's behavior was often immature and spoiled, Zoe found it impossible to imagine her life without her.

Zoe's thoughts circled back over and over again to Noah. Her final image of him buckled over in pain as they drove away from the area. With the violent deaths of Mrs. Peterson, Mr. Noonan, and Tom, Noah had to be okay. She refused to entertain even the slightest thought of any harm coming to him. The fear of never seeing him

again, of leaving so many words unsaid, even if they'd
been inspired by their close proximity to death, brought
an ache to her heart almost as painful as the physical
threat she faced.

Chapter 24

Noah felt he was reliving a nightmare. He had one main task, and that was to keep Zoe safe. In the ten minutes he'd been in the van with her, the driver suffered a bullet through his forehead, and the van transporting them came far too close to slamming into a pole with a four-foot tall, several feet thick concrete base. That they both survived with minimal injury had been a miracle. The psychological damage to Zoe, Noah couldn't calculate, but she'd need some severe trauma therapy after this.

As she had been pulled toward an unmarked police car with one of the police officers who appeared out of nowhere, she'd turned back to Noah in distress.

Another cop knocked on his window. "Stay where you are. We need to ask you a few questions."

"Can it wait? I should check on my girlfriend. She's been through a lot." He'd tried to get out from the passenger seat Zoe had just vacated, but the second officer blocked his exit from the van, asking him to be patient and wait.

That's when the realization hit him like a concrete truck. These officers arrived with an impossible quickness in an unmarked car with blue lights added. They were parked ahead of the van, which meant they either drove backward down the on-ramp, or they were already there...waiting.

He couldn't take a chance that he was right, he had to protect Zoe.

"Stay where you are." The statement promised an arrest if Noah made a move past him, but that was what Barbara was for. Bailing him out.

No police officer would keep an injured man in a van with a murder victim literally under him. He'd help him from the vehicle.

He turned to escape out the opposite door.

"Stay where you are," The officer grabbed Noah's shirt and pulled him back. When Noah saw a gun in his hand, he knew. They were tangled up together, so Noah head-butted the asshole, but received a punch to the nose in the process. Everything blurred in pain, but he managed to grab at the barrel, punching the whole weapon back into his attacker's face and hopefully breaking his jaw.

He pushed through the officer and dived behind some bushes by the side of the road. There were sirens coming closer. The fake or corrupt cop took off toward Zoe.

Noah tried to rush toward them, but the car drove off before he could get closer. As blood dripped from his nose, he was somehow able to pull out his phone and dial Jason.

"Montgomery?" Jason asked.

"They got her. Corrupt cops, if they really were cops," he tried to wheeze out the words while holding back the nausea. O'Reilly had people everywhere.

"Are you okay?"

"I'll be fine." A broken nose wouldn't kill him, just

make him miserable for a bit. "Zoe was okay when I last saw her, but I don't know." If anything happened to her, Noah would never forgive himself.

"Focus on the details. I'm putting you on speaker so Calvin and Fiona can hear."

He took a breath and coughed, spitting up the taste of the blood. "The driver's dead, shot by something long-range. Two men arrived, dressed as police, and pulled her to their car before I could stop them." He coughed again and spit out blood.

He could hear Calvin say "shit" in the background. There was definite comfort in knowing that the team had his back.

"I'm on the way. Get yourself into hiding. Do not stay at the scene," Jason commanded.

"What about Zoe?"

"Calvin's already started trying to track her down. Now go. We'll talk when I have you." He hung up.

Since every one of Jason's employees wore tracking devices when on the clock, Jason would track him down quickly. A thought hit him. Everyone wore one, including Zoe. The relief was short-lived as he struggled to push the door open and flee down the embankment into the woods, stumbling over downed trees. He continued moving until he was about a mile from the accident.

He remained hidden in the shadows behind a set of triple-decker houses. For the second time in a year, he'd lost someone he'd been entrusted to protect. The first time was with Jason's son. After Noah's failure, the team made a daring rescue mission to save him, but not Noah. He'd been in the hospital with a gunshot wound. This time, he'd lost Zoe. Frustration gnawed at his insides, a physical manifestation of failure. That Zoe had been placed in such a dangerous situation and could be hurt or worse added unbearable shame and guilt to his turmoil.

A black Explorer arrived on the road where Noah had hidden. He moved between the two houses, alerting a dog from one of the apartments. To his relief, Jason was at the wheel. Through the fading pain in his face, Noah could see the fury in Jason's expression. He climbed into the passenger seat and remained silent for most of the ride as Jason blasted orders to the team through his phone.

When they returned to headquarters, Jason took off to his office while Noah was given enough medical intervention to make him functional again. But he didn't care much about his own health. All he could think about was Zoe. Not only had she seen the brutal murder of a man that she'd been laughing with only minutes before, but then she was kidnapped by the very people that she'd trusted.

When he arrived at Jason's office, he stalled at the door. Jason was talking to someone on the phone, his hand clenched in a fist as though about to punch some imaginary demon. When he saw Noah, he told the person on the line to get their shit together before slamming the phone on his desk.

"How are you holding up?" Jason asked, his voice filled with genuine concern.

"What's going on? Have you located her yet?" Noah demanded, ignoring any worry about his own well-being.

Jason fixed Noah with a look that was hard to read. "I thought we had her location, but they found our tracker. Calvin tracked it to an empty lot in South Boston. Fiona drove there to investigate and possibly rescue Zoe, but she found the watch and several other articles of her clothing and shoes with no sign of anyone else in the area," Jason explained, his voice revealing his growing frustration.

The realization that they'd lost the lifeline to Zoe's location sent a wave of cold dread through Noah.

Her tracker had been a silver watch with a black onyx face. Elegant and more like jewelry than a technical gadget so she could wear it on the air. Without it, it would be almost impossible to locate her. That terrifying thought felt like a boulder pulling Noah down.

She'd become a needle in a haystack. At this moment, Noah's nausea surpassed anything he'd felt after being hit in the nose. He was usually someone who could come up with a dozen different scenarios with corresponding plans. Being stuck on the sidelines, powerless, ate him alive. Doubt crept in on this assignment, on his abilities, and his place at Fresh Pond Security. Two people he'd been assigned to protect, two people taken. Perhaps he was not only not qualified for this job, but his arrogance in thinking he was placed Zoe directly in danger.

He paced back and forth, frustrated and furious. Jason led him to Calvin's office. Before they entered, Jason pulled him aside.

"Noah, I need you to hold it together." Jason's voice was firm.

He couldn't hold it together, not with Zoe out there without any protection at all. Calvin had three assistants, all of whom were manically tapping away at their keyboards. Noah could see a map of Boston on one and a few live streams on another. Jason stood with his arms crossed, standing over Calvin, looking at one of his computer screens. Noah turned and began pacing again.

"Anything?" he asked.

Calvin remained fixated on the screens, which irritated the hell out of Noah. He nearly pulled Calvin back to demand an answer when he felt a hand on his shoulder. Jason. The gesture stopped Noah from pushing. He stepped back from Calvin's desk.

Calvin glanced over his shoulder at them without the slightest indication that he was aware of Noah's anxious behavior. "So far, no. Zoe has no footprint and the police car you described, unmarked dark sedan with lights in the back windshield could describe a thousand cars in the city."

Calvin's focus on finding Zoe forced Noah to place his attention back on the important details and not his own failures. "But the police are only tracking their cars, so if there's a car that's acting a bit erratic and it's not on any police scanner, etc. it may give us something to focus on."

Jason shook his head. "What are the chances?"

Calvin shrugged. "Ten percent? Maybe less?"

That was not what Noah needed to hear. His rage built inside of him and he struggled to keep it under control.

"We can check traffic cam live web feeds from various parts of the city," Calvin added. "If she's in Boston, we'll find her."

"And if she isn't?" Noah replied, his voice hostile.

Jason, stepped toward him, as though he were going to give him some fatherly advice or comfort. That was not happening. He didn't need to be calmed down like some super hormonal teenage boy. Not in front of other members of the team. He had to get a grip and act like

a field team member. He had years of experience tracking criminal organizations at the NSA, both domestic
and international. He sat in a chair next to Calvin and
shut his eyes to refocus on the situation and get his head
back in the game.

After several minutes, he remembered something everyone else seemed to have forgotten. "What about her
cell phone?"

"Cell phone?" Jason asked. "She didn't have one. We
took it into custody so no one could track it."

"You took Allison's phone, not Zoe's. We've been in
touch all day on it. Can we triangulate her phone's last
known signal? It was on when we left the zoo. I'm pretty
sure most of her location tracking was turned off to protect her."

Jason appeared at once furious and relieved. "We
should have confiscated it and replaced it with a burner,
but at this moment, I'm glad we didn't."

Calvin started typing something on his keyboard,
"Let me see what I can do. If she and her sister share
locations, we might be able to go directly into her GPS.
That would be the most accurate way to go."

"Her sister's phone is in the trunk of my car, in a Far-
aday bag to block any tracking," Jason said.

"That's going to be a problem." He'd forgotten to tell
Jason about his car being towed with everything happening.

"Where's my car?" Jason rubbed his temples.

"I don't know. Last time I saw it, it was hitched to a
tow truck and driving away from the zoo."

The room filled with a desperate energy as Jason and
Noah waited for Calvin's analysis. Noah leaned in closer
to read the data pouring onto Calvin's monitor.

"Guys, it's going to take longer than five minutes." Calvin glared at Noah. "Go get some coffee or check back in with everyone else, then come back. There has to be something else for you to do."

Jason pulled on Noah's arm. "Let's go."

Once in the hallway, Jason strode away in silence. He never liked when things went wrong on an assignment and he probably hated that this current disaster was directly related to Noah's second chance in the field. Noah followed a few steps back. They both needed some breathing room.

As they entered the kitchen, Fiona arrived.

Jason poured everyone coffee, while Fiona leaned against the counter. She rubbed Jason's arm and then stepped over to Noah.

"First," she said to him, "you need to examine this incident with complete impartiality. It wasn't your fault. There's no one on the team that would've been able to stop a bullet going into the head of the driver. Second, that spot was chosen by those butchers because of a lack of cameras in the vicinity as well as being a decent place for a shooter to hide, which is why the so-called police arrived so quickly. I went to the site before the coroner arrived while Jason went out to pick you up. The fact that you were able to stop that van from slamming into the light pole saved Zoe's life."

"How did you know it was me?"

"Dead men don't brake up an incline as steep as that on-ramp, and Zoe was in the passenger seat. I doubt her instincts would have been to hop into the lap of a man she'd only just met to stop the bus. Grabbing the steering wheel maybe, but not braking."

He didn't want compliments, he wanted Zoe back. "We can run a whole crime scene reconstruction after we get Zoe back. We don't even know if she's alive."

"Focus on the what is, not the what-ifs. We know she was alive when taken. If they only wanted her dead, they could have added a bullet to her head as well and been done with it. They didn't." Fiona had never been one to beat around the bush. She was as direct and deadly as a missile. "Third, and most important," she added, "I found something. I put a call into a friend at the real estate tax office at City Hall after you told me about Patrick O'Reilly. He emailed me a list of every property under O'Reilly's name in Boston in the vicinity, including those obscured by an LLC or trust." She waved her iPad in the air.

Jason brows lifted. "How many?"

"Over two hundred."

The volume was overwhelming, but with the right program, Noah could scan it quickly for the most likely locations. "Can you forward that to my email?" he asked. At least it would give him something to concentrate on. Doing nothing was not an option.

"Absolutely." Fiona picked up the cup of coffee Jason had made her and headed to the door. She turned around before she left. "We can both look over the addresses. Let's do this separately and then we can compare lists. Once Calvin narrows down the cell location, we can reduce the possible locations even further, although cell phone pings are notoriously difficult to trace to an exact point, especially in a city."

It didn't matter how difficult the task. Noah would not stop until he located Zoe and put an end to O'Reilly's hold on the city.

Chapter 25

Zoe followed the beast of a man through a few more rows of cars, her bare feet cold on the concrete floor, until she reached a row of offices and what looked like an employee lounge from the 1970s with harvest yellow vinyl chairs and gray linoleum worn through in places. He pointed for her to sit in one of the chairs. The cold metal of his gun caught a piece of the sun, menacing her by sight alone. She forced herself to breathe, to think. Panic would not help her out of this situation. She had to use her brain more than her self-defense-for-beginner tactics if she had any hope of surviving this.

"Noah," she whispered under her breath, more of a prayer than a request. She wondered if he knew where she was, if he was plotting her rescue. She thought of the rest of the team as well, but not once did she allow herself to think about Noah's fate at the van. The idea of Fresh Pond Security focused on her provided a bit more courage, a reminder that she was not entirely alone in this fight.

But as the seconds ticked by, each one stretching into an eternity, hope faded. She thought of her sister and all she'd done to protect Allison only to find herself caught up in the same web. She'd worked so hard to become her sister and to learn whatever it took to save her. Instead, she'd ended up in a place where her neck could be snapped, her body violated, and her mind twisted. Regret mingled with fear. She'd failed.

Her only positive had been that it was her and not Allison in this mess. She'd handle whatever obstacles were thrown at her. She might be terrified, staring at the gun, a weapon that had ripped a hole in Tom's head, but she wouldn't give up yet. The fire that had driven her to take on this mission, to protect her family, still burned within her. Even more so after seeing the level of violence these people were capable of.

"Wait here." He left her alone with the door open and she didn't dare stand from the chair to which he'd specifically sent her. When he returned, he tossed a greasy set of overalls toward her. She looked up at him with no idea what he wanted. She cataloged his appearance, burly guy in jeans and work boots. His brown hair a wavy mess stuffed under a baseball hat, but his hands weren't as calloused as the mechanics she'd known on Nantucket.

"Go ahead and put it on over your dress. It gets cold in here." Then he left, shutting the door this time.

The gray outfit was huge, made for a much larger person than herself, but she liked the idea of covering up, so she put it on, rolling up the legs and the sleeves to fit her better. While fixing the overalls, she shifted her phone to an inner pocket by her hip. There was no time to look at it, since the door opened without a knock.

She looked up to see not the beast, but an Adonis in a tailored suit stroll in, completely out of place in the grimy surroundings. His entrance commanded her attention as his eyes took in every aspect of her appearance. He scanned over her outfit and seemed to scrutinize her in a cold and calculating manner as if assessing her worth—or lack thereof. Her intuition told her exactly who she was looking at—Patrick O'Reilly.

"Sit." He pointed at her with a dismissive flick of his wrist, his voice smooth but holding an icy detachment. "Miss Goodwyn, nice to meet you." He did not attempt to shake her hand. This was a show and she was the only audience.

"What's going on? Why am I here?"

"Because I told you to stand down and you didn't."

"Stand down? I was doing a story at the zoo," she countered.

"That was convenient, but your blog says differently."

Zoe bit back her response because she had nothing to say. A blog? If Allison had recently written something about the bribes, she'd not only undercut all the preparation and risk Zoe had gone through to protect her, but she'd sent her into a deadly situation. Worse, Zoe couldn't exactly ask about the blog or risk exposing herself as a fraud.

"Who assigned you to the lion cub story?" he asked her.

"Glenn did," she replied, an easy answer after a bunch of impossible ones.

O'Reilly stepped up to her, his piercing blue eyes appearing more glacier than sky. "Did he?"

Zoe nodded.

"And yet even with something to occupy your time, you couldn't let up on the other investigation. Are your life and the lives of those you love worth so much less than this story?"

"No. I don't care about the other story." She honestly didn't. "I can promise you that I dropped that story."

"Promises are convenient words, but words mean nothing to me. Actions do and so far, you have proved to be far more stubborn than everyone around you." He shook his head as though Zoe had disappointed him in some way. He stepped toward her, something about his expression made Zoe pull back from him.

The door creaked open. The beast entered, his bulk eclipsing O'Reilly. His mere presence stilled the air in the small space, bringing the tension down. A sigh of relief escaped Zoe, more terrified of the tailored suit than the blue jeans.

"Did you get your questions answered?" He looked from O'Reilly to Zoe. His emotions remained hidden beneath surliness.

O'Reilly took a moment to consider Zoe and then frowned. "I have enough to be satisfied for now, but I'm afraid she'll need to remain here for a bit longer. There are still questions she needs to answer."

She hadn't thought he'd open the door and let her get away, not when her sister's knowledge could subject him to criminal prosecution.

"Where do you want her?"

"Put her with Maisie," O'Reilly said with wave of dismissal. "She could use a babysitter. And frankly, we've relied too much on you for such services. I'd prefer if you increase security here."

"I'm here to help in any way I can." For such a large intimidating man, he certainly kowtowed to O'Reilly.

"And I appreciate that. Monitor the warehouse and keep the facility free from visitors until tomorrow. I'll send O'Donnell to pick the kid up before bedtime."

"I understand. Anything she should eat for dinner?"

O'Reilly made a face. "I really don't give a shit."

Before Zoe had time to process anything, the beast lifted her by the arm. His grip never slipped as he dragged her further into the warehouse. She fought to get onto her own feet.

"This would be easier on both of us if I could walk," she said.

He dropped her and she fell hard onto the floor without him saying a word. The humiliation hurt more than any other part of her. She scurried up and followed him, not willing to risk an escape while the floor had a dozen men working on the cars around her. He opened an office door.

"Through here," he said, pointing.

As she stepped inside, he closed the door behind her. Although dimly lit, she could make out a wooden desk in front of her, scarred from scratches and coffee stains. The desktop contained a chaotic array of papers and Post-it notes. The vinyl of the office chair had split open long ago, its padding pushing through the broken material.

She froze and contemplated her first minute alone without someone threatening her. A soft whimper caught her attention. In the shadows of the room, a little girl sat curled up on an old sofa, dressed in a parochial school uniform, her red curly hair pulled into a ponytail, her blue eyes wide with fear. Zoe's heart clenched at the sight, her own fear forgotten.

"Hi," Zoe said softly, moving closer to the girl, her voice instinctively adopting the soothing tone she used with her students. "What's your name?"

The girl hesitated, then whispered, "Maisie. Maisie O'Reilly."

The name sent a shock through her. O'Reilly. The asshole in a thousand-dollar-plus suit who didn't give a damn about what some girl ate—this was his daughter. The realization added a layer of complexity to her situation even more intricate than she'd imagined.

Maisie watched her warily, but the kindness in Zoe's voice seemed to offer some comfort. "Are you my new babysitter?" Maisie asked, a tremble in her voice betraying her attempt at bravery.

Zoe's heart not only ached for the girl, but burned in anger. They were both prisoners, but Zoe would never allow a child to be hurt in any way if she could do something about it. She had to be the fierce one, not a woman cowering in the corner. "I think I am your babysitter. For now, anyway. I'm Miss Goodwyn," she said, which wasn't a lie. She and Allison were both Miss Goodwyns. "Have you been here all day?"

Maisie nodded. "Daddy has to work, so I stay here after school."

So he left her in a place where thugs roamed freely and the police could arrive at any moment, armed and able to use deadly force? Her anger at O'Reilly grew. That lazy jerk. There had to be a thousand other options he could afford for his daughter. This was negligent.

"When do you go home?" Zoe asked, her mind racing to formulate a plan.

"Before I go to bed."

If Zoe were a super spy, she could use Maisie as a human shield to escape, but she'd rather sacrifice her own life before ever risking the life a child.

Instead, Zoe took the opportunity to pull her phone out to call for help. She stared at the black screen. The battery was dead.

Chapter 26

While Noah waited for Calvin to get a location on Zoe's phone, he listed out the twenty places out of two hundred where O'Reilly might hide someone. His analysis wasn't perfect, but after years in the NSA analyzing the empires of high-level criminals, he had an excellent understanding of kingpin portfolios. He searched real estate in somewhat isolated locations, preferably not listed under O'Reilly's legal name, probably held under a trust, partnership, or LLC. After he finished, he handed his list to Fiona to compare to her own.

Each minute that passed put Zoe further at risk. He had managed to keep his tension under control, channeling his focus on the facts and figures Fiona had him analyze. Now, however, as he mulled over the potential locations where he might find her, his patience frayed at the edges. He headed to Calvin's space, but the tech guru ignored him, as he listed out tasks for his team to handle. Noah didn't want to disturb them, but he had to know if Calvin had triangulated her location, or even better, found her through GPS. Instead, he went to see Jason.

The atmosphere in Jason's office simmered with the strain of a ticking clock and an entire city to search. The harsh lighting cast long shadows across the room that mirrored the stormy mood that seemed to be emanating from Jason. The tight furrow of Jason's brows made Noah anxious to talk to him yet nervous over what he'd found. His boss was engrossed in a sea of maps, printouts and the glow of his computer screen. As Jason lifted his attention toward Noah, a silence stretched out between them as taut as a rubber band.

Jason finally broke the silence, his voice a controlled fury that Noah had rarely heard directed at him. "How are you feeling?"

"How do you think? I had one job. Keep Zoe safe. And now? We have no idea where she is." Noah's jaw tightened, his guilt and frustration warring within him. "I was sitting right next to her."

"How would you have known someone would assassinate the driver? That's another level of violence and intimidation."

Noah understood Jason's reasoning, but Noah hadn't been as cautious as he should have been. He'd let her be driven to the zoo without him, leaving her even more vulnerable until he'd finally caught up to her as she handled the interview. Overall, he'd made some stupid mistakes, and in reality, she should have been in the back seat in the van with him. Instead, he'd allowed her to sit up front, where a bullet might have killed her instead of Tom.

Jason leaned forward, his hands clenched on the desk. "You should have anticipated anything and everything. I gave you a second chance after Matt. You are in the field because you belong there. I would never place anyone who didn't have the skill set to handle their assignment."

The more Noah thought about it, the more he realized that Jason hadn't second-guessed his abilities, Noah had done it to himself.

Fiona burst into the room, her entrance like a gust of wind.

"Jason, listen to me." Her glare at Jason was sharp, a clear indication that she wasn't an ordinary subordinate but a force to be reckoned with. "Noah did nothing wrong. If anything, you should have had a backup following them. That was your blunder. Fresh Pond Security has taken on too many assignments, and we've all been pressed into more dangerous work with less coordination and backup."

Noah, momentarily taken aback by her assertiveness, felt a surge of gratitude for her intervention, although she had it all wrong. It was Jason providing the support.

"This isn't just Noah's responsibility," Fiona continued, her stance beside Noah a literal and figurative support. "Just like Matt's kidnapping wasn't his fault. You, Meaghan, and I were all in the same house when Matt was taken. We all failed. We win together, we lose together."

Jason lifted his brows at his wife's arguments. He sighed, the rigid lines of his body relaxed slightly. "Are you done berating me in front of my team?"

"Our job right now is finding Zoe. We don't have time to dwell on what should have been done. We'll go over all of that in the postmortem."

Jason nodded. "If you actually listened in on our conversation you'll know I agree with you. I was trying to give Noah a pep talk."

"Oh… Good." Then without a speck of embarrassment, she turned to Noah. "I went over your analysis. We had five locations in common. Your criteria fit the general workings of a criminal enterprise. My choices reflected something similar, but also integrated the area Calvin plotted as the most likely area where the phone last pinged."

"We have a spot?"

"Yes, but there are multiple factors that affect the accuracy of that spot. In the city, there's a ton of signal interference, and her cell phone was an older model, so it isn't connected to the fastest cellular network. There's a bunch of other factors that could diminish accuracy. I think we should look at these five places," she said.

The news gave him more hope than he'd felt all day. The isolation and the weight of responsibility that had threatened to crush him now seemed more bearable.

"Let me see the list," Jason said, taking over his position as leader again. "Noah, Fiona, you're both coming with me. We'll start with the closest location and work from there. Have Calvin contact the Bureau after he gets confirmation that we've located her and are going into a location." He stood and approached Fiona. "Thanks."

"I've always got your back," she said to her husband, but her glance at Noah conveyed that her commitment extended to him as well.

As they prepared to leave Jason's office, Noah felt the dynamics of their team shift, solidifying into something stronger, more cohesive. He had a renewed sense of purpose, bolstered by his continued inclusion on the team and Jason's and Fiona's unwavering support for him. "I'll tell Calvin," he replied.

When he pulled Calvin aside to tell him the plan,

Calvin stepped out of the room with him. "Listen, with the location narrowed down, our plan makes sense and I think we have a real shot at finding her." He clapped a hand on Noah's shoulder. "And Noah, you're better out in the field than you think you are. Keep your focus on the present, not on what-ifs or what happened. Your instincts were right about sneaking into the producer's office. Not only were you not caught, but you gave us more information than you realize. Without your work, we'd still be trying to figure out who was going after Allison. And those photos you downloaded from his desk provided us the connection between Glenn Morrow and O'Reilly."

"What is it?"

"O'Reilly's ex-wife is Glenn Morrow's first cousin. They're family."

Noah shook his head. "I still don't get it, why would he put Allison in harm's way?"

"When you find out, tell me."

Ten minutes later, Noah was dressed for a fight in black cargo pants, a black T-shirt and armed like an Army Ranger. He followed Jason and Fiona in his own car.

The first location was an old retail site, abandoned about three years before. He hoped she was there, safe, and mentally okay. The area was known for its crumbling infrastructure and had become a haven for unsavory characters, making it a dangerous place to search and a perilous place to be held for hours. Noah raged with a fierce and unrelenting determination. He would find her safe or he would burn the whole place to the ground.

Chapter 27

The dimly lit back office of the warehouse, with its dusty piles of folders and the distant sound of muffled voices, seemed a place where Patrick O'Reilly discarded everything he didn't care about, including his daughter. The thought broke Zoe's heart. She'd read about the fierce custody battle where he had witness after witness disparage his ex-wife. Yet, he wasn't the caring person he'd pretended to be. Without regard for the well-being of Maisie, he struck out to hurt her mother and in the process was destroying Maisie as well.

Zoe sat cross-legged across from Maisie on a small couch in the back room of the warehouse. Some extra clothes for the little girl were left on a dusty file cabinet, and a pink-and-blue comforter and a very loved stuffed puppy were on the couch. Someone had placed a pile of worn books between them, some chapter books, some a bit more advanced. An iPad offered some one-way companionship for her.

"Is this where you live?" Zoe asked.

Maisie shook her head. "I only stay here when Daddy is away or busy." A tear rolled down her cheek, and Zoe shifted over next to her, holding her in her arms as more tears fell. "He's away right now."

Zoe couldn't think what kind of monster would be fifty feet away from his daughter and not even check in on her. She absorbed some of Maisie's unhappiness. "Who watches you when your dad is away?"

"Johnny and David and Freddy."

"Do they work here?" Any and all information related to her captors would be a benefit.

Maisie nodded. "They help Daddy."

"Why aren't you at your home?"

"Mrs. Gallagher had to visit her sister." She looked up at Zoe. "She'll be dead soon."

"Mrs. Gallagher or her sister?" The words slipped out before she realized it, the strain of being manhandled and then thrown into limbo added to the stress twisting her thoughts.

"Her sister. She has cancer."

"Cancer stinks." It had murdered Zoe's mother.

"Yeah." Maisie hesitated, then began to recount her story in halting sentences. As Zoe listened, she pieced together a narrative that was heartbreaking and illuminating. The details Maisie provided could be the key to understanding the motives of her father, to finding a way out.

As they talked, Zoe's resolve hardened. She was no longer just fighting for her own life and her sister's safety; she was fighting for Maisie, for this innocent child caught in the crossfire of a conflict she couldn't comprehend.

In the dim light of the back room, Zoe Goodwyn found a new sense of purpose. With Maisie by her side, she was no longer just a teacher or a sister; she was a protector.

Maisie picked up a book, her small fingers tracing the illustrations with evident delight. "I like the pictures," she said, her voice a whisper of enthusiasm. Perhaps she'd learned that loud noises were not acceptable here.

Despite her fear, Zoe smiled, encouraged by Maisie's interest. "Do you want to try reading some of it together?" she suggested.

Maisie hesitated, her excitement dimming. "I... I'm not good at reading." Her gaze dropped to the book in her lap.

"I can help. I teach kids to read. Sometimes, it's not easy, but they all get there on their own schedule."

Maisie did not appear convinced.

As they attempted the words together, Zoe noticed the way Maisie struggled with the letters, her frustration mounting with every stumbled pronunciation. The struggle culminated in Maisie throwing the book across the room.

It hit the door, and O'Reilly's giant minion, who had locked her inside, opened the door. "Maisie? You okay?"

She nodded, but didn't say anything. He must have noticed her tears, because he rushed inside and lifted her up. "Come on. Let's get you something to eat." He glared at Zoe and then slammed the door shut, the lock clicking before they walked away.

The way he cared for Maisie made Zoe feel a bit better. Someone gave a damn about her. Not in a normal adult-child relationship, but he minded her and cared about her feelings. That show of empathy toward her wouldn't get Zoe out of this situation, but it did give her an opportunity to help her own circumstances.

She grabbed the iPad from the table and found it was protected by a password. While she couldn't get into the programs, she saw that it had an internet connection. If she could convince Maisie to log on, she could contact Noah or Allison. She placed it back on the table and sat on the couch again as Maisie returned, carrying a can of Coke and a handful of Oreo cookies. The man never came back, instead, he opened the door enough for Maisie to return and then locked the door behind her.

"Thank you, Freddy," she called out through the door before sitting on the couch beside Zoe.

Freddy.

"Feeling better?" Zoe asked Maisie, as the little girl sat in one of the two chairs at the desk.

She smiled between sips of soda. "Do you want a cookie?" Maisie held out an Oreo.

Zoe wasn't sure when or if they'd feed her, so she accepted the gift and thanked her. "Do you want to read some more?" she asked, trying to build up their trust.

"No." She glanced down at the book, a frown forming all over again.

"Hey, it's okay," Zoe replied, her heart aching for her. "Letters can be tricky. A *C* can be like four different sounds, and it takes a while to figure out which is which. They don't always look the way they sound. Words can be trickier. English is a very difficult language to learn. Many adults have trouble too."

Maisie looked up, her eyes searching Zoe's. "I thought... I thought I was just dumb," she confessed.

Zoe's heart clenched at Maisie's words, a fierce protectiveness rising within her. "No, Maisie, you're definitely not dumb. I've worked with lots of kids who see words in a different way from other kids. Have you ever heard of dyslexia?"

Maisie shook her head. Zoe explained it in the simplest terms that would hopefully encourage Maisie and not crush her under a label. "Dyslexia means your brain has a different way of looking at words than other people. It doesn't mean someone can't read or learn, they just need some different strategies to help. I bet if you speak to your teacher, they can get you tested to find out if you see the words differently too."

"Maybe I can go home if I'm better. Mom said I have to study really hard and maybe we can be together again."

Her words broke Zoe's heart. How could a man be so cruel to the woman he'd married and his child? Then again, he thought nothing of murdering Mrs. Peterson. "Anything is possible." And she meant it.

"So, I'm not stupid?" she asked, a glimmer of hope breaking through her uncertainty.

Zoe held her small hand. The connection, the human touch, fortified Zoe and reminded her of what was at stake. She needed to protect Maisie, to get them both out of this nightmare.

"Absolutely not," Zoe replied, her voice firm. "You're incredibly smart, Maisie. And I think you are brave too. Being here, away from your mom and dad. That takes a lot of courage."

Their conversation meandered then, from ballet classes to the yellow curtains in her bedroom.

Zoe reached across the couch and picked up the stuffed dog. "Who is this?"

"That's Buttons. He's my puppy." She put her arms out and Zoe brought him to her. She squeezed him close when he was in her arms. "He's very naughty sometimes."

"Naughty dogs are sometimes very smart and feel bored."

"I think he's very bored. He bites people too."

"Does he? He doesn't bite you and he didn't bite me."

"He liked you."

That was exactly the type of statement Zoe wanted to hear. It meant Maisie was building trust in her. Even though they'd only known each other an hour or so. So perhaps she could convince Maisie to let her use the iPad. One step at a time. Not too much pressure, but she couldn't wait too long either in case Maisie was summoned back to her father's house.

Zoe flopped down on the couch. She made a dramatically loud sigh. "I'm bored too. Do you have any games on the iPad?"

Before answering, Maisie jumped up and ran over to the table as though she'd forgotten that she had it. She carried it back to the couch, but by the time she arrived, she'd already put in the password. They played Minecraft, Maisie focused on building a zoo, while Zoe cheered her on. When she asked if she could try, she purposely hit the off button.

"Oh no. I think I messed it up." She stared at the screen acting as confused as possible.

"I can fix it," Maisie offered. She took the iPad back and plugged in the password—1235. Not too hard to remember. After a few minutes, Maisie banged on the door to go to the bathroom. Although Zoe felt the need for a bathroom break as well, she let Freddy lead Maisie from the room, locking Zoe inside with the iPad.

She unlocked the iPad and logged on in order to Direct Message Noah. Only she didn't know Noah's information. So she contacted Allison instead. She found a way to drop her location into the map and sent a screenshot of it to her. Her only message was "hurry, with Maisie."

Just as she finished logging out and cleaning the account, Maisie returned.

Zoe returned to Minecraft. "I think I figured out how to get a camel."

But Maisie wasn't listening. She was occupied with what sounded like a dog. Zoe tossed the iPad aside and watched in confusion as Maisie led Marlowe in on a leash. He wagged his tail and became excited at the sight of her.

"I think he likes you," Maisie squeaked. "My dad sent him to me. He said I could keep him."

Freddy stood in the door with a slight smile on his face, as though Maisie having this dog was a good thing.

If Marlowe was in the warehouse, that meant they'd found Allison and Meaghan. Zoe nearly buckled at the thought of more harm coming to her sister.

"Where did you get him?" Zoe asked Freddy, who ignored her. "WHERE DID YOU GET HIM?" she screamed out, panic filling her.

He replied by slamming the door shut again.

Maisie stared at her, her demeanor now walled off toward Zoe. Marlowe continued to wag his tail, only he rushed to Zoe's side and licked her face. Zoe rubbed Marlowe's ears and placed her forehead to his. The comfort she received helped her get her emotions under control again.

"This is Marlowe," Zoe explained as calmly as possible to avoid bursting into tears. "He's an old friend of mine." She didn't want to lie to the little girl, but she didn't want to spill the truth either. The truth being that Maisie's father was the devil incarnate. As Zoe blamed herself for how bad her charade had gone, she made a weak attempt to be happy so as not to scare Maisie any further.

"Hi, Marlowe." Maisie sat on the floor and Marlowe rushed to her, wagging and licking and hopping onto her lap. She laughed. "He's so silly."

Zoe sniffled. "He is." Never the best guard dog, but always the best companion.

Zoe held on to the hope that Noah and the others were searching for them, that they'd soon be rescued. But she wouldn't rely on that. There were no guarantees. As she played with Maisie and Marlowe, she began to make a plan.

When the door creaked open, Freddy walked in with a box of pizza and two sodas. Maisie's eyes lit up at the sight of the pizza. Zoe's stomach growled.

"How's your dog?" her jailer asked.

Maisie grabbed Marlowe and gave him a hug before saying, "He's hungry. Can he have a slice of pizza?"

"Sure." He winked at her, ignored Zoe, and then slammed the door shut, leaving them once again in isolation.

"Dad always orders pizza to eat on Friday nights. Maybe he's coming back to get me soon."

"Maybe. Let's eat," Zoe said, forcing a smile as she opened the box. Melted cheese and tomato sauce masked the smell of oil and dust.

They ate in silence, the pizza taking up the focus of everyone's attention, including Marlowe. Zoe took a huge bite and tried to figure out a way to escape with Maisie and now Marlowe too. She couldn't focus on what had happened to her sister, so she ignored the raw ache lingering in her chest. There was no proof of any foul play, besides Marlowe's presence with them. The truth was that Marlowe's presence was a glaring sign that Allison had been found and harmed, but Zoe had to believe that Allison was safe. If she didn't, she'd completely fall apart and would be no use in getting herself and Maisie out of there.

As darkness enveloped the warehouse, Maisie began to cry.

Zoe pulled her onto her lap on the couch. "What's the matter?"

"I want to go home."

"I know. Maybe your dad is just late. He works long hours."

Maisie nodded and leaned her head on Zoe's shoulder. It would be impossible to understand everything this child felt in this situation. Abandoned by her father, taken from her mother, and left to be raised with men who thought nothing of kidnapping and murder.

No light came under the door. It appeared they'd closed up shop and left Maisie and Zoe in the warehouse alone for the night. Zoe set Maisie up with Minecraft on her iPad. She acted as though she'd never played before, although she'd made it a habit to try out whatever the most popular games were in order to understand the other worlds her students visited. Maisie was more than happy to explain everything. They remained next to each other, with Marlowe curled up beside Maisie. When Maisie stopped talking, becoming more absorbed by the technology, Zoe made her move. Compelled by curiosity, Zoe rose, her movements casual as she approached the file cabinets. She didn't want to alert Maisie to what she was doing. She opened each drawer, finding files and information that perhaps they hadn't meant to leave with her.

Maisie looked up, her expression a question.

Zoe thought fast. "Do you know if there are any blank pages in the drawers? I'd love to draw something." She picked up a few files and glanced through them, making a disappointed face when she read the front pages. In reality, those first pages told her a few things that might help put O'Reilly behind bars. They had inventories of various stores throughout Boston. One of them also contained a map with some random symbols on it.

She took out the map and drew on it with a golf pencil she found under some of the files. While Maisie remained engrossed in the game, Zoe flipped the map over and examined it more closely. From the information she'd acquired from Noah and Fiona, this was a map of the properties that O'Reilly had tried to get permitting for in Brendan Quinn's district.

Maisie was still playing her game. Zoe went back to the file cabinet and flipped through a few more files. Permitting issues, zoning requirements, and other building issues had been listed out for a variety of properties. All of the addresses were located on the map.

Finally, Maisie fell asleep, the iPad dropping onto the couch bedside her. Zoe ignored Marlowe's thumping tail as she picked up the iPad and used it to take a picture of the map and some of the other documents. Then she sent them to her sister and hoped someone on the other side would receive them.

"Don't let the mobs escape," a tired voice warned Zoe.

Not quite sure what a mob was, Zoe pulled up the Minecraft screen again and handed it back to Maisie. "I wasn't playing, just enjoying your work. You did a great job."

"Thanks." Maisie put the iPad down next to her, curled into Marlowe and fell asleep again. There was nothing else to do, so Zoe sat on the other side of the couch and grabbed some sleep too.

Chapter 28

The search of the old retail site proved fruitless. The storefront had large windows boarded up and a few cameras set up around the periphery. Fiona and Noah walked around, giving a wide berth to the cameras while Jason remained in the car. They both stopped at a faint buzzing sound headed toward them. As Fiona stepped toward a dumpster, Noah dropped to the ground. He landed in a puddle that smelled like something had died there. The buzzing disappeared and Noah stood up.

"That was dramatic," Fiona said, holding back a smile.

"What was that?" He'd been attacked in the most unexpected ways in the past twenty-four hours and his body reacted to every anomaly.

"A microdrone. Jason prefers using them for surveillance when we don't know what we'll encounter. People can set booby traps in abandoned property to keep out trespassers. It's too much of a risk to go in and potentially trip a wire. Their protection systems may even *accidentally* burn the place to the ground, which would provide them with a lucrative amount of insurance funds. A win-win for them, a potential lost limb for us." She waved him back to Jason's car.

Jason's laptop, sitting next to him, showed an infrared video from the drone flying through the second floor of the building. Despite focused attention on every corner of the building, they saw nothing but abandoned clothing racks and a few mannequins.

By the time the drone returned to the parking area, Jason wore a tight frown on his face. "Cross this building off the list. Where are we headed next?" he asked, attaching the drone battery to a charger and putting the drone in a hard case.

Fiona looked at her list. "A three-building complex, former housing project, about a half mile from here. The police had been called a few times in the past few weeks for trespassers, but overall, it's pretty quiet."

Noah wanted to have some hope, but he was a pragmatist. If the next group of buildings had trespassers, then O'Reilly wasn't protecting it enough. So the chances of Zoe being there seemed low.

A sharp ring cut through their conversation, silencing them. The name "Meaghan" flashed in bold font on his phone screen. He answered her over the speaker of the car, allowing Meaghan's voice to fill the space of his Explorer.

"Meaghan, I have Noah and Fiona on the line." He gave her a heads-up of the audience.

"Good. We had a breach. Two armed men," she reported as though she'd just escaped a war zone.

The words hit Noah like a freight train. "Damn. Are you and Allison okay?"

"You should be asking about the two men. One is at the hospital under police guard with a significant bullet wound in his stomach and the other might have a broken leg, but he took off with Marlowe. Allison is upset, understandably, but physically fine."

"And you?" Jason asked, his voice tight with concern.

"I may have a bruise on my jaw, but otherwise, I'm good." She sounded a bit winded, but completely professional. "I'm in the process of finding a new location. It will be low-tech except for my phone."

"How did they find you?" Noah asked. His need to understand the entire situation was imperative to find and then protect Zoe going forward.

"Allison had logged into one of the nurse's phones that she'd stolen at the hospital. They tracked her. It also explains why they went after Zoe. Allison had agreed to stay off the investigation, but she was blogging details in order to keep herself in the story. She could have been killed. *A stupid thing to do*," she said, her voice chastising Allison, who had probably already endured a verbal backhand from Meaghan laced with annoyance and anger. She hated when clients placed others in danger.

"What about Marlowe?" Allison said from Meaghan's end. She sounded exhausted, but alert.

"Marlowe will probably be fine. If they didn't kill him in front of you, he has a decent chance of just being let go. Are you as concerned about Zoe?" Fiona's normally even-tempered voice was edged with irritation. "Your sister was out there protecting you, and you carelessly made her the target. If they saw that you're still on the investigation, and you then had announced that you'd be at the zoo for an interview, where the hell do you think a second team would be headed?"

Allison's reckless actions killed Tom and almost killed Zoe. That thought left a bitter taste in Noah's mouth. If something he did could put Elise in harm's way, he would never even think of doing it. His sister's life was worth more than anything he'd ever gain from a career.

"Meaghan, we have to go," Jason interrupted Noah's thoughts and Fiona's lecture. "We have another building to clear. Keep in touch with Calvin."

"Copy." And the phone went silent.

Noah wanted to wring Allison's neck. How selfish could a person be to put her sister at risk to get ahead in her job? That was the same BS his father would do to his own family. Everyone had to sacrifice their own needs for him to get ahead.

An hour later, they were no closer to finding Zoe. The three abandoned buildings had a few squatters living in them, but otherwise, were clear.

"Where are we going?" Jason asked as he put away his drone again.

Fiona punched up her list. "A warehouse by Andrew Station, up closer to Dorchester."

Noah already had the directions. "I'll see you there."

The drive to the third location would take twenty minutes, thirty if the lights and traffic worked against him. He could feel the clock counting down. Zoe would be exhausted and scared by now. They had to move through these next locations quicker. If she wasn't found soon, it would be more and more difficult to find her.

They drove from some bustling streets to areas where streetlights needed replacing and people seemed forgotten. The warehouse looked as large as an Amazon shipping facility, as though an entire town could be packaged up and delivered from the warehouse to anywhere in the world.

Noah slipped into the back seat of the Explorer when they parked. "What do you think?" he asked Jason and Fiona.

Fiona pointed to the cameras at each of the corners of the warehouse and over entrances, all fairly new technology. "We need to clear through that mess. But there's a light on in that small window to the right. There are also about three expensive cars parked at the building that no one would leave in view without a certainty that there was adequate protection."

Jason nodded. "I agree. Let me send the drone once around to look for anything you missed, and then we head in." He pulled out the microdrone and it circled the building just above the height of the cameras.

While he was looking for problems, Noah prepared to enter. He slipped on a pair of thin gloves that had enough of a grip to help him climb, if necessary. A utility belt held his handgun, a knife, and a small set of binoculars. By the time Jason had finished his task, they were ready to head toward the door. Jason wore asphalt gray and slid through a partially open loading dock. Fiona slipped into the darkness like a shadow, her movements more cat than human. Noah took a path that required him to navigate the unseen margins of the warehouse.

A car accident on the street in front of the building that sounded as if it crashed into a dumpster shattered the quiet of the area. Noah took advantage of the noise and sneaked through the back entrance and straight past the camera. Hopefully, if someone were watching the cameras, the accident would draw their attention just enough so he could get inside.

The interior was a maze of rows of cars and abandoned rooms. Almost no light penetrated the grimy windows. Cars in various stages of disassembly created an obstacle course. If Zoe was in the building, she wouldn't be lingering with the skeletal remains of an Acura. She'd be hidden in a side room.

Noah paused, ducking behind a half-stripped sedan, as the faint sound of voices reached his ears. He focused his attention on the movement around him. The steps and voices grew louder. He peered over his shoulder and saw shadows a few rows over.

"Check on the accident outside. Make sure the police keep their attention on it and nothing on our property," said a man with a deep voice and a body size to match.

The two men split. Noah had crouched low and remained silent as their steps faded in different directions. He waited for a few minutes to ensure that he was alone and continued toward the back wall. Lined with drywall, unlike the concrete of the main area, it would have offices and other rooms. On one end, he could see several video monitors through a small glass window in the door. The rooms next to that one had no light coming from under them, so he ignored them and continued down the line. A commotion from further inside had Noah on alert. He could rush there and risk missing Zoe, or he could leave the sound and keep moving door to door.

Chapter 29

Zoe wasn't able to sleep. She listened to the creaking joints of the old building. The door opened, and she tensed. Marlowe barked and hopped up to check out their visitor. Instead of attacking, he wagged his tail and jumped up on Freddy. Zoe was terrified the huge man would club the dog away from him, but he merely put his hand down and rubbed his head, then shifted him to the side so he could enter.

He walked over to Maisie and pulled her blanket up over her. Then nodded to Zoe. She lifted her head, about to say something, but he didn't feel threatening, so she remained where she was. Before he left the room, he picked up the pizza box and the drinks.

Zoe stayed silent until he was gone. In the silence, she noticed one very important thing. She didn't hear the familiar clip of the lock each time someone came and went into the room. Freddy hadn't locked the door after him. A few minutes after he left, she walked over and slowly tried the doorknob. It turned with ease, and she pulled it enough to peek out the door, and then close it without a sound. She took a deep breath, trying to remain calm. This was her chance to get out.

"Maisie," Zoe said, shaking Maisie's shoulder gently. "We can leave now."

Maisie yawned and stretched, and then looked at Zoe, snuggling her stuffed dog tight. "I have to stay here until I go home."

It was a Friday night. There was no school the next day. Was this jerk going to leave his daughter in a warehouse all weekend?

"And I don't wanna leave Freddy. I like him," she said.

"Freddy wants you to be safe, and that means getting out of here." She tried to reason with her, but this couldn't become a lengthy debate. Zoe felt an urgent need to move now or lose her chance. "What about your mom? Don't you want to see her?"

That seemed to do the trick because Maisie sat up and was more enthusiastic than only a minute ago. "Will you stay with me the whole time?" Maisie's waking voice was barely a whisper.

"Every step of the way," Zoe assured her. Not that she was so certain about this plan either but knew she wasn't going to be safe if she remained.

Maisie finally nodded, slipping her little feet into her sneakers. "Okay."

Zoe breathed a sigh of relief. She pulled the door open with caution and peered into the hall. It was dark and quiet inside the warehouse with none of the rustling of people working on cars or the whirring of drills and other tools.

"Maisie, stay close," she whispered, her heart pounding as she stepped into the dimly lit corridor. The little girl's hand gripped hers.

With each step, Zoe's hope grew, the possibility of escape becoming a tangible reality. Marlowe remained with her, although without a leash, she couldn't guarantee he wouldn't run off.

But as they reached the back exit, one of the men Zoe had seen earlier stood there, his hand on a holster. Marlowe rushed to him, and she almost took that chance to slip around him and run, but when the man kicked the dog, something snapped inside of her. She punched at the man's face, only he caught her fist before it made its mark. Her brief moment of hope shattered as he twisted her arm behind her back, turned her around, and walked her back to the room. Maisie and Marlowe followed, no force needed for either of them.

He pushed her into a chair, and when she tried to stand he grabbed her hair and pulled until she was seated. He tied her hands behind her back, the thin rope biting into her skin. When he left, the lock clicked behind him.

Maisie's cries filled the room, a heartbreaking sound that pierced Zoe's heart. "Daddy's going to be mad at me."

Zoe calmed herself at that statement. Her attempt to flee might have created a dangerous situation for Maisie. She might have been safe if she merely remained quiet in the room, but sneaking out with Zoe meant she could be punished.

She struggled against her bonds, her gaze meeting Maisie's tear-streaked face. "It's going to be okay, Maisie. I promise, I'll tell your father it's my fault."

As they sat in the darkness, the hope of escape became a cruel joke.

But even in her lowest moment, Zoe refused to give in to despair. She had to believe that they would be found, that Noah and the team were out there, searching for them.

Chapter 30

Noah remained crouched by one of the cars, staying hidden, but able to see down the long wall of doors. He heard shuffling feet, muffled thumps, and perhaps someone swearing in an angry voice. The sounds drew him to one of the doors toward the end of the building. He paused, frozen, as he saw Zoe pushed through the doorway by one of the guards, a little girl following her, and to his surprise, Marlowe. Allison's dog trotted in after them, his tail between his legs, and he seemed to be limping. The guard pushed Zoe into a chair, and Noah nearly sprinted into the room to destroy him. But patience would keep them safer, so he squeezed his fists and stayed put. The guard, after a quick glance around, locked the door and left.

Waiting until the coast was clear, Noah approached the door. The key was in the doorknob, able to be opened from the outside. He entered.

"Zoe," he whispered. She was a mess, dressed in mechanic overalls, with a strained expression on her face.

She looked up with surprise, then relief. "I'm so glad to see you," she said.

"Who is this?" he asked in a friendly voice about the little girl on the couch as he untied Zoe.

"This is Maisie," Zoe said, her voice tender.

The little girl looked up at Noah with tears in her eyes. He had no idea who she was, but she'd just joined their team. He wasn't leaving this building without Zoe, Maisie, and Marlowe.

"And you've already met Marlowe," Zoe said.

Noah rubbed his fingers behind the dog's ears and touched his sore leg. Marlowe whimpered a bit, but was otherwise okay. "Allison's going to be happy to know he's been found."

"What happened? I was so worried about her."

"She and Meaghan had some unexpected visitors, but Meaghan handled it. They're both safe."

Noah glanced at the rope he'd untied from Zoe's hands, then at Marlowe. In a swift decision, he fashioned a makeshift leash and attached it around Marlowe's neck. "Let's go." He waved them to follow him and Marlowe.

They hadn't gone far when the sound of a gunshot echoed across the warehouse, followed by multiple shots, and then a small explosion. The building shook lightly and smoke began to fill the air.

"Keep close," Noah commanded, leading them through the maze of crates and machinery. The smoke billowed toward them, making it hard to see, but Noah kept moving through the cars toward an exit.

Another explosion rocked the building, sending a wave of heat and smoke in their direction but it didn't slow them down. He froze when they arrived at the exit and saw a wall of flames blocking them. He turned them around and led them to another door.

Chapter 31

Despite Noah's rescue attempt, Zoe found herself grappling with a terror that threatened to overwhelm her resolve. A tower of fire chasing them down.

Maisie clung to Zoe, her small body trembling with fear. Zoe, ignoring her own distress, wrapped an arm around Maisie, offering what little comfort she could. "We're going to make it out of here," she whispered, more a promise to herself than to the frightened child by her side.

When they turned a corner around a large pickup truck, they were blocked by one of the guards. As the guy reached for a gun, Noah shot him, and continued forward, pulling Marlowe with him. There was a strange sense of relief that the man wasn't Freddy. Maisie definitely acted as though he was a friend to her. Seeing him shot would devastate her.

They ran further and Noah stopped. Between another row of cars, Jason was on the ground, his head bleeding. Zoe nearly tumbled over in panic.

Maisie knocked her out of her paralysis when she asked if he was okay.

"I'm sure he is," Zoe lied.

Noah ran back to her and handed her the leash. "Take them and go."

She wanted to complain, but the fire was moving fast, and she had to get Maisie to safety. She glanced back at Noah and Jason. Noah had rushed over to him, squatting down by his side. She couldn't do anything for them, so she ran toward the exit.

Zoe tried the door, but it was locked. Panic rose like bile in her throat, she had no idea how close another door was.

Fiona appeared from behind her.

"We can't get out," Zoe told her.

Fiona tried the door as well and it wouldn't budge. She told Zoe and Maisie to move away from the door. "I have a plan."

She climbed into the driver's seat of a forklift that was a few yards away from them. "Cover your ears," she shouted over the roar of the fire and the forklift's engine. With a determined grimace, she maneuvered the vehicle toward the door, the forks lowered like the lance of a charging knight. The impact was deafening as the forklift tore through the door. Fresh air rushed in to fill the void left by the broken door. She backed up and pointed for them to go through.

As they stumbled away from the warehouse, Zoe stopped in panic. Maisie was no longer by her side. She spun around, her eyes frantically searching the darkness for any sign of her.

"Maisie!" she yelled, despite the risk of alerting their whereabouts to their captors. With everything going on, they would not be the top priority to those men. Without a second thought, she released Marlowe's leash and turned back inside the warehouse.

Just in front of her, Noah shouted, as he carried Jason in a fireman hold over his shoulders. "Zoe?"

But Zoe was already moving back to the office, almost straight into the fire. Her lungs burned as the smoke obscured her vision. And then she saw her, coming out of the office—Maisie, coughing and scared, clutching her stuffed puppy to her chest. She'd gone back for her dog.

One of the burning cars, groaned ominously before a shower of sparks fell around them. Zoe wrapped Maisie in a protective embrace, shielding her from the falling debris.

"Zoe?" Noah's voice felt closer now. He appeared through the smoke, no longer carrying Jason. Zoe handed Maisie over to him, the child's small form curled into his arms.

They made their way back toward the exit. The heat was unbearable, but the sight of the night sky through the broken doorway urged them forward.

As they emerged from the building, the cool air eased the burn in her throat. Behind them, the warehouse groaned as the entire building erupted in flames.

Maisie clung to Noah, shaking with sobs, part relief, part terror. Zoe, her own relief mingled with the aftershocks of fear, watched as the entire area filled with police cars and firetrucks. An ambulance arrived and Fiona stood over the EMTs as they lifted Jason onto a stretcher.

Chapter 32

Under the sterile fluorescence of the police station, Zoe tried to relax, but so much had happened, she had a difficult time coming down from it all. They'd been assigned a small conference room to wait between police interviews. Noah sat across from her on the phone with Marlowe on his lap. Maisie rested on the floor with her stuffed puppy and a bag of pretzels.

"I've just spoken with Fiona," Noah said, putting his phone back in his pocket. "She's optimistic about Jason's recovery. Not a bullet, but a smack in the head by something flying through the air, probably in one of the explosions caused by one of O'Reilly's idiots sending a bullet into a generator. She's going to spend the night with him. He didn't need stitches, just a good cleaning and some bandages."

Relief washed over Zoe at his words. She'd been terrified that Jason had been grievously injured or worse. Despite the weariness that clung to her bones, she mustered a smile. "I can't thank you all enough. You came at the perfect time."

He offered her a smile in return, though it held shadows. "I was terrified we wouldn't be able to find you," he said. "If it wasn't for your phone, we'd be all over the city searching for the building."

"My phone?"

"It saved you."

She then remembered something. "I took photos on Maisie's iPad of everything I found in the files."

"Do you have it?"

She nodded and pulled it from her overalls. "Should I hand it over to the police?"

Noah thought about it and shook his head. "I think the person who hired us should have first dibs at that information."

She wouldn't argue. She trusted him completely.

"We should try to rest," he suggested, his voice a calm anchor in the storm that had been their night. "It's been... quite a night. And tomorrow isn't going to be any easier."

Zoe knew he was right. They were all running on fumes, and Maisie, the young girl who had become an unexpected responsibility, needed rest more than any of them. "You're right. Maisie, sweetheart, we're going to get some sleep soon, okay?" Zoe said, turning her attention to the child who had shown remarkable resilience in the face of fear.

Maisie's small voice broke the heavy silence that had resettled. "Did...Freddy make it out?" she asked, her eyes searching Zoe's for reassurance.

She leaned toward her, her voice gentle. "I think everyone made it out of the building, even Freddy." Although she really had no idea. But Maisie had been through enough, and she didn't need another thing to stress her out.

"Okay," Maisie said, and she took another pretzel out

of the bag and bit into it. Her arms squeezed her stuffed dog a bit tighter. Someone from Social Services had already determined that Maisie wouldn't be returning to her father's custody, as the probability of him being arrested was high.

The conference room door burst open and a woman with long blond hair tied back in a ponytail rushed in. She scanned the room until she saw Maisie. The recognition was instantaneous, and Maisie's reaction was ecstatic.

"Mommy!" Maisie screamed, her voice echoing through the hallway as she jumped up and ran into her arms.

The reunion was a burst of raw emotion, the mother enveloping Maisie in a tight embrace, tears streaming down her cheeks as she whispered words of love and reassurance into her daughter's hair. Zoe watched, her heart swelling with a bittersweet joy at the sight of their reunion, feeling a sense of loss and relief as Maisie found solace in her mother's arms.

As the initial wave of emotion from their reunion eased, Maisie's mother, her eyes red from crying, turned to Zoe and Noah. "Thank you. I don't know how to ever repay you for bringing her back to me."

"Seeing you two together is more than enough," Zoe said. Then, remembering the discovery she'd made during their captivity, she added, "Do you mind if I ask you something?"

"Sure."

"Have you ever had Maisie diagnosed for reading difficulties?"

Maisie's mother frowned. "I haven't had any say in Maisie's education."

Zoe had seen plenty of parents use custody battles in an attempt to harm their former spouse, end up hurting their child instead. She nodded. "I understand. I'm a teacher, third grade."

"Really? I thought you were in law enforcement?"

"No. I just had a wonderful opportunity to stay with Maisie." She picked the stuffed puppy off the floor and handed it to Maisie as she sat on her mother's lap. There was never an easy way to tell a parent something like this, so she just stated her belief and hoped for the best. "I think Maisie might have dyslexia. It could be why she's been struggling in school."

The revelation seemed to take Maisie's mother by surprise. This often happened when Zoe discussed learning disabilities. "Dyslexia?" she repeated, her gaze shifting to Maisie, who looked back with a mix of apprehension and hope.

Zoe nodded, her voice soft but firm. "Maybe. I wasn't able to truly diagnose her with four books and a few hours, but it's a possibility. If she does have it, it doesn't mean she can't learn or succeed. There are strategies and resources that can help Maisie be a great student. It might be challenging, but she's so smart and brave, she can conquer anything."

A glimmer of hope replaced the fear in the mother's eyes. "Thank you," she said again, her voice steadier. "I'll make sure she gets the help she needs. I… I had no idea."

Glenn Morrow, Allison's producer, stood by the door and watched the reunion. His face seemed pale without the bravado he'd exhibited at the newsroom. He walked up to Zoe and apologized. "Patrick O'Reilly wanted you out of the picture. I had to follow his orders or he threatened to harm Maisie."

Zoe didn't bother explaining she wasn't Allison. Instead, she nodded toward him and then turned back to Maisie, giving her a huge hug. "Be good for your mom."

"I will," she said, wearing a smile that declared that she was finally home,

As Maisie's mother gathered her daughter to leave, Zoe felt a pang of emptiness. The adrenaline that had sustained her was fading, leaving exhaustion in its wake. She wasn't ready to face the solitude of her own home—not yet.

Turning to Noah, who had been a constant presence by her side, she hesitated a moment before speaking. "Noah, I...would it be okay if I crashed at your apartment again tonight? I'm not quite ready to go home and I don't want to stay at Allison's place."

Noah's response was immediate, his warm smile reaching his eyes. "Of course, Zoe. My place is your place, for as long as you need."

Zoe felt a wave of calm at his words. The idea of a quiet space to process everything that had happened, away from the echoing emptiness of Allison's apartment or the guest room at headquarters, and before she boarded the ferry back to Nantucket, offered some comfort she hadn't realized she needed until now.

Chapter 33

In the soft glow of his waterfront apartment, Noah found himself sharing a peaceful moment and another grilled cheese with Zoe. They had been through a whirlwind and Zoe had to be exhausted. She'd held herself together and Noah was convinced she'd been strong for the benefit of Maisie. If she'd fallen apart, the little girl would have been far more traumatized after witnessing a death and outrunning a raging fire.

As they settled into the comfort of the living room, the tension that had accompanied their adrenaline-fueled day dissipated.

"I was so incredibly proud of you today," Zoe said, her voice low and sincere. She moved closer, her presence a calming force. "And I… I care about you, more than I thought possible in such a short time," she admitted, her gaze locked with his, vulnerable and searching.

Their fingers intertwined naturally, as if meant to fit together all along. The distance between them on the couch gone.

The softness of her fingers and the sweetness of her breath forced him to acknowledge how bad he wanted her. He felt a shift within him. The barriers of their professional relationship, now gone, left them standing on new, uncharted ground. "We're not working together anymore," he said, the reality of their situation dawning on him, both liberating and daunting. "But, our jobs, they're still...complicated."

"I'm willing to make sacrifices if you are," Zoe whispered.

"Definitely," he replied. "I refuse to let you go. Not without exploring what this is between us." He'd have to speak to Jason, but there must be a way to stay in the field and still be a part of Zoe's life. A significant part.

She traced his lips with her finger until he bit it lightly. "I'm hoping it goes further than *The Princess Bride*," she teased, pulling his shirt over his head.

"And *John Wick*," he replied, doing the same to her shirt. She had on a simple white bra underneath. Despite his urgency, especially after the hell of a day they'd both had, he wanted to respect her pace.

Noah's breath hitched as Zoe stood, her movements deliberate and unhurried. She slipped out of her sweatpants, letting them pool around her feet and, with a soft sigh, unhooked the front of her bra. Her eyes never left his as she approached, the intimacy of the moment making his heart pound.

She straddled his legs and leaned in to kiss him, her lips tender and searching. Noah held her hips gently, his touch reverent as he pulled her closer. The world outside ceased to exist; it was just them, wrapped in a bubble of mutual longing and unspoken feelings.

Zoe let her head fall back, her body instinctively moving against his. Her vulnerability touched him deeply. He had intended to take things slow, to savor every moment and focus on her pleasure first. But the urgency in her movements spoke volumes about her needs, and he found himself matching her pace, his own desire heightened by the depth of their connection.

"I've been wanting this since the first time I stayed over here," she whispered, her voice trembling slightly. "I need to feel close to you tonight."

Noah cupped her face in his hands, his thumbs gently brushing her cheeks. "Whatever you want, Zoe. I'm here."

Their kisses deepened, growing more passionate, as they shed the last of their clothing. Every touch, every caress, a silent promise of love and devotion. Noah took his time exploring her, memorizing every curve. Zoe responded in kind, her hands roaming over his skin with a tenderness that made his heart ache.

When they finally came together, it was a culmination of all their unspoken emotions, the love, the fear, the relief of having survived. Their movements were slow and synchronized, a dance of two souls finding solace in each other. He held her gaze as he whispered her name like a prayer.

Zoe's breath caught, her fingers digging into his shoulders. "I love you, Noah." The words hung in the air, wrapping around them like a warm embrace.

"I love you too, Zoe," he replied, his voice thick with emotion.

They moved together, their lovemaking a gentle exploration of their connection. It was more than physical; it was a merging of hearts, a silent conversation of love and trust. They took their time, savoring each moment until they both found release, their cries mingling in the quiet room.

Afterward, they lay entwined in the delicate shimmer of the moonlight filtering through the curtains. Noah held her close, his fingers tracing idle patterns on her back, while she nestled against him.

As he drifted toward sleep, a sense of peace settled over him. They had found each other in the most unlikely of circumstances, and now he couldn't imagine a life apart. The night was still, the only sound the gentle thrumming of the waves on the rocks below.

Zoe broke the silence. "What happens next?" she asked.

He kissed the top of her head, a smile playing on his lips. "Something wonderful."

"Can we talk about the elephant in the room?" she said, her fingers caressing his arm.

He turned to face her, noting the seriousness in her eyes. He nodded. "What would that be?"

"The fact that your job has you jet-setting to who knows where and dodging fists and bullets, while I'm teaching third graders how to spell *Mississippi* on an island that barely gets cell service."

Noah smiled, appreciating her attempt to inject humor into their dilemma. "Sounds like the plot of a bad romantic comedy, doesn't it? *The Spy Who Taught Me*."

Zoe swatted his arm. "Be serious for a minute. I admire what you do, Noah. I saw you in action, saving us, being the hero. And I want you to thrive in your career, but I'm scared. Scared of the danger you face and scared of being left behind."

Noah took her hand, the gravity of her words settling

over him. "I think you're the bravest person I know. You faced danger without any training, saved Maisie, and you still managed to locate enough evidence to put O'Reilly away for a long, long time. You're my hero."

"But that's just it, Noah. I don't want to be a hero, I just want to be with you. And I'm terrified of what your job means for *us*," Zoe confessed, her gaze locked with his. "Which is ridiculous, because you can't have an *us* after a week."

He squeezed her hand, his mind racing for the right words. "I won't lie and say my job isn't dangerous, not after you had bullets flying over your head, but the question of whether you and I can be an *us* is determined by...us. We can label this whatever we want."

Zoe sighed. "So, what do we do? I teach by day, you dismantle criminal organizations by night, and we meet in the middle for the occasional heart-stopping make-out session?"

Noah laughed, the tension between them easing. "I like the sound of that."

Their eyes met, a silent understanding passing between them. They were navigating uncharted waters.

"So, we take it one day at a time?" Zoe suggested, her voice steady.

"One day at a time," Noah agreed, pulling her into his arms.

In the quiet of the night, with Zoe's steady breathing as his only comfort, the reality of their choices settled around Noah like a heavy fog. He understood that for them to continue their journey together, they'd have to endure a mountain of challenges, but the thought of facing the world without Zoe by his side was unimaginable.

Chapter 34

Zoe lingered in the doorway of Allison's apartment and smiled. Allison, her leg encased in a cast and elevated on a pile of cushions, had a makeup artist dabbling blush over her cheeks. Despite the constraints of her injury, Allison had transformed her living space into a make-shift newsroom, her commitment to journalism undeterred by physical limitations.

"Allison, you're a force of nature," Zoe remarked with a mixture of admiration and concern as she stepped inside, closing the door behind her before a hyper Marlowe escaped for a run down the hallway.

Allison's face brightened at Zoe's presence and she waved away the makeup artist to speak to Zoe alone for a minute. "Now that I don't have threats hanging over my head, I've got a story to tell, and a broken leg isn't going to stop me." She was still determined to complete her story about the city councilman being bribed by the Irish crime boss. O'Reilly didn't care about Allison's investigation anymore. He had far bigger problems. The documents Zoe had taken pictures of provided a crucial link in his illegal financial dealings. And there had been an undercover mole inside of his group. Zoe was convinced it was Freddy, a gentle giant, who had been a guardian angel to Maisie. In addition, their investigation helped get the mole in the FBI field office as well, one of O'Reilly's own men. The only negative for Allison had been when two other news stations broke the story. Allison, refusing to give up a scoop, had decided to make her own ordeal into a story. Zoe thought that was a brilliant way to get some credit for it, but warned her to not reveal Zoe's part. Allison promised, not that Zoe held her breath. She'd never trust her sister the way she had in the past, and in a way, that freed her from her complex over Allison's purported perfection. When push came to shove, Zoe wanted to be Zoe, not her sister.

She moved closer to Allison, sitting on the arm of the couch. "I know you'd do anything to get your story out. But remember, to think about collateral damage," she said, reaching out to gently squeeze her sister's hand.

"I will. And I'm sorry for everything." She seemed remorseful enough.

Their conversation was interrupted by a knock, followed by an assistant peeking in. "Allison, the crew is ready for you whenever you are."

"All right, give us a few minutes, please," she replied, turning her attention back to Zoe as the assistant disappeared.

A quiet resolve settle within Zoe. She'd decided to remain in Boston for a few days to assist her sister and spend her nights out with Noah. They could enjoy some time together before they had a separation. Summer camp began in a week and soon she'd be on the ferry home. Noah had to find out his next assignment, which could take him anywhere. But they had committed to merging whatever time they had free.

Their father had also moved in to help Allison for a few days, although he wanted to return to his boat and heal after the death of his best friend, Mr. Noonan. Living in a close community would provide him with support and take some of that burden off Zoe. They both had healing to do, and being surrounded by friends and neighbors who cared would make a huge difference. She couldn't wait to get back to their house and felt better with her dad living with her. Allison took their imminent departure well. Her college roommate would move in to help until she got the cast off.

"It won't be quiet when Dad and I leave."

"I prefer pandemonium. It relaxes me," Allison said with a smile. Then her expression softened, the gratitude in her eyes clear. "Zoe, thank you. I don't know what I'd have done without you."

Zoe smiled, warmth spreading through her at the thought of being able to give back to her sister. "I can't say placing my life in danger was fun, but I did enjoy being on camera for two days. It was so much fun. And I also had fun being your courier when you came back to your apartment. And your stylist, chef...whatever you needed."

Allison stared at Zoe's sweatpants and tank top. "Stylist?"

"Okay, maybe not that."

The mood in the room lightened. Their relationship wasn't perfect, but maybe it could be strengthened over time.

When the crew finally entered to film Allison's segment from her makeshift home studio, Zoe watched from the sidelines, pride swelling in her chest. Allison was a natural. Zoe, however, was done with her broadcast work. She wanted to return to her classroom full of children. Her only regret would be leaving Noah behind.

A few hours later, Noah arrived with their father. They'd bonded over their worry for Zoe, a very annoying thing for them to bond over in Zoe's opinion.

"I'm going to miss you, John," Noah said to her father.

"It's only a short ride over to the island. When you come, I'll take you out on the boat." He slapped Noah's arm, and while Noah smiled, there was something in his expression that told Zoe he might not be around enough to ever get out to the island. He had a meeting with Jason about his next assignment in the morning. For all Zoe knew, he could be flying off to Asia for three months. The thought made her stomach ache. The problem was that neither of them belonged in the other person's world.

"Sounds great," Noah answered in a noncommittal way.

She walked him to the front entrance so they had a moment alone. They chose to take a quick walk up to the State House and back, hand in hand. The black sky had a glitter of stars and probably satellites overhead. The hustle of the city had slowed a bit as people drifted back home and headed to sleep. They strolled along, step by step. Zoe couldn't think of any words to say to him that wouldn't make her overly emotional.

He spoke instead. "Have fun in summer camp next week."

She laughed. "It will be fun. Four weeks and then I'm

preparing to be back in my classroom. You could quit your job and be one of my assistants."

"Sounds great, is the pay good?"

She shrugged. "Minimum wage."

"I'm ready. I'll tell Jason tomorrow." He squeezed her hand and her heart broke.

He turned to face her, pulling her into his arms. "I plan on coming by after my next assignment. I might not be able to travel there by private jet, but I'm sure I could catch a ferry easy enough."

"I'd like that, but promise me you'll stay more focused on your job than on me, because I know how important and dangerous it is." And the idea of anything happening to him…it scared her.

He drew her close, their breath mingling in the chill of the night air. The city stood still for a moment, the weight of the goodbye, even if temporary, drowning out their surroundings. His hands framed her face, as though he could imprint this moment into his memory forever. She closed her eyes and absorbed his touch. And then he kissed her, a whisper of love, a tenderness of care, a restrained passion. Perhaps in a year or two or three, they could find a way to make it work with less time apart and more time side-by-side.

He paused and rested his head against hers. The connection giving her a false sense of security. He'd been in her life for such a short time and yet she considered him home. His thumb brushed away a tear from her cheek.

He studied her face, tracing all of the contours with such a soft and gentle touch. "It's all going to work out."

"How?"

"It just will. As far as I'm concerned, we belong together, so we will be."

"That's profound."

"It's the truth." He kissed her again, his lips pressing softly against hers until she parted her lips. The gentle caress of his tongue against hers made her crave far more for the night and her entire life. She leaned into him as his hands held her close and refused to let go.

When they finally separated, Zoe tried to pull herself together but feared time and distance would keep them apart. She stood outside for several minutes after he drove away and let the tears fall.

Chapter 35

Noah found himself staring at Jason on a computer screen. Jason's injury didn't allow him to get back into the office yet, but he insisted on running everything until his partner, Steve, got back in two days. He was in a sweatshirt in bed, with his wound covered and his whole face swollen. The air between them was charged with an unspoken understanding of everything they'd endured together and Noah's stepped-up belief in his own value on the team. Jason, looking as worn as any man who had been hit hard in the head, leaned forward, locking eyes with him.

"I haven't always supported you as a full-fledged member of the team. Perhaps it was your lack of on-the-ground training and experience. Ironically, Fiona, whose opinion I respect more than anyone, believed in you from the moment she met you. You not only put your life on the line for Matt, but you acted as both field agent and analyst in finding Zoe. Not many on our team could handle both roles simultaneously. You did a great job. Brendan Quinn is under arrest, as is the entire top tier of the O'Reilly crime family. Not only did we get them on conspiracy and bribing a government official, but the

DA is also holding O'Reilly on kidnapping, murder, and assault charges. A lot of this is due to your vigilance. I should never have faulted you in Matt's kidnapping," Jason began, his voice tinged with regret. "It was my fault for leaving the team unprepared, and you…you took a bullet on top of it. I owe you for that and for this…" He gestured vaguely, encompassing the recent ordeal with Allison and Zoe Goodwyn. "You handled yourself on this case exactly as I'd hoped you would when I hired you years ago."

Noah absorbed Jason's words, a mix of surprise and appreciation warming him. "Thanks," he said. "I appreciated the opportunity to prove myself."

Jason didn't hand out compliments easily. That alone was enough to keep Noah happy in his work. Not one hundred percent happy though. He was missing something in his life…love. The job, however, wouldn't make having a relationship easy. He had to travel often and might work round the clock for days, weeks, and even months at a time, only then earning enough free time to have a normal life for a week or two. The unpredictability of it made for a difficult dating life. He'd seen both Sam and Meaghan experience the downside of their random hours on their relationships. Noah had never tried to fit someone into his life, but now that he'd met Zoe, it was all he wanted.

Since Jason spoke so highly of him, perhaps this was the best time to broach the subject of a different work schedule. No matter what happened between him and Zoe, the decision for more of life than he'd had before had solidified in the wake of recent events. Their conversation was abruptly interrupted by the sound of a door swinging open. Fiona, a woman with no understanding of hierarchy, barged into their meeting, her presence filling Jason's room with her intense energy.

"Sorry to interrupt, but I wanted to add to any praise Jason should have given to you." She practically pushed her injured husband out of the computer screen to speak to Noah. "Your analytical skills are near perfect, but your fieldwork, is top-notch. I'd have you as my partner anytime."

"I appreciate that."

"She's right. You're one of the best people we have in the field." Jason leaned back in bed. "I hope you're ready for something international, because we have a CEO of an AI company that could use some backup when he flies to Southern France."

"For how long?"

"About three months."

Three months was a lifetime when the woman he loved only had the summer free. "I'm glad you see my value because I've been thinking," Noah said, ignoring Fiona and focusing on his boss. "I'd like to step back a bit to have some more free time." His voice stayed steady despite the uncertainty of how his request would be received.

Jason's expression tightened. "Your timing is poor. We have more and more government contracts every month. We need all hands on deck."

"I work part-time, why can't he?" Fiona interjected, her tone challenging and playful, a smirk playing at the corners of her mouth.

Jason sighed, running a hand through his hair in exasperation. "That's different, Fiona, and you know it."

Fiona, unfazed, leaned against the wall, her gaze shifting between Jason and Noah. "Maybe it's time to think outside the box. If Noah needs the space, we should find a way to make it work. He's too valuable to lose."

Jason looked at Noah, his mouth open to say something, but nothing came out. It was good to see him struggling, because it meant he wanted Noah at Fresh Pond Security and Noah certainly wanted to stay.

"I have no plans on leaving, to be clear," Noah said to fill in the space left by Jason. "But I do require a different schedule."

Jason shook his head. "We're down to a skeleton crew as it is."

"Why don't we reach out to Finn? He left because you hid information from the team, Jason. But maybe it's time to beg and bring him back into the fold." Fiona's suggestion nearly knocked Noah over. It had been his wish for Finn to return, but it wasn't his decision, and every time they spoke, Finn didn't sound as though he'd ever come back. Being a good friend, Noah refused to broach the subject, but the prospect of Finn rejoining their ranks made him second-guess his own request to step back. Finn had been one of the most valuable assets on the team, his departure a loss that diminished Noah's work satisfaction. Yes, Noah loved his job, but he loved it more when his best friend had been with him. But would he be willing to forgive Jason for lying to him?

Jason seemed to consider Fiona's suggestion, the gears clearly turning in his head. "Finn, huh? That might just work," he conceded, the hint of a plan forming behind his eyes. "I suppose I'm the person who needs to reach out to him. Although I can't guarantee I'll have any luck with it."

"Until you grovel to him, which is precisely what needs to happen, you won't know what his decision is," Fiona said.

Noah remained silent. Perhaps he could put in a good word for Jason to Finn, or he could stay out of it. He didn't know which path would help Finn return.

"Is there a way I could have some time off this summer before we learn about Finn's potential return?" Noah asked.

"Anything's possible," Fiona replied.

Jason closed his eyes for a second then nodded. "Okay. I'll ask Meaghan to head to France," he pointed at Noah, "and you can look after one of the Kennedys on Martha's Vineyard for a week. Then you can take a few weeks off before Zoe's classes begin."

"How do you know I…"

Jason lifted a brow. Noah stopped his question because Jason knew everything. Besides, it wasn't as if he'd done a great job hiding his attraction for Zoe.

"Can you handle that?" Jason asked.

"I definitely can. Thank you." One week and then he could breathe.

Whatever the future held for him professionally, he knew that the connection he had forged with Zoe was something he wanted to pursue.

As the meeting drew to a close, Noah left with a sense of cautious optimism. Only time would tell if Finn would be willing to return to the team. Even more important, he had a schedule that just might turn his relationship with Zoe into something much, much more.

Chapter 36

Nantucket had always been home for Zoe, but now she felt a strain on the island since the death of Mr. Noonan. She'd spent the past few weeks getting back into her old life, although the sleeves no longer fit and the waist was too tight. Her father had melted back into his day-to-day activities as though he hadn't lost his best friend and almost lost his daughters, although the retired cop had always faced adversity, such as the death of his wife, by working harder. He replanted some of the flowers trampled by first responders, polished his boat, and hung around at the police station offering wisdom for the price of a cup of coffee and some company.

Zoe buried her own trauma by surrounding herself in the laughter and energy of summer camp. She loved working with children outside and away from the rigidness of books and testing.

As sun filtered through the trees bordering the local park, casting shadows on the play fields, she organized a game of soccer among a group of enthusiastic children. Her laughter mingled with theirs, a sound of pure joy that felt worlds away from the tension and danger that had nearly killed her.

She paused to catch her breath, and a familiar figure caught her eye. Noah Montgomery, casual and relaxed, strolled up to the edge of the play area, watching her with an affectionate smile that made her heart skip a beat. His board shorts and Salt Life T-shirt had him blending in to the summer island crowd.

She turned to one of the camp assistants, a young woman helping some of the campers paint small rocks into ladybugs and spiders. "Hey Lori, can you take over on the field for a minute?" she asked, receiving a nod and a smile in response.

As Lori stepped in to continue the game, Zoe led Noah away from the laughter and toward a quieter spot under the shade of a large oak tree. He placed a wicker picnic basket on the ground. The coolness of the shade was a welcome respite from the summer heat, a secluded enclave where they could speak freely.

"I came to tell you in person that I've told Jason I need a break from security work," he said.

His announcement confused her. She'd been sure that he'd finally felt as though he had become part of a valuable team at Fresh Pond Security. Leaving now didn't make sense. "I don't understand. You're quitting your job?"

"No. I do love my work, but after everything that's happened, I think it's time I stepped back and found some balance. I'm working on an assignment by assignment basis. I figured I could up my workload when September comes and you return to the classroom."

Zoe's eyes widened. She'd expected to see him for a few days in the next few months. Instead, she'd have him for the whole summer. "Really? That's awesome. I can't think of anyone who deserves a break more than you do." She'd never thought they would be able to work out a situation where they'd be an actual part of each other's lives.

"I don't see myself at the beach for days at a time. I'd rather spend my time wisely," he said, his gaze locked on hers. A ball rolled over to them, and he kicked it back to the children. "Are you looking for assistants?" he said, his voice carrying over playful shouts.

"Only if they can pass a rigorous background check," she teased.

Noah chuckled. "I don't think that'll be a problem," he said, his confidence evident in his easy stance.

"Are you sure being a camp counselor would be a break?"

"I can't think of anything better than being right here...with you."

The intensity of his words, the promise they held, filled Zoe with an overwhelming sense of happiness. She stepped closer, wrapping her arms around him in a hug that felt like a coming home.

"I'd like that," she whispered against his shoulder. The simple admission lifted the heavy weight she'd carried on her shoulders since the last time she'd seen him.

As they pulled back, their eyes met, and in a moment of mutual understanding, they leaned in for a kiss, simple and sincere. It was a kiss of new beginnings, of summers filled with possibility, and the promise of countless tomorrows.

When they finally broke apart, the world around them—the laughter of children, the rustle of leaves in the gentle breeze—seemed brighter.

Zoe pointed to the basket he brought. "What's in the basket? Is it a gift?"

"It depends? Can we consider this our first date?"

She glanced over at the children and the other counselors. She was on the clock, but everything for the moment seemed under control. "A quick first date."

"That's doable." He opened the lid, and pulled out two wrapped grilled cheese sandwiches and a tub of Chocolate Fudge Brownie ice cream.

"This is a pretty serious first date," she said, her voice light with laughter.

"I'm told it's the perfect lunch to capture the heart of a potential bride."

She nearly blushed at his remembering her statement about this meal on a first date would make her seriously consider marrying the man. She reached past the sandwiches for the pint of ice cream and then wrapped her arms around him again. "It sure is."

* * * * *